ORCHARD
OF MY EYE

A Novel

Mark Canter

ORCHARD
OF MY EYE

ISBN 978-1481183819

To Carl Sagan
&
All the Eye-Openers

"If the doors of perception were cleansed, everything would appear as it is: infinite."

William Blake (1757-1827)
English poet, artist, mystic

1

Nat Colt lost control of his insides. He puked. Flushed. Stepped to the sink and scrubbed his face hard with cold water and rinsed his mouth twice with mint-flavored Scope. He let out a ragged sigh.

"Therapy" they called it: poisoning your whole system while hoping the cancer croaks before you do.

In the dim glow of a nightlight his face hovered in the mirror, a lean dark shadow with darker holes for eyes and mouth: a death skull. Quickly he looked away. Through tall windows moonlight seeped around the edges of an anvil-shaped thunderhead. "Silver lining?" he said aloud. "Or is that chromium?" A big storm had threatened all day, and now, well-past midnight, the black cloud's belly bulged with pent-up rain.

Nausea wormed through Nat Colt's gut. He stepped over to the toilet and lurched forward, racked by heaves. But nothing remained to be ejected from the empty fist of his stomach.

At last the sickening ache slithered away. Nat remained slumped over in a fog of exhaustion, hands on knees, resting his chin on his chest. "You can handle the poison," he told himself in a hoarse whisper, "but the tumor can't."

He wiped a mustache of sweat from his upper lip and crossed to the sink to again splash cold water on his face.

Droplets beaded on the wooly mat of his chest hair. The three-quarter moon appeared through a rip in the clouds and gazed down upon the lone man. Nat stared upward through the window as if straining to find a heartening beacon from a distant lighthouse knifing through the gloom, but only a light like watery milk fell upon sinewy arms and hands.

His mind wandered the past, always back to Roan.

He recalled in lucid detail the first time he met the woman who would become his wife, Roan McKenzie. He had been seventeen. In his memory he slung water from his hair and stepped dripping out of a shower room into a locker room. A tall, teen-aged woman with red tresses was standing before a row of dark blue lockers peeling off a one-piece silver swimsuit.

Nat remembered ducking back inside the shower room, face flushed hot with embarrassment. *Damn!* His first week at Gulf Coast University and he had somehow blundered into the women's locker room—the kind of screw-up doomed to become an instant school legend. He glanced around the shower room. Only one exit.

He was trapped, condemned to be mortified in his freshman year. And worse, it had to happen with *this* woman; this gorgeous, statuesque redhead.

Nat snapped out of his reverie when a child appeared in the bathroom doorway behind him, silhouetted by the amber glow of a nightlight. At nine, Jasmine Colt already flaunted a glorious red mane like her mother's.

"Daddy?"

"Yeah, Jazz. Daddy's okay. Hop back in bed. I'll be there in a few minutes."

"Why don't you turn the light on?" She flipped the switch.

Brilliance from a row of white globes above the mirror stabbed his optic nerves and he winced. *Soft-white, my ass.* He shielded his eyes and squinted. These days glare hurt. *Is that an effect of the chemotherapy or the tumor?*

Jasmine came up behind and gave her father a hug. Nat's big hands covered her little hands.

"Thirsty," she said.

Nat ran cold water and filled a glass from the sink faucet. Then he bent his head low to the sink and drank in gulps.

Father and daughter reflected stark contrasts. Jasmine, an advertisement for health: smooth skin the color of cocoa with cream; emerald-green eyes, big and shiny as shooter-marbles; dark red hair braided in corn-rows; she looked like a colorful blossom unfurling from the richest soil on Earth.

Nat looked like compost. Cancer in his brain and toxin in his bloodstream had leached the vitality from his ebony face. He had dropped twenty pounds from a hard, slender body that didn't have extra fat to lose. High cheekbones that had been one of the features of his Belafonte good looks now emphasized his gauntness. He ran a hand over his head. What remained of his wooly black hair looked like a moth-eaten sweater.

3

"Should I shave my head?" He tugged at his scalp and a clump of hair came loose in his fingers. "I could look like a soul version of Mr. Clean."

"Who's Mr. Clean?"

"Some bald white guy on a household cleaner."

"Handsome like you?"

Nat smiled. "What a smoothie." He pulled down on a bruise-colored bag beneath a bloodshot eye. "Think I'm handsome? I look like doggie-doo."

"You look okay to me," she said. "Not as good as when you had more hair, but it'll grow back."

Nat glanced down at green eyes blazing with faith and hope. Jasmine seemed to him a dollop of pure, concentrated light wrapped in yellow flannel pajamas. If he did believe in God, it would have nothing to do with theology; it would be because of beauty like this.

"Think so, sport?" he said past a lump in this throat.

"Know so."

"Okay, tomorrow, you can help me shave my head."

"Cool!"

"Go back to bed now, sweetie."

She smiled. "Night, Daddy. Love you." She tugged his pajama leg and he bent and kissed her red hair. The movement of his head triggered a sudden flood of nausea and he patted her bottom and scooted her out the bathroom just in time to shut the door and lunge to the toilet. Violent

4

cramps. A geyser erupting. The water from his stomach sloshed into the bowl.

Nat returned to the sink. Flipped out the lights. Gripped his dizzy head. His body felt like a raisin, life-juice dried up. "Die, you fucking cancer cells. *Die!*"

Bitter anger brewed in his heart at the injustice of the situation—the random, meaningless, bad luck of it. To be hit with inoperable brain cancer seemed about as arbitrary as strolling along campus and getting gunned down by some madman hiding in a clock tower with a sniper rifle.

Shit happens. That's the cold, Zen bones of it. But what hurt him most was that such shit had to happen to his daughter. Odds are he would soon be non-suffering carbon: ashes to ashes; stardust to stardust. But how cruelly unfair for Jasmine! First her mommy, murdered. Now her daddy, battling one of deadliest of the deadly—*astrocytoma*—sounds like a condition astronomers get from sitting too long on their asses gazing at stars.

Nat gazed at his dim reflection in the dark mirror. *Who knows how long I can beat this?* He choked at a sudden tightness in his throat, but no tears came.

"I'm so close to a breakthrough," he said with a soft Southern twang. "So close." He imagined he could hear game-show music ticking off the seconds that remained to his life's work on an artificial vision system for the blind.

"And the blind shall see." He glanced down at the drain. "If cancer doesn't kill me first."

Nat jerked his head up as the first lightning bolt bombed the dark pasture below. Electric fire lit up a stand of pale dogwoods atop a knob flanking the hollow. The thunder crash rattled shutters and incoming waves of hail strafed the windows.

The cancer gods are angry. They require a sacrifice.

Horses in the stable. Jasmine in her parent's bed. Seeker asleep in the hallway. Roan beyond all harm. Nat alive, for now.

All accounted for.

"Screw you," Nat told the moaning storm. "I'm not going anywhere tonight."

2

Aria Rioverde lay on her back, awaiting thunder.

She reclined on the bare oak floor of a one-room bungalow on Dogfish Key, near Tallahassee. Cedar stilts raised the 20-by-20-foot cabin above the grip of surge tides and made the structure a crude tuning fork even in ordinary thundershowers, and tonight, a ripping tropical squall burbled and brewed in the cauldron of the Gulf of Mexico.

Aria had spent the whole day teaching a Caribbean Rhythm and Dance workshop to members of the FSU dance faculty. Then she straddled her Honda 750 VFR crotch-rocket and zoomed from the downtown Tallahassee campus to her beach getaway on the tiny barrier island. Sea wind had gushed through her helmet, hot and damp with the breath of coming rain, and cumulonimbus clouds had chased her, billowing in rearview mirrors like black pirate sails. She had outraced the storm and started up the cabin stairs just as the waterfall burst free. In the seconds it took to reach the door, turn a key in the lock and dash inside, the Niagara of rain had soaked her T-shirt and jeans and plastered her short mop to her scalp like black syrup.

In the cabin's closet-sized bathroom, she wrung out her dripping clothes in the shower stall and hung them on the curtain rod to dry. The bathroom smelled musty, of mildew. One of these days she needed to get around to scrubbing the shower curtain with bleach. She grabbed a sweatshirt from a wicker laundry basket and used it to dry her hair and skin. One of these days she would have to get around to doing her laundry.

After she climbed to her sleeping loft and put on a purple cotton dance leotard, she sat at the top of the ladder and felt the cabin quiver in the gusts. A fusillade of rain pelted the tin roof and the air in the room trembled sympathetically like strings of a sitar.

Below her, a mirror with ballet bar covered one wall of the former fishing shack, and polished oak planks served as dance floor. In one far corner, four concert-sized stereo speakers and a stack of audio equipment crowded next to plump throw pillows and a bookcase made of pine planks laid between stacked cinderblocks. To the left of the front door, a narrow counter with a small steel sink hugged the wall; on it a Coleman camping stove perched beside a stash of canned soups and boxes of cereal; a miniature refrigerator nestled below near the only furniture in the cabin, a wooden bar stool.

She descended the stairs unhurriedly, enjoying the buzzing liveliness of the room and everything in it. Physicists had it right, she mused, nothing is solid—all is vibration—rhythm and flow.

Sliding glass doors dominated the wall facing the ocean. Through the flowing curtain of rain, Aria could not make out the waves rushing in a few hundred yards away, but she heard and felt their steady drum roll along the beach just beyond the dunes and sea oats.

Aria reclined on smooth, cool floorboards, anticipating the thunder's touch. She smelled Murphy's Wood Soap, sea salt, and the warm fragrance of her own bronze skin.

Lightning skewered the night sky. The sheet of rain on the glass doors flashed like a neon sign. Aria closed her eyes and shivered. Whisper-fine hairs stood in expectation on her bare legs.

The thunderclap tore loose and the whole cabin shuddered with the boom, buzzing through the floorboards and along her spine.

Another blast of energy stabbed down, branching into a hundred offshoots like a burning river delta. The cabin shook like an air horn when the sonic boom plowed through it. Aria laughed. "Shiver me timbers."

The tempest grew heavier, more violent. Thunderbolts spiked electric signals along nerve paths linking sky and sea and woman. Each megavolt pulse quaked the cabin on its telephone-pole stilts, and jolted Aria's body lying on the floorboards.

A memory leapt up from her girlhood on the Caribbean island of Curacao, thirty-eight miles off the northwest coast of Venezuela. She was about six years old, gawking at the spectacle of Carnival: people yelled and sang in Papyamentu, Dutch and Spanish; steel drums clink-clanked calypso rhythms; congas pounded a throbbing rhumba. Aria succumbed to the hypnotic sounds and jumped into the streaming swarm of revelers parading down the street. Her mother and aunts had nearly died of fright until they had found her, one hour and one

9

mile later, sweaty and still dancing, as intoxicated by the music as if she had been sipping *Curacao*, the eponymous orange-peel-flavored rum liqueur. After that initiation, Aria had devoted herself to studying dancing and drumming, and had made a career of her love of the music of diverse cultures. *Ethnomusicologist* was her professional title, her Ph.D. earned at Columbia: a fancy label for someone who can't stand still when Carnival dancers parade past.

Now she clearly saw how the same power that had entranced the little girl was contained in the music of storms. Placid lakes did not suit her. She was the girlfriend of gales and wild seas. Her symbol was crashing waves. And lightning. Thunder. That was her true-born nature, the spirit that made her real to herself.

The spirit she felt terrified of losing.

The thunderstorm swept overhead and retreated steadily into the distance like a drum corps marching over the dark sea swells toward the horizon.

Aria pressed warm hands over her face and wept.

Last year, she lost all vision in her left eye. An inherited retinal disease had blinded her grandmother, a great uncle, an aunt and two cousins—all in their forties. Aria was forty-five.

She heard her trembling voice put words to her fear:

"How will I dance when I'm blind?"

3

The thunderstorm spent its passion and weakened to a lazy drizzle. Nat Colt dragged himself into the bedroom and climbed into the king-size bed beside his sleeping daughter. Glowing digits on the alarm clock read 3:24 a.m.

Seeker padded into the bedroom in a three-stride gait. The dog's silvery-blue marbled coat marked it as a blue merle Australian Shepherd.

Nat had owned dogs since boyhood, mostly hunting dogs, nearly a dozen in all. And counting the various hounds that passed through his dad's veterinary office and the dogs of hunting buddies, Nat had personally observed a good-sized pack of purebreds and mutts over the years. None of them could come within a buck's jump of Seeker's intelligence. Best of all, Seeker was a loyal family member. The dog had nearly been fatally wounded defending Nat's wife, Roan, from her murderer. And by tearing a sizable chunk from the killer's hand the dog had provided the only evidence that the house fire that turned her body to charcoal was no accident. That raised Seeker's status immeasurably in Nat's eyes.

"Hey boy," Nat said affectionately. "Lonely? Wanna sleep with your pack mates?"

Before his words were out the dog had hopped onto the foot of the bed. It made an exaggerated yawn and curled up at Jasmine's feet. Seeker now devoted himself to Jasmine with the same fierce fidelity he had bestowed on Roan.

Nat Colt rested in bed beside his daughter and his wife's three-legged guide dog—the remnants of his family.

When Roan was murdered the arson fire had destroyed the southern wing of the Colt home, a taupe-colored Spanish stucco hacienda with a corrugated roof of brick-red ceramic tiles; it perched on a wooded knob overlooking the rolling horse pastures of Hilltop Ranch. Nat had inherited the 90-acre spread from his father, James, who had inherited it from his grandfather, Thomas, who built it.

The fire-ruined wing had been torn down and rebuilt and smoke damage in the rest of the ranch house had been washed away, but the ravage caused by memories proved indelible. A red-haired beauty haunted each room, invisible but present, like a trace of perfume. Friends had advised Nat to move away but he couldn't bring himself to leave. He had been born in the house, which had been in the Colt family three generations. And Roan had loved the site. Besides, if he relocated it would amount to one more loss, chalked up to the killer who robbed him of his wife.

Jasmine had just turned eight when her mother was murdered. Ever since, she had insisted on sleeping next to her father. The precocious and formerly independent tomboy now did not like to be separated from Nat even during normal schooldays. Nat needed her company, too. Father and daughter had done a remarkably good job rescuing each other from the panic of feeling abandoned and alone.

He snuggled close. For the thousandth time in the past month, Nat thought with dread of what would happen to Jasmine if he trailed her mother to an early grave. Nat and Roan had each been an only child, and both sets of Jasmine's grandparents were dead. A terrible guilt turned Nat's heart to lead when he dwelled on the possibility of deserting Jasmine with no one left in the world to love her as he did.

She deserves so much more. He took a deep breath and closed his eyes. He wondered if this was one of those moments when it would be easier to be a Christian. Or a Jew. A Muslim. Hindu. Zoroastrian. *Anything* other than a highly educated cynic on the subject of religious faith. He had been a devotee of hard science since boyhood. He had no idea how to pray; and no confidence in the method in any case.

Open all hailing frequencies, he tried now, and managed to chuckle. *Hello? Beam down the miracle healing rays. Nat Colt wants to live.* Science News: Desperate Atheist Prays to Deity in Whom He Has Never Believed. "And while you're at it, let there be world peace," he added. "Amen."

He remembered something he once read about non-believers: how when an atheist feels truly humble and grateful, he doesn't know whom to thank. But Nat, who often felt grateful, and lately—felled to his knees in front of the toilet bowl—could hardly be made more humble, did not suffer an inability to let his thanks be felt by the people in his life. No, it was the other way around: When an atheist feels really pissed off at the randomness of

13

the universe; the churning, murderous chaos of it all, he has no Maker to blame—no one at whom to scream.

Nat Colt knew what he would yell right now. "You call this a *plan*?"

Jasmine's warm head smelled sweetly of coconut-oil shampoo. The fragrance dug into Nat's heart and un-bottled an intimate memory of his departed wife. Julia Roan McKenzie, the Celtic goddess; Roan of the red, red hair.

Again, Nat's thoughts reached back to the morning he and Roan had met.

He saw his sturdy brown body reflected in segmented squares of shiny white porcelain shower tiles. Naked as a dolphin. Bath towel across the room in his locker. By now she was naked too. *Pray she doesn't take a shower*. If she stepped into the shower room she would scream her head off and he would die from terminal embarrassment.

He stared at the drain in the shower room floor, wishing he could vanish down it. *How do I get myself out of this?*

Suddenly he remembered the wall at the far end of the steel lockers. *Wait a sec*. He risked a quick peek around the corner of the shower room to double-check. *Yes!* A half-dozen urinals stood against the wall, marking the place as male territory.

He mentally sighed with relief. *Men's locker room. At least it's* her *mistake, not mine*. But the problem remained: how to gracefully escape the goofy situation without making them both feel mortified.

Long, wavy, red hair—wavy like the mane of Boticelli's Venus, but deeply scarlet. He had tried not to glance as her swimsuit slipped to the floor, but the red delta between her thighs signaled to him like a flash of fire. Her face must be beautiful, he knew, though she had been looking down and he had not seen it. Some deep symmetry of nature would be disturbed if a figure like hers were joined with everyday eyes and an ordinary nose and plain mouth. One glimpse had impressed all that upon him.

Nat was sure she had not noticed him. He waited, listening. So far, she wasn't heading toward the showers. Now he heard the sound of a towel rubbed across skin. *Just stay put, sister; dry off, get dressed and leave.* He tried to breathe as quietly as a paper fan waving in church.

Suddenly she spoke. "Hello?"

Oh shit. He squeezed his eyes shut and grimaced.

"Why are you hiding in there?" she said. "I don't bite. Come on out—you're spooking me."

"Uh... sorry... don't be alarmed," Nat said. "Everything's cool, but you're in the wrong locker room."

He heard a little gasp.

"Uh... look... I didn't see anything," he said. "I've been in here the whole time and I'm going to stay put in here and wait for you to leave."

He listened for her reaction. Would she make a mad dash out the locker room? He peeked around the corner of the shower entrance. The impact of her beauty swept over him with almost

15

physical force. She had wriggled back into her one-piece swimsuit and was pulling up the straps over muscular shoulders. Her pale skin was custard-smooth, with freckles sprinkling her shoulders and breasts like nutmeg. The metallic silver swimsuit gleamed with feminine curves, bringing to mind *Spirit of Ecstasy*, the chrome hood figurine of Rolls-Royce. In place of backswept wings, he imagined her long red hair trailing like ribbons of flame in the slipstream.

"I'm in the men's locker room?" she said. "I *knew* it didn't smell right in here! But the layout's the same, how I got fooled."

"Ha. Sorry. It's the kind of goof I might have made." His voice warbled and he cleared it. "It's okay, believe me. I didn't look."

"You said that already. Which means you looked."

"But just until I saw you...I mean—"

"If I hadn't heard you, what then? Why didn't you say something?"

"Sorry. I was only trying to save us both from feeling ridiculous. Honest."

She smiled sheepishly. "I shouldn't get mad at you... my mistake... I'm just embarrassed, trying to save face, I guess."

"It's all right," Nat said. "Really. Like I'm glad it wasn't me in the women's locker room. I do stuff like that. By accident, I mean."

Her shoulders relaxed a bit. "Well, aren't you going to come out?"

"I don't have a towel to wrap around me. It's in my locker."

"Doesn't matter," she said. "I'm blind."

"No way." Her eyes shone green from across the room. *How could such lovely eyes not see?*

"Way," she said, nodding. "Believe me."

Slowly he stepped out from behind the tiled wall. "You really can't see?" Her eyes followed him as he crossed the room to his locker and then he knew he had been tricked.

"Damn it, you're not blind. This was a set-up, right? Goof on the freshman, right?" His sudden anger overcame his shyness. "Big deal. Naked guy. Three billion of us on the planet, underneath our clothes."

He threw open the locker door and it banged against the adjacent locker and rattled on its hinges. The humid room reeked of male sweat mixed with Pine-Sol cleaner and generous overtones of Brut cologne and Right Guard deodorant. Nat grabbed a pair of red cotton Jockey shorts and stabbed his legs through the holes.

"Don't get pissed," she said. "I *am* blind."

"Oh yeah?" Nat tugged Levi denim jeans over slim hips. "If you're so blind how come your eyes followed me as I walked over here—how come you're looking straight at me now?"

"Right, sorry." She took on a blank look and let her eyes wander, staring into space. "I'm supposed to look like this, right? Like Patty Duke in *The Miracle Worker*. Gimme a break. My eyes naturally track and focus on a sound source. Actors are always overdoing it when they play blind people. It's insulting."

17

"Okay, if you're blind, how'd you see Patty Duke play Helen Keller?"

"I was blinded in an accident when I was fourteen. I remember a lot."

Now he stared into her bright green eyes for some subtle clue he hadn't detected before. No visible damage. Her eyes shone emerald clear. Yet he believed her. And with the certainty she was blind came a rush of sympathy.

Nat pulled on a royal purple T-shirt over his muscular chest. *It wasn't me they set up, it was her. Or maybe we've both been dumped on.*

"Hey. I apologize," he said. "Let's start all over again." He plopped down on a wooden bench. "My name is Nat Colt. Let me put on my shoes and then I'll walk you over to the women's locker room. I think this whole thing was a set-up, somebody's idea of a practical joke."

"Cindy," she said.

"Hi, Cindy."

"No, it was Cindy—Cindy Warrington— who pulled this prank," she said. "My name is Roan McKenzie."

"Roan. Beautiful name to go with the rest of you." He couldn't believe he had just said that. Normally, he was too shy to flirt, and given he had just spied her in the nude it seemed inappropriate to tell her she was beautiful. How had those words slipped out? But her name fit perfectly. Red hair streaked and highlighted with strands of natural blond, copper and cinnamon, like the beautiful roan-coated quarter horses on his family's ranch in

18

Tallahassee. He checked for a reaction to his blurted remark and was relieved to find the hint of a smile.

"Do you come here often to swim?" she said.

"How'd you know I was swimming?"

"Your bathing suit is dripping on the floor over there: plip-plip-plip. And I heard you swimming laps."

"Heard me?"

"There were only three of us in the pool. The other one was Cindy. I heard a swimmer with the same body size as you. You swam at least a mile."

"Mile and a half. Geez, what do you use, sonar?"

She laughed. "Sort of. Sounds give me pictures sometimes. So do textures, flavors and smells—they combine to form images. Sometimes it's so vivid, it's almost like I can see."

"Wow. Interesting." Probably the wrong thing to say, but the scientist in him had been switched on. "They say blind people develop their other senses more acutely. They've done studies: The part of the brain that normally processes vision gets involved with hearing and the whole sensorium."

She nodded. "I was in one of those studies three summers ago—Johns Hopkins—and it's true; for me at least. I use more than just my temporal lobes to process sounds—PET scan showed I also hear with the part of the brain you see with."

Nat thought about that. With such a keenly sensitized brain, he wondered what it would be like

19

for her to make love. Had she already found out? She looked a little older than him; at seventeen he was still a virgin.

"So who's this Cindy?" he asked. "And why's she got it out for you?"

Roan sighed and shook her head. "Last semester I blew the curve on an organic chemistry final by making a perfect score. The next best score was seventy-one. Now I'm on everyone's hate list. They'd been begging me, you know—"

"To turn it down a notch? Don't show off? I got that all the time in high school—and it was supposed to be a high-ranking school, for the sciences anyway, a place where kids didn't consider you a nerd just because you were smart."

She continued his thought for him. "But the whole school ended up treating you like a threat from Planet Brainiac. Even some of the teachers—am I right?"

He nodded. "Most of the teachers. But I had an awesome physics teacher last year. She got me a scholarship—

"Hey, are you National Science Foundation?"

He hesitated to admit it.

"Cool," she said. "Me, too. So you're the other mutant on campus. A danger to grade curves everywhere."

Nat broke into a grin. "Really?" He couldn't believe his good luck. Roan McKenzie, the luxury-car-ornament-in-the-flesh, was his intellectual counterpart. Last year, as a high-school junior, Nat had been granted a prestigious four-year National

Science Foundation scholarship. Now he was an early-entry college freshman. He had been told another NSF scholar was attending Gulf Coast University.

"That's so cool," he said. "I was supposed to meet you at an orientation dinner tonight."

"This was a bit more intimate than chatting over roast beef and mashed potatoes, don't you think?"

He blushed. "Sorry."

"I'm teasing."

"But now I get it," he said. "See? They're hazing both of us at the same time. Punishment for you, a warning to me. Someone found out I swim every morning before classes." He shook his mop of wooly hair. "What a drag."

She frowned. "Cindy was totally bent out of shape after the final. She's in pre-med, wants to be a surgeon like her dad. Then today she acted like all was forgiven, invited me for an early-morning swim, then showed me to the door of the 'women's locker room'. I even said, 'This isn't the same door I used,' and she told me it was a different entrance. I didn't suspect anything when she didn't follow me in because she said she was heading outdoors to catch some rays."

Nat tied yellow laces on red Converse sneakers. "You didn't suspect anything because you don't go around supposing people will be assholes. Oh hell, don't tell me this is going to be *deja* high school—or worse."

She turned her head toward the door. Even heavy with dampness, her red tresses undulated

21

down her back like rippling heat waves. "I'm sure they're busting a gut outside laughing at how they got us."

"They did us a favor. I'm glad." It *was* more intimate than chatting over roast beef and mashed potatoes.

"Got an idea," Roan said. "Will you help me get out of this stupid stunt with some dignity intact?"

"Absolutely. We're in this together."

"Let's hold hands and stroll out of here smiling, like we're old lovers."

"What about your clothes? I'll walk you to the *real* women's locker room."

"No need. Look." She opened her locker wider and inside he saw a red-white-and-blue gym bag emblazoned with the logo of the U.S. Olympic Diving Team. "One of Cindy's co-conspirators brought my bag here and put it in the same locker relative to the room's layout. She wanted me to feel comfortable getting naked and strolling to the showers."

How thrilling! Nat thought. "What a bitch!" he said. He glanced back at the shower room. "Okay. I'll wait in a shower stall while you get dressed, and I promise I won't peek."

"I'll get dressed later," she said. "C'mon. This is too good to pass up."

Nat gazed at the tall redhead in the gleaming chrome swimsuit and figured pretending they were lovers would give him wet dreams for a week. Already his body was responding to the gush of hormones she set off in his bloodstream. He tucked

22

his T-shirt into his jeans and covertly adjusted his swelling erection. Could she pick up *that* on her sonar screen? He stood, smiling. "Sure. Great idea. I'd be flattered, but... " He wavered.

"What?"

"Well... does it make a difference to you that I'm black?"

"I'm blind, not deaf."

His arched his eyebrows. "My voice?"

"Either you're black or you're one of the Righteous Brothers."

He laughed. "I'll take that as a compliment."

She flung her damp hair across her bare back and smiled wickedly. "Does it make a difference to you that I'm taller than you?"

"You can tell *that* from my voice?"

Her turn to laugh. "Based on angle and direction, I'd say you're two or three inches shorter than I am."

"My mom's really petite," Nat said. He hoped that hadn't sounded apologetic. It's not like he was a midget or anything. She looked six feet, maybe taller.

"My mom was a giantess," Roan said.

"I believe you. What happened, she shrink?"

"Died."

He winced. "Oops."

"It's okay, you didn't know." She shrugged. "Let's go."

He offered his arm. She took hold with long, elegant fingers tapered like candles. Nat wondered if she played piano; if not, the loss was to Baldwins and Steinways.

23

She gave a little squeeze to his bicep and instantly he felt stronger and warmer all over. Just the pretense of being her boyfriend sped up his heartbeat and again his manhood obeyed hormones over willpower. How's that brain response light up on a PET scan?

Maybe this wouldn't be like other schools he had attended. Maybe this would be the beginning of a new, luckier stage of life. About time, he thought. He was past due for a break. It'd be terrific to have a friend—girlfriend?—with a gifted IQ. Conversations about science and stuff that mattered, without having to dumb himself down! And it didn't hurt one bit that she was beautiful.

Together they strolled out of the men's locker room. They pretended not to notice the huddle of students loitering in the hallway that ran alongside the indoor swimming pool. As they ambled past the group, Roan snuggled her arm around Nat's waist, bent her head and kissed his cheek.

The snickering crowd hushed and every jaw dropped as by signal from a choral director. Nat spotted a bleached blond woman meat-packed into a white Speedo swimsuit a full size too small. As Nat passed by arm-in-arm with Roan, the other woman's lips formed an aghast O.

"Think I found Cindy," Nat whispered in Roan's ear. The aroma of swimming pool chlorine, wet hair and warm skin stirred his feelings like fine perfume as Roan McKenzie walked beside him the very first time, down the gymnasium hall and out into the freshness of a new golden day.

24

In the subtropical light doves cooed from magnolia trees studded with white blossoms big as Easter baskets. Though the couple had strolled well beyond the gym, Roan did not withdraw her slender arm from Nat's. That simple fact—and the promise implicit in her touch—meant more to Nat with each step. He looked at Roan and read pleasure in her smile.

Suddenly, from out of the bright sky, shadows swirled over the plaza. A flock of ravens appeared above their heads, circling and cawing menacingly. The soft mewing of the doves turned to screeches of warning. Broad black wings orbited, red eyes glared, orange beaks snapped. Like the doves, Nat felt instant dread. He drew Roan closer and glanced wildly about for the nearest sheltering tree. No safety. The trees were halfway across the world.

Abruptly the ravens swooped down and attacked. Wings churned the air, beaks and talons ripped at clothing and flesh. Nat frantically tried to shield Roan from the slashing assault, but she fell to the sidewalk wrapped in a squawking shroud of killer birds.

From out of nowhere, an Australian Shepherd dog leapt into the squirming black hive, snarling and snapping at wings, tearing one rooster-sized bird to tatters. Then a blur of talons gashed the dog's leg like a stiletto.

Nat yelled, "Roan!" and reached, reached out for her, his best friend, his lover, his wife. But her trembling fingertips were impossibly distant as he stretched out his hand from the far side of the planet.

The squawking grew impossibly loud and hot. Black feathers fluttered like smoke and the ravens erupted in orange-red flames, a mixed fuel of beaks and eyes, the color of murder. A roiling ball of heat blasted Nat backward. The sidewalk buckled and cracked. Roan screamed and her voice caught fire.

Nat awoke bellowing.

"Daddy!" Jasmine yelled and shook him hard. "Wake up! It's just a dream. Wake up! You're having another bad dream."

Nat opened his eyes and bolted upright in bed. A hand-colored lithograph of Tuko-See-Mathla, a black Seminole war chief, faced him from the bedroom wall. Next to the nineteenth-century litho hung a framed wedding photo: Roan McKenzie and Nat Colt at Maclay Gardens, thick garlands of carnations and roses draped around their necks.

Nat groaned. The homicidal ravens were gone, vanished into the ether-realm of dreams. But vanished also was the woman of his dreams who had shared his waking life for so brief a season.

Jasmine's eyes were big with worry and sadness. Seeker hobbled across the mattress and licked Nat's face.

"It's okay," Nat said, patting the dog's thick coat. "Just a nightmare." He squeezed Jasmine's hand. "I'm all right now."

"You called out Mommy's name."

Nat understood why it sounded like an accusation. He had gotten to see Mommy again, while Jasmine had not. She began to whimper and tears started down.

"Shhhh." He pulled Jasmine into his lap and squeezed her whole body against his bare chest. "Shhhh. It's okay." He rocked her like a baby. "I was dreaming about the day she and I met."

Jasmine looked up and managed a smile. "In the men's locker room?"

His eyebrows shot up in mock surprise. "Who told you about that?"

"You did. A hundred times."

"That's because you asked me *two* hundred times."

"Tell me again."

"You know it by heart now, sweetie."

"Please?"

"You really wanna hear that old story all over again?"

She nodded and snuggled under his chin.

Nat took in a deep breath and let it out slowly. Asking for stories about her parents was a ritual Jasmine had fallen into since her mother's death. Nat believed it was her way of keeping the memory of her mother alive; and not just mother alone, but the great dynamic of Mommy-Daddy: the magical strength of The Duo when it was still intact. He felt tempted to begin his narrative with, "Once upon a time," for his love affair with Roan had possessed the grandeur of a fairy tale and had flourished nearly twenty years before her killer destroyed "happily ever after".

27

Nat began his account to Jasmine: "I stepped out of the shower in the men's locker room and found a gorgeous redhead standing there in a silver swimsuit." In the version he told his daughter, Mommy was not peeling off her silver swimsuit, nor did Mommy's sleek nakedness jolt Daddy like an electric shock. But any other details he omitted, Jasmine added in.

When Nat had finished, Jasmine held his gaze. He knew intuitively what she would ask next, and he dreaded the moment of truth.

"Daddy, are you going to die?" Green eyes searched his soul.

What the hell was he supposed to say? *'Fraid so, darling. Daddy is probably gonna be dead within the next half-year—and that's only if he's lucky enough to double the doctor's prognosis.*

"I'm trying my very best not to, baby," he said in a hoarse whisper.

"But are you?"

He saw his reflection in her wet and shiny pupils. Gaunt. Haggard. Yet somehow he didn't feel that it was possible to die. How could he leave her? From the bottom of his heart he needed to tell his daughter that he absolutely would not desert her.

"We're going to be all right," he said. *Somehow.*

"Promise?"

"I promise."

"With a Vulcan handshake?"

He smiled and split the joined fingers of his hand into a V. She did the same and her little hand fit into the king-sized version, interlocking fingers like a dove joint.

"Live long and prosper," Jasmine said, and giggled.

"*Live long*...and prosper," Nat affirmed.

The words had never meant so much to him.

4

Roan McKenzie shoved away a plastic food tray. The rice and beans were cold, like everything else in the air-conditioned hell that had become her life. In the past week she had hardly touched her food, too downhearted to feel hungry. She stood from the meal table and ran her fingertips along the cinderblock wall till she reached her workstation. She flumped into a seat at a desk to face another day in a hidden bunker buried deep inside a nightmare.

The desktop computer was loaded with text-to-voice and voice-to-text functions and additional software and hardware features designed for blind users—most of them Roan's patented designs under the Insight Corporation trademark she shared with Nat.

Her computer spoke to her in a deep male voice that sounded uncannily human: "Happy sunrise, orchard of my eye!" It had been Nat's daily greeting to her, and Roan knew he meant it from his heart, day after day.

She sighed and thought for the hundredth time that maybe she should not have programmed the computer to echo her husband's words. It hurt too much. But to not hear those words of love every morning stole a treasure from each day.

Nat and Jasmine believed she had been killed in a fire. No one suspected the truth and no one was searching for her. Her captors had impressed upon her that rescue was out of the question. They had played for her audiotapes from various news networks reporting on the "tragic death of a remarkable young computer scientist." The anchors' voices grew appropriately solemn: "The blaze killed Julia Roan McKenzie, 40, whose research with a radically new type of computer chip had been expected to earn her a Nobel Prize in physics." A sound bite from one of her former professors described Roan as "a fabulously gifted mathematician who had not allowed the loss of her eyesight to halt her tremendous contributions to the field of computer design."

The report called her case a homicide. No suspects. Roan figured her abductors had substituted a corpse that fit her build, dressed it in her clothes and burned it beyond identification. Her kidnappers had probably planned the house blaze and death to appear accidental, but they'd screwed up somehow and the police had recognized it as murder and arson; but no one had seen through the rest of the hoax. *The whole world thinks I'm a homicide victim.*

Roan thought of Nat and Jasmine and her guide dog, Seeker. Tears filled her eyes and she gulped at a lump in her throat the size of a plum.

At times it was Nat she longed for most; long conversations about science and a thousand interesting things; his rough chin against her cheek; his man-smell; his deep, sonorous voice at kiss-close range. At times she missed her daughter most of all; Jasmine's giggles like tinkling finger cymbals; the simple intimacy of braiding long hair into pigtails or cornrows. And yes, at times she even

31

missed Seeker most; his abject devotion; tail-less body trembling with canine love just to hear her say, "Good dog."

When she thought of her guide dog, tears spilled down. Seeker's furry companionship and seeing-eyes had provided her with untold comfort. Why couldn't they have allowed her the company of Seeker? Dogs tell no tales about secret bases.

Roan wiped her wet cheeks with the back of one hand.

Will I ever hold my family again? Will I ever touch my home, sense the world that is mine? Or will my life end here? Alone.

"Wherever the hell *here* is," she said aloud.

5

Nat glanced at the alarm clock: 4:02 a.m. Jasmine had drifted off to sleep again.

The median basilic vein of his right forearm stung where the IV puncture had dripped chemotherapy solution into his bloodstream this morning—no, *yesterday*—Monday morning. Spaceship Earth had sailed along into Tuesday while Nat lay awake, seasick from the spin of the cosmos, worrying about his daughter.

In a couple more hours, when the alarm buzzed, he would feel like reheated road kill; he would languish in bed all day with a blue plastic basin on the mattress beside him. Wednesday he would feel a bit better; he would get himself up and drag his body around the house like a zombie lurching through some shantytown in Haiti. Thursday, his vitality would begin returning; but he would still feel hollow and dizzy—like a boozer recovering from a lost weekend. Friday, he would begin caring about eating meals again; he would take an evening stroll or easy bike ride around the neighborhood. By Saturday, he would feel ready to romp with his daughter, visit friends, play sax, read, write, think, plan his biophysics experiments— maybe even go out to a restaurant. Sunday he would feel fine—almost like his former self—except for knowledge of the tumor spidering through his brain. Sunday evening he would stay up late, late, late— listening to his stack of jazz CDs, composing on piano, sculpting with clay, watching his beautiful daughter asleep on the sofa near his reading chair, watching the red and white carp flit through the garden pond, watching the stars coil over the horizon, watching carrots grow in the backyard vegetable patch—*anything* but lying down in bed to sleep—to waste these premium happy moments of his abbreviated life.

Then Monday morning, he would take a cab to Tallahassee Memorial Regional Medical Center for a fresh round of poison. Cab home. And the plunge into the dark night of the soul and the week-long ascent to the world of the living would begin again, another creaking turn of the wheel.

Cozying next to his daughter now, he breathed her aroma deep into his heart. Jasmine Amelia Colt: the most precious incarnation in the cosmos.

Jazz, how can I promise to be here for you?

A smothering sense of powerlessness pressed in. He struggled to breathe. It seemed he teetered on a brink and stared down into a bottomless maul. After a time he understood he wasn't staring at death—but at fear and depression—the fate of quitters.

Nat sat upright in bed. *To hell with this. I've always been a fighter. There's no damn use giving up now.* "I'm not dead yet," he said aloud.

From a bed stand he grabbed a pen and notepad he used for jotting middle-of-the-night flashes of inspiration related to the study of human visual functioning. In the faint glow from a nightlight he wrote at the top of a blank page: LIFE

GOALS. Then he scratched that out and wrote: FINAL GOALS.

After that heading, he hesitated, realizing it was tough to rank his deepest desires. Which goal took priority? Over the last few weeks, depending on the emotions of the moment, any of several objectives vied for the lead. Nat glanced at Jasmine and decided his most heartfelt aim was to make sure she would be taken care of by someone who loved her—yes, definitely that was his top goal. He nodded earnestly as he wrote it down. The rest of his objectives followed. The list read:

Find a mommy for Jazz.
Nab Roan's killer.
Develop fully operational cyber-optic
implant.

He longed terribly to accomplish each of those ends, but forced himself to admit he wielded almost no control over the first two goals, and perhaps not enough lifespan left to succeed at the third.

He blew out his breath in a loud sigh and stared at the list, thinking.

Life had a way of yanking the rug out from under your feet. Only in his case it felt as if the whole house had been ripped out from beneath him—floorboards, foundation and all. Ironic how a colleague had spoken of "the gravity of the situation" after Roan had been murdered. Gravity was exactly what Nat had suddenly lacked. He had felt as if he were floating in shoreless space, tethered to his daily life by a fragile line that threatened to snap and send him tumbling into nothingness, adrift and lost, beyond return.

Only Jasmine, with her child's innocence and grace, had kept him sane through those first months of unspeakable grief and loss and guilt. It had taken about a year for Nat to begin to sense solid ground beneath his feet. His body returned to life slowly, like a tundra awakening in spring. One morning Nat noticed the smell of the sun-warmed damp Earth after a rain and he knelt in the wet lawn and wept mindlessly, casting off leaden shrouds of sorrow. When he finally stood, he had accepted the message of the sun and rain and leaves of grass: *Life goes on.*

In the past several months, Nat had returned to his lab with a redoubled intensity, immersing himself in the research he believed would bring vision to the blind. And lately—beyond his expectations—he had felt, not happiness, but at least a sense of acceptance that gave him an inkling of peace. His work was his anchor, strong and righteous as a religious calling, and he was the father of a wonderful daughter who *said* something, *did* something, *made* something every day that brought him pride and delight. He had never bothered about dating or finding a new mother for Jasmine. Overcoming raw grief was one thing, but a year wasn't nearly enough time for Nat to get over the kind of companionship he had lived with Roan.

Then eleven weeks ago, Tom Mercer, an oncologist and friend, diagnosed Nat's inoperable brain cancer—and the turd hit the turbine. Now, a purpose that had not before even been a consideration topped Nat's goals list: to find a mother figure to love and care for his daughter, so when he died Jasmine wouldn't feel as if her lifeline had snapped and she was marooned alone in emptiness.

Nat's other two goals—to track down his wife's killer, and to create a cyber-optic interface for the blind—had at times felt as urgent as bodily needs, like dire thirst or hunger.

Find Roan's killer. God, how he longed to!

One year, one month and twenty-two days ago.

Jasmine was staying overnight with a school friend and Nat was jetting to Australia to attend a medical engineering conference. Roan had been home with only her guide dog. The cause of the blaze had been made to look accidental: faulty wiring in a surge protector. Had it not been for Seeker no one would have suspected foul play and the fire department investigators might not have pressed on until they discovered the evidence of arson.

But Seeker had torn two fingers and a fat wedge of meat from the killer's left hand, breaking out two of his canine fangs in the process. At some point in the fight the intruder had stabbed and nearly severed the dog's right front leg.

The wounded dog's howls alarmed a neighbor who phoned 911. The firefighters were forced to subdue Seeker before they could approach the blaze because the snarling dog would not let anyone near the house.

Hours passed before a member of the TPD homicide division bounced a signal off a satellite to the other side of the world to reach Nat's cellular phone. In an awkward but professional tone, the detective introduced himself and declared it his "painful duty to regretfully inform you, Dr. Colt, that your wife is dead," and that "homicide is probably indicated."

Roan murdered.

Nat had dropped his cellphone. In the instant it took the phone to fall to the lobby floor and smack the polished marble, his pole star was torn out of his sky and every compass smashed.

For the first hour he had been too shocked even to weep. He made it back to his hotel room, but didn't recall getting in the elevator. Slumped on the floor leaning back against the bed, he telephoned the parents of the friend with whom Jasmine was spending the night, because in the morning they were going to drop her off back at home. "You can't tell her over the phone," the friend's mother had said. "Hurry back. We'll keep her safe from the news until you get here." After hanging up, he had labored through an earthquake of vomiting and diarrhea.

The earliest flight back to Florida left the next morning. Nat had stared through the Jumbo Jet's window in a stupor as crestfallen clouds draped the wrinkled sea. For hours, he rehearsed telling Jasmine the impossible. When he finally arrived in Tallahassee he had not slept for two days and he looked and felt subhuman. He could not recall a single word of his tragic conversation with

38

his daughter, but he still winced when he remembered Jasmine's anguished screams.

Nat had officially identified Roan's charred body by means of melted lumps of jewelry found with it: necklace, bracelet, wedding ring—and the engagement ring that he had planted for her to find inside a fortune cookie on Valentine's Day, back when she was twenty-two.

Nat had ordered Roan's corpse to be cremated—completing the job the killer started—reducing it to ashes and tiny chips of bone. Then with a ceramic urn holding her remains, Nat and Jasmine had shoved off for a morning sail into the gulf aboard the 28-foot sloop, *Redheads II*.

Sitting up in bed now, a year later, Nat remembered the most incongruous thing—how weightless Roan had been on that day. It had felt unreal. Not at all believable that a woman who had made such an impact on his life—as John Lennon had meant by his lyric *She's So Heavy*—could have been reduced to a few pounds of calcium phosphate. Roan had been an athlete, six feet tall, a virago, and Nat had many times borne the weight of her astride him—*"O happy horse!"* as Shakespeare put it. During her pregnancy Roan had gained forty pounds—her belly had bulged as round and full as the planet Earth—and after she gave birth to the world's most beautiful baby girl, she had dropped only fifteen of those extra pounds. She had worried about her love handles until she realized there was not an ounce of her 185-pound body that Nat did not honestly adore. Yet on that morning aboard the sailboat on the gulf, the cold ashes of Julia Roan

McKenzie had weighed no more than the hole in the center of Nat's world.

Nat and Jasmine had not been given the chance to tell Roan goodbye. On the sailboat they said their good-byes to ashes. Roan of the fiery mane, reduced to gray flakes sifting through waves. And the water did not even sizzle or steam.

What a joke. He had wanted to laugh. He had wanted to hurl the empty urn into orbit around the moon. He had wanted to topple into the green water with the anchor cord wrapped tight around his neck.

Now as Nat sat in bed thinking of his wife's murderer his heartbeat pulsed hard in his throat, a two-thump meter like a ticker on a time bomb. Finding the killer seemed next to impossible. The crime scene had burned to charcoal and the only living witness was a dog. In one year since the crime occurred, the police hadn't gathered enough clues to fill up a Post-It note.

Nat and the cops had never even come up with a motive. Roan simply didn't have enemies. And the purpose of the break-in wasn't burglary— or at least the burglar was too stupid to recognize valuable property when he saw it. The bulk of Nat's inherited collection of black cowboy and buffalo soldier artifacts and memorabilia had been left untouched in three glass display cases, to be ruined by water and smoke damage. High-end stereo equipment and two computers had been ignored and had melted into blackened paperweights; a hand-me-down Cohn tenor saxophone, which Nat's late uncle had played in a thousand New Orleans gigs and which bore autographs scratched on the inside of the bell by Charlie Parker, Gene Krupa, Louis Armstrong and John Coltrane was left behind, heat-forged into a brass ingot.

What had the killer wanted? What was the goddamn point?

"*Why*?" Nat whispered. The question had burned down to a soreness in his soul. The pain never went away, but only slumbered with one eye open.

To hell with it. Finding Roan's killer demanded a skilled detective team with plenty of time to invest in the case. Nat had no such expertise, and time had become a coin too precious to spend on justice—or revenge. *What difference would it make ultimately? Nothing can bring Roan back to Jazz and me.*

On the notepad Nat scratched out the second goal. Two ambitions remained. The only objectives left in his life that truly counted and could make a real difference. Finding a maternal figure to provide a home with love and security for Jasmine. And creating a technology to bring vision to the blind.

He understood achieving these aims meant surviving brain cancer unfashionably longer than the statistics foretold. At its present pace the tumor would whittle him down to a toothpick before he made it to his thirty-ninth birthday.

How? How can I do it all?

How to accelerate the design and testing schedule at his lab, while wiped out most of each week with severe nausea? How to meet a woman-friend, a mothering type to love his daughter, just when he looked and felt, not like Mr. Clean, but Mr. Contaminated.

He wondered if he might achieve his aims by sheer force of will. He was headstrong, he knew, some would say stubborn. In academics and sports, teachers and coaches had praised his determination, focus and persistence.

But he shook his head. *No way.* He felt utterly drained. The nausea was too much. When it struck, all the will-power in the world couldn't stop his guts from revolting and taking his mind offline. No, he would never be able to concentrate and work intently, much less carry on any semblance of what passed for dating these days. Chemotherapy was his nemesis.

Suddenly, the solution stood out plainly. *That's it. Stop the treatments. No more chemo.*

After all, Tom Mercer was not guaranteeing the chemotherapy would cure Nat's cancer. Far from it. Nat got the feeling his longtime racquetball partner—now his oncologist—had prescribed the poison to keep from feeling professionally helpless in the face of a stricken friend with a devastating illness. Nat had gone along with the program in his desperation to live. Without the treatments, the fatality rate for this type of cancer was one-hundred percent—but the survival rate *with* chemo wasn't anything on which to plan a retirement party.

The crucial thing now was to fulfill his life's mission—not merely to skip the scythe for another year or two. If he obtained his goals his life would be a success no matter what the calendar said. *If I halt the chemo treatments I just might buy myself enough clear-headed weeks—maybe months—to make the right things happen before it's all over.*

Nat signed his name at the bottom of the list, folded the document and put it back in the drawer along with pen and notepad. Then he settled back in bed and a sense of relief eased his mind like a cool cloth on a fevered brow.

Nat laid his hand on his daughter's back. Through cotton pajamas he felt her small, strong heartbeat against his palm. "I'll make it right for you, Jazz," he vowed. "I'll do it, or die trying."

Dawn blushed the bedroom walls a soft rose. The pink wash gradually took on a brightening tint of gold. Wrens and larks began a sunrise song and Nat heard again the everlasting lyrics: *Life goes on.*

He punched the radio alarm clock before it sounded. "Jazz, it's six-thirty." He gave her a gentle shake. "Good morning. Time to get up for school, Swee' Pea."

Nat swung his legs off the bed, pushed to his feet. He wobbled and supported himself against the night stand until he gained balance. The nausea felt all-pervading, as if it extended beyond his body and filled the room and the world with queasiness.

Jasmine watched him, frowning. "Aren't you still sick, Daddy? It's only Tuesday. Stay in bed."

"I feel like a coughed-up hairball, Sugar Babe, but Daddy's got a lot of work—a *lifetime* of work to get done."

6

Underground. Roan knew that much. No sounds of birds or nature down here, and often she heard elevator doors swooshing open and closed outside her room. She had been allowed a few brief escapes outdoors for an exercise walk along a beach, but only at night, and far too infrequently for her sanity. Those trips to the surface had required an elevator ride, but she had not been able to closely estimate the number of floors; she guessed there were at least three or four, but there could be a dozen if it were a high-speed lift.

Roan heard the air-conditioning system kick on and a polar wind poured down from a ceiling vent, fluttering strands of long hair against her shoulders, mocking what she longed for: a warm ocean breeze to comb her tresses. She thought again about cutting off her hip-length mane because, here in hell, it was harder to wash and condition and take care of it. But Nat adored her long hair; somehow, clipping it short would mean she might never see her husband again.

Roan tugged a sweater off the back of the chair and pulled it on atop the hospital-style scrubs that were hell's daily garb. She wondered at the color of the shirt and drawstring pants—medical-staff green or more suitable to her current status? *Roan is modeling a simple cotton leisure outfit, zebra-striped, in a bold, black-and-white prison-inmate motif.*

She had named her mystery locale The Dungeon. "Please don't think of it as a prison," her handler, a man who went by the name John, had said. "We've tried to make it like an apartment. We'll do everything we can to make your stay as comfortable as possible."

Roan had fumed. "Get it straight: This is not a vacation resort and I'm not here as your goddamn guest. I'm your *prisoner*. So you can cut the crap," she spat back at him. "You try being cooped up underground for months on end. You've stolen me away from my family. It's a goddamn dungeon, all right. And I'm your prisoner. Your slave."

"But I *do* stay underground," he said, "and I'm away from my family, too."

"Don't make me sob for you. Tell me, does your family also think you're *dead*?"

He had hesitated. "Actually, yes. They do. I was a college senior when I got, uh, recruited." He paused again. "They...my folks...think I overdosed." He had said no more that day, but turned and left, locking the door to her room from without.

Roan sorted and rotated and flip-flopped every piece of information that came to her, trying to fit the puzzle pieces together into a recognizable picture. She had made an educated guess at the prison's location after John had unwittingly provided her with a clue in the form of fresh flowers he brought to her room. Roan's mother had been a floral gardener, with her own greenhouse. After Roan lost her vision she learned to identify many species of flowers by their shapes and

45

fragrances. John had brought her cuttings of red jasmine blossoms, from which perfumers derive the strongly sweet fragrance called frangipani. She believed the telltale red jasmine and the warm, arid climate she encountered on nighttime walks placed her island prison somewhere within the tropical latitudes of the West Indies—but *where*? The Caribbean Sea was a long blue drink.

In moments when she felt hopeful, Roan reminded herself that her captors had purposefully concealed their identities and her whereabouts—and this was good. If they were actually planning to set her free in exchange for her cooperation—as they had repeatedly promised—they surely wouldn't reveal who they were, where they were, or their master plan. In fact, if they disclosed such details it almost certainly would mean they intended to kill her.

But in fits of despair she doubted this logic. How much longer they kept her alive depended on one simple factor: how much longer she proved useful to them. After all, look what they'd done to the woman whose body had been switched for hers when they'd set fire to the house. Why had they killed that woman? Had she run out of things to offer? Or had they simply murdered her off-the-rack because the victim had the terrible luck of having the same height and build as Roan?

Roan listened through the dark, aware without seeing that video cameras followed her every move. She took a few deep breaths to fight down a wave of claustrophobia. It seemed to her she possessed no life experience of any help in this

46

bizarre predicament; not the slightest idea how to play the game.

In her teens, before her diving accident, Roan had devoured fat technical manuals on advanced computer programming; and when she squeezed in time for books unrelated to computers, she leaned toward romance novels and hard science fiction. How could she have guessed she should have been studying spy novels and James Bond flicks to prep for her future in international "black ops" intrigue?

Roan sighed and rested her head in her hands. Trapped in an underground room, disappeared from her familiar world, she recalled a bumper sticker Nat had read aloud to her in Tallahassee: IF YOU'RE NOT PARANOID, YOU'RE NOT PAYING ATTENTION.

At the time, she had smirked at the raw cynicism. "What's the driver look like?" she had asked.

"A bit like Franz Kafka," Nat had said. "Dark bags beneath manic eyes. Painfully skinny."

"Really?"

He laughed. "Nah. Just a college student, probably. A pierced woman of the black clothes and purple fingernail tribe."

Roan had smiled and then cheerily sang lines from a Simon and Garfunkel tune. *"You said the man in the gabardine suit was a spy. I said, 'Be careful, his bowtie is really a camera.'"*

Roan's trusting nature had kept her from feeling overly suspicious of anything or anybody in those days. Back then, if she bothered to give a

47

thought to CIA, KGB, Mossad, secret agents—all that Spy vs. Spy shit—she would not have believed such operations would ever affect her daily life in the slightest degree. To the extent such machinations were real and not just meal tickets for Hollywood scriptwriters, they happened in another world, far from Roan's Tallahassee home and family.

But her simple faith in a simple life had gone up in flames a year ago. Nothing could ever feel ordinary again.

When her captors broke into the ranch house Nat's grandfather had built, Roan had been alone in her office going over the design for a revolutionary computer information storage and retrieval device, she called a data-cube. Micro-circuitry arranged along three axes mimicked the layout of a neural net in the human brain. The arrangement permitted information to be written-to and read-from points anywhere within a 3-dimensional grid. In theory, the cubic design would surpass the data processing capacity of an ordinary computer chip by mind-boggling factors of speed and volume. It would permit powerful computers to be shrunk to one-hundredth of their present size.

"You've poured the Pacific into a goldfish bowl!" Nat had said when she explained the data-cube's architecture.

Roan had designed the circuitry wholly in her mind's eye. Working in this way was akin to deep meditation; it required unwavering concentration for her to visualize the various elements of the design without benefit of pencil and

48

paper, turning its three-dimensional surface and interior through mental space.

Her focus had been so intense, she never heard Seeker barking, snarling, until it was too late. She had been drugged without a struggle.

Waking up in a sightless void, smelling and touching an alien environment, Roan had at first felt too numb with disbelief to feel afraid. John, with the husky voice, had promised they would release her as soon as she gave them what they wanted: a working model of the computer cube floating in her head.

The panic set in later. It built its nest in her bosom, never far from her attention; always ready to cramp her chest and choke off her breath if she dwelt on her situation.

Roan was terrified to assist her captors. Who were they? What did they intend to do with the technology they'd already killed for? What scheme had she become a part of?

The quandary forced Roan to squarely face the potential military uses of her invention, a problem she had naively pushed out of her awareness in the past. Weapons controlled by such computers would be much more than mere smart bombs—they'd be genius bombs. You could program a thinking land mine to destroy only a vehicle with a certain government license plate, deliver a deadly virus through a subway turnstile according to the DNA of the commuter who pushes past, or break encrypted missile-launch codes and explode ICBMs on their pads—the possibilities went on and on. Cyber-War could get really imaginative, really quick; then all previous high-tech weapons would be as outmoded as flint knives.

On the other hand, it had occurred to Roan that her kidnappers might not be spies with military goals. An alternative scenario could be that this whole caper had been funded by a private corporation motivated by plain old greed—to reap obscene profits from advanced computer design that would annihilate the competition.

In fact, two years ago a South Korean businessman had written letters, made a dozen phone calls, and finally showed up, uninvited, at INSIGHT Vision Research Corporation, the lab Roan and Nat managed together. He had introduced himself as Kim Il Cho, head of a videogame company, Chullima Computer Entertainment Corporation. He said he had read of her theoretical computer designs and felt her research held strong promise for commercial applications in electronic gaming and virtual reality. The man had offered INSIGHT Corporation a mountain of money in exchange for certain exclusive rights and shares in the patents.

"I appreciate your interest in our work," Roan had said, "But our goal is one-pointed: To create an artificial vision system for the blind. We're not interested in pursuing non-medical applications for the device."

"But I can fund you with millions, possibly even billions of dollars in research grants," the man had said, "and I can provide a design team with dozens of top designers and fabricators to work under your direction. With that kind of assistance you could forge ahead with your vision project. The design elements my company ends up applying to computer gaming would be a by-product of your success. It would be—how do you say it?—a win-win situation."

"Fortunately, our lab is not in need of sponsors," Nat had answered for her. "And we like the way we do things—at our own pace. We've intentionally maintained this project as a small and strictly-controlled enterprise. We don't want military types or corporate types looking over our shoulders." Nat had put his arm around her waist. "So far, only Roan knows the design for the data cube. We want to keep it that way."

The Korean had persisted, becoming a major pain. Nat had grown defensive and finally, angry. At last, Nat had taken the guy's arm and escorted him to the door. Roan could hear the swish of Kim Il Cho's suit coat as he bowed and turned to walk out. She and Nat had never bothered about him again.

But the guy had offered vast wealth and a design team. A man with those resources would easily be able to hire agents to grab Roan and wring the knowledge out of her. Or maybe Cho himself was a secret agent. Maybe he had just been there to scope out the lab and plant bugs, tiny hidden cameras. He had, in fact, excused himself to use the toilet; that Roan remembered clearly.

Paranoia. Boy was she good at it now.

South Korea. Which, of course, might really be North Korea. Same language, foods, customs, same looks, right? Easy enough to fake a passport.

51

North Korea had become isolated from the rest of the communist world, Roan thought. The USSR had slumped over and died with vodka on its breath. Cuba was wheezing on its last cigar. And the new, improved China now had its own country club of capitalist millionaires. All of which left North Korea stranded, alone, a guppy among sharks. North Korea was desperate. A desperate government will go to great lengths to save its economy and power, its face. Roan was learning.

But although she had spent many hours obsessing about it, the enigma was still intact.

Who are these phantoms and what are they planning to do with my data cube?

Roan had never thought of herself as a heroine, but it was hard not to concede that the patriotic thing to do would be to tell her captors to take a flying fuck at a rolling won-ton. She didn't trust their promise to release her anyway.

But when they'd recited a complete schedule of Jasmine's school days, including her friends' names and addresses, piano teacher, riding stable—everything—Roan took them at their word to torture her daughter to death if Roan refused to cooperate. In the past year, she gave the team of scientists everything they asked for. She had managed such consulting via conference calls, talking to men and women with digitally-disguised voices. They took their cloak-and-dagger roles very seriously in Nowhere Land.

A cursory knock at the door broke her reverie. Without waiting for an invitation an outer lock turned and the heavy door slid open on silent hinges.

7

"Good morning, doctor." The man with the hoarse voice. John.

She did not turn in her chair to face him. "Is it a good morning? I wouldn't know."

"Most definitely."

He came and stood beside her at the desk. He wore his habitual cologne. Roan would recognize the fragrance anywhere for the rest of her life, she thought, and it would probably make her inwardly shudder as it did now.

"Today I have great news," John said, "something special to present to you—a working model of the cube, manufactured from your design."

A spark of hope flared in her chest. "I see. You've been busy."

"Ha. Not me. I wouldn't know a computer chip from a buffalo chip. But yes, three teams have been working on the project round-the-clock."

Roan turned up her face toward his voice. "John, if it's finished then let me go. I gave you what you needed to make a data-cube. I want out of this, I want to go home."

"But you know we can't do that yet," he said, and placed a hand on her shoulder. She repressed a flinch. "The project is just beginning. The cube must be implanted. We've got to make it work in a human subject. Then we can let you go."

Roan recoiled as if an invisible hand had slapped her hard. *"What?"*

54

"We need you as consultant until we can be sure the data cube functions in a human brain."

She shot to her feet. "You're going to implant it? But... for what?"

"As part of an artificial vision system, of course."

Roan gripped the armrests of her chair, dizzy. Nothing was making sense. All this mayhem—kidnapping, burning a corpse to fake Roan's accidental death, imprisoning her for a year—for what? To create an artificial vision system? The very same goal toward which she and Nat had been striving. Since when were government agents intent on aiding the blind? These murderous bastards cared about visually-impaired people? Or...what? Money? Money from medical-engineering patents? But there was much more money to be made in weapons and entertainment than in enabling the blind to see.

"I'm confused," Roan said shakily. "Why are you doing this? Was this your plan all along?"

"Yes. I'm not at liberty to disclose more. But yes, we wanted to perfect an artificial vision system. We learned that you and your husband had made a quantum leap with your design. So we...borrowed your expertise."

Roan shook her head and sank to the chair.

"Now we need you to evaluate its performance. We've followed very closely your husband's successes with blind chimpanzees. We're going to skip all that and implant the device in a man. Fine-tuning may be required. We trust we're close to the optimal design, but it may be a matter

55

of a few trips back to the drawing board." He touched her arm again. "And frankly, doctor, your mind *is* the drawing board. So you're far too crucial to this mission to let you walk away just yet. I mean that, most sincerely, Roan—as a compliment."

His voice had changed tone, in the way it sometimes did. She hated it when he called her by her name. Roan sensed his eyes undressing her and it made her feel exposed. Both the scrubs shirt and sweater she wore had a deep V-neck and she knew her ample cleavage showed. Did John select her wardrobe? She wished she wore a high-collar Victorian-era blouse with the top button fastened under her chin; hell, she wished she were draped in a *burqa*.

"You're a ...brilliant woman," John said and began to gently knead her shoulders.

Roan shrugged off his touch, pushed away in the rolling chair and spun to face him. "I don't feel brilliant. I feel homesick. I'm sick down to my soul of this dungeon you've stuck me in. I want to be with my family, my *husband*."

"All in good time."

"Yeah. Fuck you, too."

God how she longed to hear the birds and insects, smell something more earthy and alive than paint, stainless steel, Lysol spray and filtered air.

"Look, can you at least let me out of here briefly, for a stroll?" Roan said. "Just let me breathe some fresh air, feel the sun and wind on my face. I'm going nuts. I can't even remember what the sea smells like, let alone concentrate on microcircuits."

56

"What about your exercise station?" John said. "You hardly ever use it. It's got a treadmill and—"

"Go stick your dick in the gears of that treadmill, I'll hit the START button." She spun in the chair to turn her back to him. "Before I was 'borrowed' from my home, I used to swim laps, several miles a day. Got a lap pool handy?"

After a pause he said, "I might be able to arrange another night walk along the beach."

"The sun!" she said with quiet intensity. "The sun!"

"You know we can't allow—"

"I mean it!" she screamed and jumped up and shoved a tape recorder off the desk. The plastic console bounced off the cinderblock wall and smacked the tile floor with a splintering crunch.

"Okay, okay—just take it easy," John said, "I'll see what I can do."

"Let me out into the daylight." *You fucking asshole.* "Today and every day from now on. Or I'll not be able to help you one bit. My concentration is shot. I'm burning out down here in this dungeon, get it?"

"Give me an hour. I'll get back to you. Stay put."

She smirked and rolled her eyes. "Duh."

After an extra-long hour, John returned and escorted Roan up, up into open air and sunlight. The ankle-sting of windblown sand. Crying gulls. Wind caresses and seaweed-breath and the susurration of breaking waves.

57

John absolutely refused to let her go swimming. But he allowed her to slosh barefoot through surging foam. Her long hair billowed in the salty breeze. Her skin could breathe again.

A couple hours later—*paradise lost*—John led Roan back up the volcanic mountain trail toward the vault-like entrance to the underground quarters. At one point he grasped her upper arm and she recoiled from his touch.

"I know you take pride in being independent," he said, "but this spot isn't safe." He took her arm again, more firmly, and guided her past an area where the trail had turned to smooth rock.

An abrupt change in air-currents told Roan they were crossing a break where trees no longer hugged the rocky slopes on the seaward side of the trail. Waves boomed far below, rolled back gurgling loudly, then *kashoom*, tons of white water slammed the island again at the base of the mountain and sea spray misted her cheeks.

"A cliff?" Roan drew back farther from the ledge, afraid.

"About a hundred feet, straight down to the sea. Reminds me of those sheer cliffs in Acapulco where the locals do those suicidal dives for the tourists."

Kashoom. Seawind whooshed up from below, tousling Roan's tresses. She pictured in her mind the long vertical drop to the water and shuddered. More than two decades had passed since the diving accident blinded her, but she had not gotten over her post-traumatic fear of heights. It

58

was hard to remember the teen-age girl who had thrilled to dive from high places, who thought the 10-meter platform wasn't daring enough and ventured with her dive-team buddies to the cliffs of the local limestone quarry to plunge into deep cobalt water from 50 feet above. She even had dived from an 80-foot ledge. Once. It turned out to be more scary than thrilling.

Those were the highest dives she had ever braved. Then she watched a documentary about the professional divers in Acapulco, Mexico—soaring like swans off the 125-foot cliff at La Quebrada. At fourteen, she had vowed that one day she would dive at La Quebrada herself. But now, just knowing she was close to a cliff scattered her courage like the shore-break sends the sandpipers darting. She hurried on past the place of danger.

A quarter-hour later Roan and John arrived at the passage back down to the Underworld. "Where do you guys keep Cerberus chained?" she asked.

"*Who*?"

"You know, the three-headed guard dog. Greek mythology."

They passed through the security gate and entered the short tunnel that led to the elevators. "What the hell are you talking about?" John said.

"*This* hell. I'm talking about *this* hell." The elevator doors shut behind them, pinching off the sounds of wind and sea. "Cerberus guards the gates of hell." The floor fell away for an instant as the car started its descent.

That night, in her lonely chamber buried under dunes and lava rock, cut off from the fragrant breath of the living Earth, Roan's hair yearned for the sea wind to come calling again with its caresses and sighs.

8

Aria Rioverde lounged on a comfortable, if somewhat battered, olive-colored leather couch in the office of INSIGHT Vision Research Corporation. Her gaze wandered the small room and found its masculine decorum strongly appealing. She wondered if that spelled trouble. It might be tough to get her message across firmly if the guy she was waiting to confront turned out to be a hunk with excellent taste and natural charm.

She rolled her eyes at the thought. Damn horniness! Ten months without a boyfriend had begun to gnaw at her independent spirit. Daily, her female hormones posted chemical messages in the primitive pathways linking brain to crotch. *Urgent* messages. And for nearly a week now a tune had been stuck in her head: "I Want a Man with a Slow Hand."

Girl, use your own *hand.* She chastised herself for sinking to a teen-age level of emotional vulnerability. *So you're lonely and horny. Just don't add dumb.*

Besides, Aria told herself, chances were good the man she was waiting to go up against would turn out to be a nerd with vinyl pocket protectors, tri-color ink pens, mechanical pencils—the classic dork in a lab coat. She had promised herself the next time she got involved with a citizen from Mars—from where men are rumored to hail—the Martian would be required to exhibit a fully functioning personality: body, mind and heart.

Aria smoothed a yellow silk dress over her thighs, opened a manila folder in her lap and glanced at her notes. Nat Colt, M.D., Ph.D. She had downloaded the first few pages of his fat resume off the internet: medical specialties in neurology and ophthalmology, doctorate in medical engineering, full-time research physician. Studied psychology and physiology of perception at Johns Hopkins; postdoctoral research at Schepense Eye Research Institute, Harvard; former editor, *Journal of Mathematical Psychology*; former director of the Vision Group at NASA Ames Research Center. All that, and the guy was five years younger than her.

She whistled low. This guy made the average genius look like a slacker. He was a fellow of The Israeli Academy of Neuroscience, The European Conference on Visual Perception, and a dozen other international science societies from which he had received numerous honors and awards.

Author of *CYBER-OPTICS: A Heuristic Approach*; *Dimensional Modeling of Human Visual Processing Via Hierarchical Computational Structures*; and *Thresholds for Wavelet Quantization Error in Neuro-Cybernetic Imaging*.

Neither of those titles struck Aria as a great beach read. Nor did the next batch: *Fuzzy Logic in the Encoding of Human Vision*; *Interpolating Holonomic Data in Stereo Photogrammetry*; and *Image Interpretation Strategies for Artificial Sight: A Cognitive Architecture*.

"English, please." She chuckled. Yep, he'll probably look like Bill Gates' long-lost twin—with an even goofier haircut. On the other hand, she made a mental note not to be intimidated by a brainy scientist who might raise a shield of jargon-speak as soon as she introduced herself and the reason for her visit.

But as for Dr. Colt's taste in furnishings, he could decorate her little bungalow anytime. For starters, he didn't own one of those gargantuan mahogany desks, like some dictator of a banana republic; furniture designed to emphasize the importance of the person enthroned behind it, while robbing significance from the supplicant perched before it. Rather, a small rattan desk held a single black *raku* vase with an *ikebana* flower design: two delicate purple-and-gold orchids supported by a thin shoot of green bamboo. Lovely, Aria thought. Subtle.

The walls weren't decorated with traditional duck-hunting prints of camouflage-garbed men with shotguns blasting migrating waterfowl out of the sky. Instead, to one side of the desk hung a framed sepia photograph of a Native American squaw nursing her baby while weaving a blanket on a loom. Twin buns of black hair perched over the woman's ears, and a hammered-silver-and-turquoise necklace rested above bare breasts. Aria guessed the Indian was Navaho or Zuni. Like the flower arrangement, the antique portrait was graceful and understated.

The feminine touch of the flowers and photo art was balanced by the decidedly macho display of two six-shooter handguns in an oiled teakwood rack on the top shelf of an oak bookcase. A brass plate read: Nat Love's 1875 Colt .44 Frontier & 1878 Colt .45 Peacemaker.

Guarding the guns from the top shelf of an adjoining bookcase stood a foot-tall bronze figurine of a black cowboy, shoulder-length hair spilling from beneath a sombrero, a randy look of toughness on his square-jawed handsome face. The miniature man wore a rodeo shirt and neckerchief, jeans, fringed chaps and boots with spurs. A low-slung holster belt with cartridge slots hung from one outthrust hip. A Western saddle lay on the ground in front of him, rope coiled around the pommel. He stood with one hand on his pistol grip and the other holding a repeating rifle. A baseplate identified the figure as Nat Love, Black American Cowboy.

Aria pictured herself the size of a Barbie doll standing on the top shelf all gussied up like a dancehall queen in a décolletage ruffled blouse and hoop skirt. She sashayed over to the dangerously good-looking cowboy named Love. *What if he insisted on having his way with me? Those muscular arms would pull me close, those full lips an inch from mine, those veined hands reaching up under my skirt...*

She chuckled at herself. "There you go again, girl. Geez Louise."

She switched her focus back to the manila envelope. Who was this researcher she was about to engage in battle? No pictures of the guy.

Aria stood and peeked at two framed photos on the desk. The smaller of the two held a candid shot of an adorably cute mixed-race girl playing at the seashore and grinning widely, revealing two missing front teeth. The larger portrait showed a stunning redhead whose emerald eyes and facial features announced she was the girl's mother. Aria realized the president of INSIGHT must be of African heritage, and he was married to a Caucasian woman. *Interesting.* Score ten respect points for the doctor. As a person of several blended races herself, Aria naturally felt drawn to people who lived and loved as if color-blind.

She noticed that Dr. Colt had jotted notes on a coffee-stained Mister Donut napkin and on a flattened white paper bag from Taco Bell. His scribblings struck her as further examples of an unbreakable cipher.

On the unfolded napkin he had written:

- *Complexity constraints imposed by natural retina on geometric mapping in visual cortex?*
- *Robust feed = Solution to neural morphometry problem?*

On the white paper sack, he had scrawled:
- *How much data can be compressed/decompressed via computer-neural interface?*
- *Upper limits for data input/processing?*
- *What would patient SEE?*

A man's deep voice surprised her. "See any potential for a bestseller?"

Aria looked up, feeling guilty. "Oh. Sorry. I'd been waiting a while…"

Damn. First rule of confrontation: Don't let them catch you off guard.

He smiled. "Didn't mean to spook you." He extended a broad hand. "Nat Colt."

"Hello. I'm Aria Rioverde." She grasped his hand and gave him a quick study. His strong hand felt warm and good. Not a nerd. Not a hunk. Though certain clues told her Nat *had* been a hunk in better days. Now he looked really haggard, as if he had suffered the flu non-stop for a year or two. Wooly fuzz sprouted on his recently shaved scalp; he definitely wasn't the type who looked great bald. But he did have sexy eyes, shiny black as obsidian; a straight bold nose like she had observed in tribal peoples in Ethiopia; and a voice as deeply sonorous as a stringed bass. He wore no polyester lab coat, but rather, a deep red cotton T-shirt over faded blue jeans and lived-in boat shoes.

"How can I help you?" Nat asked.

"Are you the author of this paper?" Aria reached into her manila folder and slapped down on his desk a reprint from an article in *Visual Neuroscience*. The paper was titled, *Cyber-Optic Brain Implants: Trials in Six Blind Chimpanzees.*

Nat glanced down at the reprint then fixed his gaze on her. "What's this about?"

"How can you bring yourself to do that?" Aria demanded, tapping the paper with her index finger.

"Beg your pardon?"

66

"Chimpanzees are sentient beings. They have feelings, just like you and me. Yet, in the name of science, you blinded six chimps to conduct your tests. That amounts to torture."

Nat's face hardened. "I see. Who do you represent, PETA?"

"I'm president of the local chapter of SPARE." *Not to mention, its secretary, treasurer and sole member.*

He shook his head and shrugged.

"Society for the Promotion of Animal Research Ethics," she said. "We're a less militant organization than PETA, so you ought to be glad I came across this article first. If I represented PETA, we wouldn't be having this chat. There'd simply be a break-in after midnight, and your lab animals would be liberated."

"Then I'm glad it was—"

"Doctor, are you aware that ninety-eight percent of our human DNA is identical to the genetic code of chimpanzees? We at SPARE consider ourselves the 'Voice of the voiceless'—"

"Wait." He held up a hand. "Before you launch into your spiel, I want you to know I didn't blind those chimpanzees."

She frowned. "Then who did?"

He waved away the insinuation. "Chimpanzees suffer congenital and accidental blindness just like humans. You said yourself— they're a lot like us. I've got ads in a dozen exotic-pet trade sheets around the U.S. and Canada. When a zookeeper or breeder comes up with a blind chimpanzee, he ships it to me." He half-smiled. "I

67

could never blind a chimp; I'm way too soft-hearted. Really." His eyes met hers and she instantly believed him. "And you're absolutely right about lab animals deserving to be treated ethically, humanely. It really pains me to see—"

"But you placed implants in their brains," Aria said. "Brain surgery. What about that? Did you ask their permission?"

Nat gestured toward the olive-colored couch. "Won't you please have a seat? I'd like to tell you a little about my research. Let's try to understand each other's position a little more clearly." The tone of his resonant bass voice conveyed patience and tolerance, a genuine willingness to communicate.

Aria had already awarded him respect points when he said he had not blinded the chimps. Now she gave him more respect points for not getting defensive or abusive, something she had encountered plenty of times, even from public relations flacks at big corporate labs. And this guy handled his own P.R. She guessed the entire operation of the small lab was a one-man show. She sat on the leather couch, knees together, and smoothed her yellow silk dress with both hands. *Should have worn something more formal, businesslike. Yeah—as if I owned such an outfit.*

"Can I get you anything to drink?" Nat asked. "I've got Coke and iced tea in the fridge, and it wouldn't be any trouble to brew a fresh pot of coffee."

"No thank you. I'm here to talk."

He sat at the other end of the couch, angled to face her. "Let me begin by saying I don't wish to make myself sound purely innocent," he said. "Years ago, when I was in grad school I performed experiments on live animals that make me cringe now when I look back. I'm not sure how I justified it at the time, or if I even tried. It's what my professors were doing and expected of me, and I went along with it."

"That's the plea of German soldiers at the death camps," Aria said. "'Just following orders.'"

His eyes flinched. "We weren't exterminating the animals out of genocidal hatred, surely you must see that. We were learning how to surgically repair congenital retinal defects. We learned a great deal. Our research has restored the eyesight of hundreds of newborns."

"I'm sorry," Aria said. "That wasn't fair of me. That's the kind of crap PETA spouts—why I dropped out of that group."

Nat's features softened and he touched her hand with his fingertips. It was a simple and genuine gesture of peace. She liked it. A lot.

"I suppose that in some ways the comparison is too close for comfort. Hurts to hear it." He sighed. "I'm not sure what woke me up to empathy for the animal's plight. I believe it had to do with falling in love with my wife, Roan." For a moment his eyes turned slightly inward, toward a well-lit memory. "A lot of what's best in me has to do with her," he said quietly, more to himself than Aria.

69

Nat looked up again. "Anyway, Roan was the quintessential animal lover." He smiled warmly, teeth bright in a gaunt, brown face. "She would've supported what you're doing here today."

Aria raised her eyebrows, questioning.

"She passed away about a year ago."

"Oh, I see. I'm sorry."

He nodded. "In any event, I can assure you I really do my best to see that the animals in my lab don't suffer. I always use anesthesia and sterile technique. And post-surgically I use sterile dressings and antibiotics and pain medication. Exactly as if the animals were human patients in a hospital setting. Also, I have a fenced-in acre so the animals can play outdoors. I treat them well—fresh fruit, vitamins, clean water, plenty of fresh air and sunshine, care for their illnesses; I even give them pet names—"

"Yes. But they don't sign consent forms," Aria said, "and I doubt they *want* to be operated on."

He sighed again. "What you say is true, Aria, but here's the dilemma: Do you leave the animals alone—in this case, blind chimpanzees who'd be put to death by pet store suppliers or zoo owners. Or do you allow them the opportunity to contribute something meaningful to life, to not die in vain?"

"Meaningful to the chimpanzees?"

He smiled. "*You* said they're sentient. I swear to you, some of these animals are so sweet-tempered I believe if they could understand and talk they'd say, 'Yes, let me have a chance to help blind people around the world to see.'"

Aria felt unconvinced. "There could be a lot of money in developing such a device, no doubt."

"No doubt."

"Millions of dollars."

He nodded. "Billions."

Aria waved her hand around the office. "So why aren't you in plush corporate digs, with hot and cold running lab assistants?"

"Let's just say I don't like the way the big labs treat their animals—human and otherwise. I need freedom to go with my intuition and try new, radical ideas, without having to explain my every move to execs in five-hundred-dollar business suits. They don't seem to grasp that failures are as useful, as informative, as successes. And besides, I can't stand all the politics and paperwork, and..." He blinked. "Sorry. You got me started."

Aria shook her head. "I get the hunch there's more to it than that," she said. "Something about this research is very personal to you. That's why you've got to do it your own way, because the whole thing carries so much..." She closed her eyes, looking for words to describe her insight. "I see your quest as almost religious—an individual resolve—like the vow of a monk."

"What is this, the psychic hotline?"

She opened her eyes and read his face. *Bingo.* "Call it what you want, I'm right on target."

He brooded for a moment. "Okay. Yeah. You're right about the personal quest." He stood and faced her, leaned back against the desk. He was

71

silent for a long pause. Aria waited, sure he was about to reveal his heart.

"When I graduated from college," he said quietly, "I married a woman I'd met there as a freshmen." He smiled. "Julia Roan McKenzie. She'd been a talented young diver on a fast-track to the Olympics. But at age fourteen she slipped on a dive from 10 meters...remember when Greg Louganis hit his head on the dive platform in Seoul?"

Aria nodded. "Ouch!"

"Same move. Reverse take-off, struck the back of her head. The concussion knocked her out and she slammed the water face first. When her teammates fished her from the bottom she was in a coma. The medical personnel were so busy keeping her brain from swelling and draining water out of her lungs that no one noticed the impact had detached both retinas. By the time she woke up and they discovered the injury, it was too late to save her sight. They tried surgery, it failed. She remained blind."

Aria felt stunned. "Your wife..." She glanced toward the desk. "The gorgeous redhead in the photo?"

Nat nodded and pride showed in his black eyes.

"That's so tragic."

"Yes. But Roan had a great spirit. She never complained. Never cursed her fate or hated life. She spent her energy living." He looked at the back of the wooden photo frame on his desk. "Roan was...she *is* my inspiration."

72

"And you dedicated your career to developing the means to restore her sight." *God, how romantic!* Major point-bonus.

"She worked on the project, too. She was a great theoretician. Mathematician. But…well, she didn't live long enough for us to find a breakthrough." He turned and picked up the framed photo and gazed at it. "To me, that's the real tragedy," he said softly.

Aria swallowed past a lump in her throat. "I'm so sorry for you."

"I'm a year late. But I'm ready now." It seemed to Aria that Nat spoke the words to his dead wife. "I've done it."

"Done what?" Aria asked.

Nat turned toward Aria and pinned her with a piercing gaze. "Do you believe in synchronicity? Fate? Karma? That sort of thing?"

"Sure. Happens to me all the time."

"Well, funny thing is, I don't." He gave a little laugh. "In fact, I once wrote an article for *The Skeptical Inquirer* in which I debunked such notions. Called it wishful thinking. Humbug." His eyes continued to bore into hers. "But then again, here you are."

Those bright black eyes. Aria couldn't tell if they merely reflected light or positively emitted it, only that they shone with a contagious intensity. "What do you mean?"

"Just when I need you, you show up." He whipped out a penlight from his desk drawer. "May I take a closer look at your eyes, please?" Without pausing for an answer he bent close and aimed the bright beam into her left eye.

Aria did not blink.

"You're blind in this eye." It was a statement, not a question. He said it as if the liability was her best asset.

"Yes," she said. "Since seven months ago."

"Macular degeneration."

"That's right." It felt strange to Aria to permit this male stranger to peer deeply into her eye as if it were an open window—if not a window of her soul, then at least, of her genes. His lips were only inches from hers, as if poised for a kiss.

Nat stood and turned. "One moment, please." From an equipment cabinet he retrieved some type of magnifying scope attached to a plastic headband. He put on the band and flipped the scope over his right eye, clicked on a bright point of light, adjusted the lens. Again he stared into her left eye. After a moment he examined her right eye. When he stood and took off the headband, a thin smile played at the edges of his mouth.

"Have you had lunch?" he said. "I know a little health food hut near FSU campus, students rave about it."

Her guard went up. "Lunch?"

"I'd like to tell you of a way you can help spare the chimpanzees. No more animal experimentation."

A mix of hope and caution stirred in Aria's chest. "What are you getting at? How can I help?"

"Let's discuss it over food. I'm famished. Come on." He took her hand and helped her to her feet.

9

The Rainforest Cafè on College Avenue was dim and cool inside like a grotto, crowded with university students and faculty. Sunrays from a central skylight gilded a three-foot cascade gurgling into a carp pond surrounded by an indoor jungle of ferns and peace lilies. New Age piano music trickled from speakers like Valium through an IV drip. To Nat Colt, the restaurant's ambience seemed designed to sedate a sloth, but Roan had liked the healthy food.

Aria Rioverde strolled with Nat to a glass-topped wrought-iron table with padded wrought-iron chairs. She moved with a lithe, sleek grace, as if she were a member of the cat family.

Aria was as dusky and petite as Roan had been fair-skinned and towering. Smooth skin the rich color of caramel, and almond-eyes that suggested an Asian fold at their inner corners. Irises shone clear, dark yellowish-brown, the tint of strong-brewed Darjeeling tea. Nat guessed Aria's driver's license listed her eye-color as "hazel", but in expensive paint-sets the color was labeled "Burnt Umber." Her straight, broad nose complemented high cheekbones and a neck as long and regal as Nefertiti's. The sum of Aria's features fairly sang her mixed ancestry.

Nat could see Aria's heritage included Asian and African roots, and he suspected her high-ridged nose flaunted Hispanic genes. Her black tresses reflected a bluish sheen—thicker than Asian and straighter than African hair—yet somehow a luxuriant hybrid of the two. She wore a longish pageboy haircut with bangs that swept asymmetrically down one side of her face. Nat was an enthusiast of hip-length red hair, but he found Aria's short hairstyle appealing; it dramatized the flawless sculpture of her face.

A sleeveless yellow dress emphasized slender, muscular arms. Her breasts were small enough to behave without a bra; in the deep V of yellow cotton Nat noticed their soft slopes overlying hard muscle. He wondered at her age and was stumped. Body-wise, she could pass for a fit, athletic college co-ed, but the crinkles around her eyes betrayed her true years as—what? Late thirties?

Nat considered Aria uncommonly beautiful and poised, but he also recognized that their styles did not match. She wore a tiny diamond stud in one nostril, elaborate shell-and-bead ear rings, and a necklace of exotic *rudraksha* from India— decorative seeds the size of plum pits. On the rounded muscle of her left shoulder a tattoo of three intertwined carp, red, blue and yellow, swam in an eternal triskelion of primary colors. The tattoo struck Nat as oddly familiar—a Shinto design, he thought. Had she gotten it in Japan?

Nat had not forgotten his urgent goal of finding a mother figure for his daughter, but Aria was definitely not a candidate for that role. Too young, whatever her actual age, too artsy-cool, too independent, too...*hip*. Not the mommy-type.

77

A waitress arrived, wrapped in a personal cloud of patchouli oil. She wore an oversized, black cotton men's shirt, tied at the waist, and a black leather miniskirt over black Doc Marten boots. She had platinum quarter-inch spiked hair, and sterling silver studs through eyebrows, nose and lower lip; her earlobes were decorated top to bottom with stacks of silver rings and charms. When she bent to pour iced water, her unbuttoned shirt sagged open and Nat glimpsed silver bars through both nipples. He suppressed a wince. *Ouch.*

The waitress, tinkling like a charm bracelet, dropped off menus at their table and hurried to the next table balancing a tray of cinnamon-sprinkled cappuccinos.

Nat studied Aria again. In comparison to the waitress, she now looked as staid and demure as the Black Madonna—with a diamond nose-stud.

"Aria Rioverde," Nat said, as if tasting her name on his tongue. "What's your middle name?"

"Carmen."

"Your parents were opera buffs?"

"Of course."

"But your accent is—what?—West Indies?"

She nodded. "Curacao. Dutch island in the Caribbean Sea."

"Off the northern coast of Venezuela."

"Very good." She poured on her accent thickly: "So you say, mon, dat we Rasta be too clot for de opera?"

Nat felt sheepish. "Sorry. A culturally biased assumption."

She laughed. "I'm teasing you," she said. "My mother sang contralto in the Operà Nacional de Venezuela, my father was a cellist in the national symphony in Caracas. But my aunts and grandmother raised me on Curacao. Everyone I knew growing up was into reggae, ska, calypso, salsa, mambo, American rhythm and blues, jazz and soul music. Personally, I don't connect with opera. Too stiff for my blood. I love to *dance*."

"Then I take it you're not a big fan of this music they're medicating us with now." He glanced up at ceiling speakers. Synthesizer notes from Kitaro drizzled on their heads.

Aria snorted. "What do you get when you play New Age music backward?" She paused. "New Age music."

He laughed. "Perfect." He swigged the ice water; it had sprigs of spearmint floating in it. "Well, you certainly look like a dancer. Feline. Either a dancer, or a panther."

She smiled. "Thank you. I like that. I've been dancing professionally since I was fourteen. Actually, for about twenty minutes, I was even married to Randy James."

Nat shrugged. "I'm not familiar with the dance world."

"He was a very big name in the fields of ethnic dance, ethnomusicology: a major choreographer and performer."

"Was?"

"Randy died of AIDS."

"Oh. Sorry."

79

She nodded. "That was...twenty-one years ago. We'd been divorced six years by then."

"So you married him when you were—what?—four years old?"

She gave a pretty laugh. "Eighteen."

He shook his head. "My math is botched. You *can't* be forty-five."

"Says I am on my driver's license. But thanks for the compliment."

She sipped her water and plucked a soggy spearmint leaf from her full lips. Her eyes had focused inward. "Randy was my mentor and a good friend. I miss him. I never should have married him, really; we were married less than a year. He was just a great buddy. Funny and charismatic and *so sexy,*" a corner of her mouth turned up in a crooked smile, "to both men and women."

"You dance still? Professionally, I mean."

She nodded. "I'm guest faculty at FSU this whole year. Caribbean folk dance. And I consult with their music department on West Indian and Afro-Cuban rhythms and music. It's fun. I love my students."

"Any kids of your own?"

She shook her head. "How 'bout you?"

"We have—*I* have—a beautiful daughter, Jasmine. She's nine."

"I can see you adore her."

"Can't help it. She's smart and sweet and cute—all-around terrific." He almost added, *Just like her mom*, but kept the sentiment to himself. "I'm curious," he said. "What's your heritage?"

"Racial or cultural?"

80

"Well, both."

"Would you believe there flows in this five-foot-tall body the blood of the Dutch, Spanish, Portuguese, African, British, Indian and Chinese?"

He smiled. "And it's not hard to guess you've just told me a history of the peoples who settled Curacao over the centuries."

"Exactly. My family incorporates the genes of Spanish conquistadors, West African slaves, indentured servants from India and China, English pirates, Portuguese farmers and Dutch plantation owners. And I've always assumed I'm part Caiquetìo, the island's aboriginal natives, though I don't know that for sure."

"And I would add that you're possibly part Arabic," he said, "in that you're part Spanish, and the Moors conquered Spain in the Eighth Century."

Her eyebrows went up. "An American who knows geography and history. That's rare."

"Maybe you've even got some Scandinavian genes—the Vikings invaded Spain in the Tenth Century."

She smiled. "I'm sure it goes on and on. Just look at me. At home we call it *krioyo*, meaning 'mixed,' but it's known abroad as the 'Curacao cocktail.'"

Nat chuckled.

"But we're *all* related, right?" she said. "People have a hard time living that truth. I read there's a greater range of genetic differences *among* the world's black people than *between* blacks and whites."

81

He nodded. "I read that, too. Look at us." He held out his arm and she placed hers next to it: his skin color was dark mahogany and hers was rich caramel. Their warm flesh touched and unexpectedly the gesture felt erotic and Nat hastily withdrew his arm. Aria's eyes told him that she had felt the sexual charge as well.

"I'm impressed, by the way, that you married a woman of a different race. I'm sure that made for some tough times."

"Uh, different than I expected," he said. "Her parents were comfortable with it from the outset. That was my first surprise. But my mom went ballistic—thought I was putting her down along with all her soul sisters. 'Since when is a black woman not good enough for you, baby?' That sort of thing... My dad worried I was marrying Roan out of pity—being too nice for my own good. But...well, they were both wrong. I wasn't trying to make any statements at all."

"I understand. It wasn't a planned thing...you just fell in love."

At first sight. He nodded deeply and took another swig of ice water. "So tell me about your cultural heritage."

"Well, let's see. I grew up speaking Dutch, the official language of Curacao. And I speak Spanish—"

"—and excellent English."

That earned him a bright white smile.

"Also, in the Leeward Islands—Curacao, Aruba and Bonaire—we speak a patois called

82

Papyamentu, which is a blend of Portuguese, Dutch, Spanish, English, Amerindian and African."

"Sort of a Caribbean Esperanto."

"Right." She took a sip of water. "I was raised on fish and guava and casava-bread, and Island-style Catholicism."

"Island-style?"

"Yeah, you know—a bit of Santerìa, voodoo and Carnival thrown in, along with the votive candles and supplications to the saints."

Nat suddenly recalled the smell of the Sunday School classroom at the African Methodist Episcopal Church he had attended as a boy: chalk dust and mildew mixed with perfume and hair-straightener. Sunday School for him had felt like sitting for hours in front of an unplugged radio.

"Sounds like fun," he said. An image arose of Aria dancing the mambo down a lantern-lit street at Carnival in a costume of exaggerated grandeur and voluptuousness, all rhinestones and feathers. From that scene he abruptly found himself in the stained-glass-blue Caribbean Sea with her, swimming nude like dolphins, beneath a white-as-coconut moon. A flare of guilt halted his fantasy, followed by a swell of sorrow.

Uncomfortable, he turned from his reverie and focused on the menu. "Guess we better order."

Every meal listed seemed to him some version of *tofu with mung-bean sprouts*. After a moment the waitress returned. Aria ordered a "wilderness salad" and Nat ordered a tofu-vegie burger because it was the one thing on the menu that contained the word *burger*.

Aria drank tea and caught Nat's eyes. "You're not a vegetarian are you?"

"Nope. Figured you were."

She smiled and shook her head and her bangs bounced prettily. Nat wanted to reach out and touch her hair. Silky and shiny. Nothing more—just touch her jet-black hair.

"I eat all kinds of food," Aria said. "But I do like vegetarian cuisine a lot. I've eaten here before."

They sat awhile in silence. Nat still felt awkward. He looked down at the paper placemat that showed endangered species of Amazonia and listed rainforest facts. *Didn't they have to cut down trees to make these?*

By the time the waitress brought their meals, he was grateful to have something to do.

He took a bite of tofu-vegie burger, then peeled back the seven-grain sesame bun and scraped off the thatch of alfalfa sprouts. The patty looked greenish, flecked with orange bits of carrots. Good nutrition, no doubt. And plenty of roughage. Delicious? Not so much.

Nat ate without conversation, growing more and more uncomfortable. What was he going to say to this beautiful woman? He needed her. Not for sex or romance or any of the things for which most men would feel drawn to her. He needed her to fulfill his life's purpose before he died.

"You didn't take me to lunch for the pleasure of my company," Aria said, as if reading his mind. "What did you want to tell me?"

Nat wiped his mouth with a napkin before he began.

"Since we were teen-agers, my wife and I had been thinking, dreaming and studying about technologies that might someday enable the blind to see," he said. "And for the past eighteen years we worked fulltime on research we called Project V.I.S.I.O.N." He paused. "It stands for Visual Input System, Implanted Oculoneural Net."

She blinked. "Layperson's terms or you'll lose me."

"It's a system that uses implanted artificial retinas that transmit visual data to tiny computers in the brain."

She nodded. "I think I read about that somewhere—a camera mounted on eyeglass frames, something like that?"

He shook his head. "No. That's not our design," he said. "That's an approach Harvard and MIT and everyone else in this field has been working on since the eighties."

"Okay."

"Their system—the one you probably read about—uses an external video camera that captures and digitizes visual information and beams it by laser to an electrode array implanted in the eye. The electrodes in turn stimulate the nerve cells of the retina, which fire a signal through the optic nerve to the brain."

Aria nodded. "Sounds awful clunky, walking around with a camera perched on your brow."

"The camera?" Nat held up thumb and forefinger to show a little gap. "Smaller than a breath mint."

85

"Oh."

"Yeah, miniature camera technology just keeps getting better," he said. "A guy I met in Japan has made a robot using a micro-camera mounted on a headless, living cockroach. Got a computer chip where its head used to be. Calls it a *bug-bot*. By remote control he can send the bug scurrying on reconnaissance patrols."

"Through greasy spoon restaurants and tenement buildings?"

He laughed. "Whatever."

She shook her head in disgust. "I believe all life-forms—even cockroaches—have an inherent right not to be tampered with, experimented with, turned into biological freaks. Especially for military purposes—because you know that's who'll buy the cockroach patrols. The Army, CIA, secret police."

"It wouldn't just be used for spying or security surveillance. Bug-bots could help in rescue work in the wake of earthquakes or other disasters—searching through collapsed buildings for survivors, that kind of thing."

"Ugh. Rin-Tin-Thin, the insect-hero. It's creepy," she said. "Not to mention, unethical."

"Are we talking insect rights?"

"*Human* rights. Play Dr. Frankenstein with bugs, and next it's with dogs and cats, then chimps—then we're next."

"The slippery slope scenario."

"Exactly."

They sat in silence for a while, eating their meals. *Should've taken a Dale Carnegie course in* How To Win Medical Volunteers and Influence

86

People, Nat mused. *How well am I blowing it, so far? Damn. She's my only chance.*

"We were talking about artificial vision research," Nat said, "then I started yakking about tiny cameras, I got off track."

Aria nodded. "Go on."

"Okay. All the big names in the field are experimenting with some version of the external camera system."

"Right."

"That approach is relatively crude," he said, "but at least it has the virtue of seeming to be possible, doable. In fact, we started off developing a very similar system. But everyone's results so far have been meager: You end up with formerly blind patients who can now detect blotches of light—say, point to the location of a window or an open door. Or if someone lit up a Christmas tree, they'd be able to identify it by shape." He shook his head. "It was too disappointing, and we were very impatient."

She nodded. "Your wife…"

"Our dream was for her to truly *see* again. We both believed that dream was achievable." He sighed and looked down at his plate, strewn with alfalfa sprouts and half of his burger. "Among scientists, a rare few possess a strong faith in miracles. Roan was blind," he said softly, "but she was a visionary."

"You believe in miracles?"

"Sure. As long as the miracles express the laws of physics. I have great faith in the power of knowledge and applied technology."

87

Nat felt Aria studying him and remembered he looked ragged, with a fuzz-covered scalp and bags under bleary eyes. And *her* eyes: Asian jewels of dark amber. He wondered how his words were coming across. *Sweet Jesus, she's stunning. Probably thinks I'm an over-educated geek.*

"Anyway," he said, "We reached the conclusion early on that the eyeball is just too perfect at what it does. No camera of the next hundred years will be able to duplicate the eye's task of capturing and encoding complex data."

She touched her left eye. "But our eyes are so fragile..."

"True. But in Roan's case, as in yours, the retina alone is damaged. The rest of your eye is intact and healthy. In other words, only a single part of a wonderful, high-tech camera is broken. Think about that."

She shrugged. "That fact doesn't make me less blind."

"Yes, but if only the retina is damaged, why not design a system that skips the external camera altogether and continues to use the eyeball as camera? Create an artificial retina only, not a whole replacement camera system—that is, not an entire artificial eye. Using the eyes as cameras retains all the advantages of natural seeing, like muscle-tracking of moving objects, binocular vision, depth perception, automatic exposure, automatic focus, automatic lens cleaning and scratch protection—"

"And skipping the dorky eyeglasses," Aria said. "Smart. So why didn't anyone else think of that?"

88

"Because, unlike the camera-laser-electrode-array approach, our approach had the stark disadvantage of seeming to be impossible. No bureaucracy worth its red tape and hoops to jump through would grant funds for such far-fetched research. You'd have to believe in miracles." He smiled ironically and jiggled the ice in his water glass, took a sip.

"Why impossible?"

"Trust me, it would take half the afternoon just to list all the problems that had to be overcome."

"Are you saying you've *done* it? Succeeded?"

"Yes," he said, and did his best to project a look of utmost confidence. He watched her face for a reaction. She seemed wary and noncommittal, or else was doing a great job faking constraint.

"I—" He paused, suddenly feeling sad and needing very much to acknowledge Roan. "*We*, I should say—my wife was foremost in all of this, every step of the way…"

Aria nodded. "You were a team."

He swallowed. "A team…*we* succeeded. Since her death I've gone on to complete the final elements of a true artificial vision system." Using his fingers as counters he began to list the elements. "First off, an implantable photoreceptor array—the artificial retina—that doesn't need batteries to power it or a laser to stimulate it," he said. "Five years ago, we managed to find the material we needed from a colleague in Tokyo. He had created a high-temperature superconductive film, so thin it bends like a balloon's skin and can be shaped to fit the retinal wall."

"Back up. You're over my head."

"What?"

"The film—whatchamacallit?"

"Superconductive. Okay, right. When electricity flows through most materials, the electrons bump into all sorts of impurities and flaws that interrupt their motion. It's called electrical resistance. Produces heat by friction. You have to supply continual energy or the electric current fades away. Superconductors are materials that conduct electricity without resistance—you can even shape the conductor into a ring and get electricity flowing in a circle forever, without decay."

Aria nodded. "Gotcha. Sort of."

"Started out, superconductors were metals that didn't do their magic until they'd been cooled to extremely low temperatures using liquid hydrogen. But we keep getting better at making stuff that works at higher temperatures. This new material my friend created is based on a compound made from buckyballs."

Aria frowned. "Dare I ask?"

"Buckyballs—carbon-sixty. Big molecules built of sixty carbon atoms in a new structural form. Called buckyballs, or fullerenes, after Buckminster Fuller—because the molecules have the same architecture as the geodesic domes Fuller invented."

"Knew I shouldn't have asked."

"Geodesic domes, you know—hippie mushroom homes—you've seen them."

"Oh. Those. Okay."

"Or the soccerball-like domes that surround radars dishes at airports."

"Right."

"Buckyballs look like that. The carbon bonds are the spokes and the carbon atoms are the hubs. They superconduct. And my old college buddy, Matsuo Ishikawa, managed to formulate a substance with buckyballs that superconducts at body temperatures."

"So...that's good, I guess?"

"Good? It's a triumph. He won the Nobel Prize in physics for it. For me, it means the photoreceptor I've built doesn't need batteries. Runs on sunlight, electric light, any kind of light energy—much like a living retina."

She nodded her head slowly, digesting what he had told her. "Light powers the artificial retina."

"Yes."

"Without energy loss."

"Exactly."

"All right. Go on."

"Another major hurdle was adapting the retinal implant so the body won't reject it outright, and eventually, the eye's ganglion nerve cells will grow links with it."

Aria wore a slight frown of concentration as her fingers twirled at the dark swoosh of hair that fell like a shadow over the side of her face.

"Researchers at Cal Tech painted a computer chip with certain peptides to coax the neurons of a fetal rat to grow connections to it," Nat said. "It worked. So I took the idea a step farther."

Aria coiled her dark locks with slender fingers, let the coil spring loose. Nat found the unconscious habit so sensual he had to look away.

"The breakthrough involves growing a layer of undifferentiated human fetal cells over the implant's surface," he said. "Early-stage fetal cells seem almost magical—they naturally develop into tissue compatible with whatever tissue they're placed in contact with. No rejection. So when nerve cells in the retina grow links to the fetal-cell-coated implants, the fetal cells actually *turn into* nerve cells. It all becomes one living circuit—a bio-computer."

"How long?"

"That little problem took four years to solve."

"No, I mean, in the eye—how long does it take to grow the connections between the eye's nerves and the computer chip?"

"Oh. Not long," he said. "A few weeks, though the interface tends to get richer, more endowed, over time. Keep in mind, each of the brain's one-hundred-billion neurons is linked to thousand others, forming hundreds of trillions of connections—so you can imagine the superabundance of neural networks buzzing in our heads. The artificial vision circuitry should keep growing richer for—well, we don't really know—for months, anyway. At least that long."

"Wow. Okay."

"A couple years ago my wife came up with a tremendous breakthrough to the project's biggest obstacle—a problem she'd been wrestling with from the outset."

"How to finance all this research without grant money?"

He laughed. "Astute. But no, that's not it," he said. "Roan's parents were old-money, Boston Brahmins—you know, Beacon Hill and all that—they left her a very substantial fortune. And I inherited an antique Western gun collection from my dad that was absolutely world-class. Museum pieces. I've sold them all except three to help finance this project."

"I saw a couple of them—in your office."

"Actually, those are reproductions. Fakes. I keep the real guns in a secure place. I've already spent nearly six million dollars on Project VISION, and I may need to cash in those pistols—the real ones—soon."

Aria arched one coal-black eyebrow. "You've spent six million of your *own*?"

"Close to it."

"But haven't a thousand temptations and distractions tagged along with that kind of money?"

"Ha. You bet. Hey, I'm no saint, not even close." He laughed at the notion. "Yes, I drive a '98 Volvo station wagon; but if I didn't have this obsession I'd be sailing out to my Monaco oceanfront retreat on my new Oyster-50 yacht with self-reefing sails and black walnut interior."

Aria's turn to laugh. "I see you've given it some thought."

"Daydreams don't cost a dime," he said, smiling. Then his expression turned sober. "Truth

93

is, my wife and I invested all our time and money into fulfilling this goal of ours together. Now it's my aim to see it through alone." *Before I die. Please, before I die.*

"I respect your commitment—a lot," she said. "I really do."

They didn't speak for a while. Nat glanced down at the half-eaten burger and pushed away the plate.

"Guess I got you off track," Aria said. "You were about to explain your biggest challenge."

He nodded. "Our eyes are more than cameras. They're *computerized* cameras—the finest on the planet, in fact. They do more than just passively capture patterns of light, they *encode* those patterns as electrochemical signals and transmit the data deep into the brain, to the visual cortex—" he patted the back of his head, "that's an area right in here—where the brain decodes the data to produce the energy-state called 'seeing'."

She nodded. "It's the brain that actually *sees*."

"Sure. But how?" He gestured with his hand. "How do we see white sprouts on a red China platter upon a glass tabletop?"

She shook her head. "I wouldn't even know which questions to ask."

"Ahh, that's the point. Where do you start?" He measured a sliver of space with his thumb and forefinger. "For years, discoveries in the field have crept forward, bit by hard-earned bit, because the human visual sense is extremely complex. *But*—and this was Roan's big breakthrough—it turns out that

94

the whole manifold process is built upon tangled layers of exquisitely *simple* algorithms of differential geometry—a modeling of three-dimensional objects in relation to four-dimensional space-time."

She waved at him. "Hey, whoa. You're looking at someone who has a hard time balancing a checkbook. Can we fast-forward past the math?"

"Sorry." He shifted in his chair, drew a hand across his fuzzy scalp. *Damn. You can't afford to alienate her by talking over her head.*

"Basically..." she prompted.

"Sure. Basically," he said, "Roan designed a supercomputer the size of a sugar cube to be implanted in the visual cortex. The computer translates the signals from each artificial retina into a geometric language the brain understands."

She furrowed her brow. "Wait a minute. I don't pretend to be a computer whiz—I mean, to me, they're just magic boxes. But I have a girlfriend who works with supercomputers. She explained how they crunch a huge problem by breaking it into a hundred-thousand parts and solving all the little problems at the same time."

"Exactly. That's called massive parallel processing. Performed by several million microprocessors at once."

"Yes, but I've seen those computers—they're way bigger than refrigerators. How'd you squeeze all that inside a sugarcube?"

He smiled. "Summer before last, my wife invented a revolutionary microprocessor. Roan worked out the math, the design. I built it. It's not a

95

chip, it's a *cube*. It imitates the anatomy of the brain by writing and reading data in *three* dimensions, not two. Every point along three axes is a potential data bit, so it allows for access to a constellation of information recorded in space—a data *hologram*. Mirrors the workings of the brain's own neural nets."

He paused for emphasis. "Think about it. Inside this protective traveling case"—he tapped his forehead—"floats a three-pound biocomputer with a volume of just fourteen-hundred CCs but packing up to a *quadrillion* neural connections—and who can guess how many pathways are possible through that universe of wiring? The factory-standard human brain makes the greatest supercomputer seem like a counting stick—and it's a helluva lot smaller than a refrigerator."

"Gee. Right now I'm feeling humbled by how little use I make of all that brainpower." She laughed. "This data cube...how do you plug it in?

"Batteries included," he said. "Two of them, inserted under the scalp at the back of the head. They're the size of the cells that power wristwatches, only much more potent, and fully externally rechargeable from a unit you can wear in your pocket."

"I meant how do you plug it in—you know, inside the brain?"

"Same way as the artificial retina. You coat the cube with fetal stem cells, which rapidly conform to tissues in their environment. You surgically implant one cube in each of the two lobes of the visual cortex at the back of the brain. The stem cells turn into healthy nerve cells—no tissue rejection—and the brain's nerve cells grow links to the cubes, as they would to any other neural nodes in the brain."

"But that remains to be seen, right?" She quickly added, "No pun intended."

He leaned forward and lowered his voice. "Aria, I can take you back to my lab and show you six chimpanzees, all born blind, that can now catch a ball, jump from limb to limb—they can *see*."

Her eyes widened and her mouth dropped open.

"The system *works*," he said, pleased that he had penetrated her guardedness.

Aria stared at Nat. In the dim forest lighting of the restaurant her amber eyes glowed like backlit honey.

"And now," she said slowly, "the punch line..."

Nat reached for a swig of water. Ice clattered in the empty glass.

"I'll say it for you," she said. "You need a volunteer—a human guinea pig."

"The system works," he repeated. "It's ready for a human clinical trial."

"Six chimpanzees...that's it?"

"I've had only a year. Since the breakthrough, I mean."

Aria took a deep breath and let it out slowly. "Listen, Dr. Colt—"

"Call me Nat."

She nodded. "I believe you're a brilliant and sincere man, and as scientists go, you've got a lot

97

more heart than what I had expected. But I'm not interested. I'm not ready. I prefer to go on with my brain not tampered with for a while longer."

She stood to leave. "Thank you for lunch, Nat. I enjoyed meeting you."

He jumped up, nearly knocking his chair to the floor. Patrons turned to stare. "Wait, please," he whispered. "Sit down again. Just hear me out." He held up his palms in a pleading gesture. His hands trembled. "Hear me out on this."

She hesitated.

"Please?" he begged.

She sighed and plopped into her seat.

Nat sat slowly, never taking his gaze off her. "Macular degeneration," he said. "Have you any idea what the chances are of your other eye failing?"

"Yes I do. My grandmother went blind. My favorite aunt. Runs in my family."

"The system I've described *works*." His whisper rose to a hiss. "I can *help* you."

"Then let me ask you this," Aria said. "If I were your sister, your daughter, your wife—and blind in just *one* eye—would you recommend this surgery to me?"

Nat looked down. "Roan *was* my wife."

"But Roan was totally blind," Aria said. "I can see with my right eye."

He looked up again, black eyes misted with tears. "For how long?" he said. "Another year, another month? You're already past the age when your grandmother went blind, am I right?"

"Yes, and I choose to interpret that in a positive light," she said. "I'm three years past the age when she went blind because I'm not going to go blind." She reached across the table and took his hand. "Or let's say, in another five or ten years, I do go blind. By then, your system will have been tested by dozens of others. The bugs will be worked out. You'll know how it holds up over time." She smiled politely. "To be honest, it's way too scary to be the first on something like this, okay? I'm not that desperate yet."

Nat pressed his hand over his eyes. He squeezed the muscles of his chest to squelch the hopelessness that threatened to overwhelm him. Anger was his weapon over sorrow, and suddenly, he boiled with rage.

He looked up. "I don't have five or ten fucking years!" he said, overloud. "I'm dying of cancer!"

Aria clapped her hand to her mouth.

A buzz went up in the restaurant and people stared and fidgeted. Nat got the impression some of them edged away from his table.

"And you don't have time, either," he said quietly, regaining some control. "I examined your eyes. As an ophthalmologist, I wouldn't bet my sports watch against your chances of saving your vision another five or ten *weeks*." He held out the wrist that bore a black plastic watch. "And it's just a cheap Timex."

She clenched her jaw and stood suddenly. "I've got to go."

"Will you take my phone number?"

99

"No."

"Take my number." He jotted it on a paper napkin and held it up to her. "Please. Just so you'll have it."

She reached for it then drew back her hand. Nat stuffed the folded napkin into her dress pocket. Aria turned and strode out of the restaurant without looking back.

Nat slumped in his chair, feeling the crowd's prying eyes. Half-moons of sweat stained the armpits of his T-shirt. He had been off chemotherapy for three weeks, yet he felt the urge to puke his tofu-vegie burger all over the air-conditioned Wi-Fi rainforest.

10

Aria moved around the perimeter of the single open room of her beach bungalow arranging four bathtub-sized black cabinets. Each held three speakers: tweeter, woofer and bass. A Roland 7000 digital percussion system stood at ground-zero, at the hub of the inward-facing speakers.

She sat on a padded drummer's throne and made a final check of the computer programming for the array of black nylon drum pads. By striking the electronic pads in different zones, each pad could play back the sound of three different percussion instruments. One pad played back digital samplings of a snare drum and two tom-toms; another pad sounded the electronic equivalent of a set of three kettle drums; another pad sang like a trio of timbales tuned in descending pitch; two other pads played back six types of cymbals—crash, sizzle, splash, ride, chime and gong; and foot pedals kicked two pads that boomed like double bass drums. In addition to these sounds, she had programmed her own digital samplings of an African djembe, a Brazilian tongue drum, a set of Cuban congas, Indian tablas, woodblocks, *agogo* bells and a cowbell.

Aria thumped the bass drums and turned up the volume from five to eight. She closed her eyes and placed her right hand over her sternum, feeling inside for her heartbeat. Da-*doop,* da-*doop,* da-*doop,* da-*doop.* She nodded her head in time to the natural metronome, stuck a samba whistle in her mouth, picked up a set of hickory Jazzmaster drumsticks.

And began to play her heart out.

Each beat bombarded her ears and flesh as a distinctive pitch-vibration. The bass drum pounded a low-frequency pitch that registered in her belly; the cymbals and higher frequencies she sensed as padded marimba mallets tapping her skin.

She hammered the drum pads and a tide of pulsing sound rolled over her. Reflections rocked and shimmered in the cabin's glass windows from the percussive volley. On Dogfish Key on a weeknight she had no neighbors but ospreys and owls. She hoped they liked thunderstorms as much as she did.

Sweat flew from muscular arms. Her damp black hair bounced to the beat. After a half-hour percussion solo she stopped playing, set down the drumsticks and quickly moved the electronic drum kit out of the center of the ring of speakers, freeing up floor space. Then she switched on the digital recording of the drum solo she had just made and cranked up the loudness to a level rivaling a buffalo stampede.

Music, for Aria, was touch as well as sound. She slid off her purple dance leotard to be naked to her self-made thunder, to better feel its signals in her body. Her mocha skin became the skin of the drum heads. The timbales and cymbals from the bugle-shaped tweeters penetrated her muscles; the boom of tympani from the 24-inch bass speakers penetrated her bones. The avalanche of rhythms prodded and tugged.

Move, it sang. *Move yourself whole. Become the music made flesh.*

She began to dance, bare feet over smooth oak.

She was still warmed up from her afternoon faculty dance class at FSU, and almost immediately, Aria surprised herself with fresh, untamed moves. Like a veteran sax player invents new riffs without having to think of each note's fingerings, Aria improvised patterns in space with the instrument of her body without having to think about choreography.

Sound became touch, and touch spontaneously became motion. No resistance to the energy flow. "I'm a superconductor!" she yelled, and laughed. Music in, dancing out.

But after a time the recording ended and Aria was abruptly plunged into a vacuum of silence. She came to a stop, breathing hard. She walked over to the mixer board, switched off the amp and sat on the floor, her back against a speaker case.

The terror rushed in again. *How will I dance when I'm blind?*

Aria jumped up and walked close to the mirrored wall behind the ballet bar of her one-room bungalow/dance studio. Diamonds of sweat glistened on smooth bare curves of her compact figure. She smelled like a spice garden after a rain.

On Curacao, she had been considered beautiful, like all the women in her family, but not especially exotic-looking. Mixed-race people were the norm there, and every day one saw dozens of combinations of skin and eye and hair color and

103

texture—even among siblings. But in North Florida, her appearance was anything but common, and strangers often goggled at her, as if she were a walking ad for United Colors of Benetton. Women stole glances, men stared with open desire, little kids pointed, but the attention of strangers only made her feel more lonely.

She stepped closer until her nose nearly brushed the mirror, peering deeply into her own eyes. It was impossible to tear her mind away from the meeting with Nat Colt earlier in the week. He had really gotten to her. He seemed so sure her vision would soon fail.

She closed her blind eye and gazed at the room with her right eye.

It seemed the gray smudge near the center of her sight had spread, darkness encroaching on light. She walked over to the counter and grabbed a white grid paper she used to calculate the rate of macular degeneration.

She stared at the chart and her heart lurched.

Fuck. No doubt about it. The dark gray blotch was larger; her visual field was shrinking, and the pace of loss was quickening. Already, she probably shouldn't be driving her motorcycle. If she were to re-take the driver's license eye exam now, she would flunk.

She felt helpless. Furious. No way in hell was she willing to give up all the things she loved to do. Motorcycles, sailing, windsurfing, surfing, dancing—hell, scrambling a couple eggs, for that matter. *Every damn thing.* So much would be sacrificed outright, and the rest would have to be

104

relearned. Simple tasks like shopping for groceries...

How do blind people do it?

She knew herself as a sensualist, a reveler in the ecology of her own female body, and the body of Earth, and all the organs of experience, including mind. She couldn't bear to give up any of it, not in the middle of her life, after being an artist drunk on the physical world for forty-five years.

Aria climbed the ladder to her bedroom loft and groped in the pockets of her yellow dress, crumpled in a small pile of laundry in one corner. She found the note: Dr. Colt's home and office phone numbers, pager, cellular, fax, and e-mail. *He sure as hell wants me to contact him.*

She watched lightning flash in the night sky far out over the gulf, mirrored in the glass-smooth sea like golden tracery in a dark cathedral window. Beautiful to behold. *To behold!* Colors, shapes, textures, patterns. Deep pleasures.

"Wish I had a cigarette."

She hadn't smoked in a dozen years. But right now, she craved to inhale a long, hot drag on an unfiltered Camel. Oh yeah.

Finally, Aria sank onto her back on her futon mattress. Took a full, deep breath without cigarette smoke. Made herself pick up her cellphone. Flipped it open. The keypad lit up. She wavered. Flipped it closed.

Took a deep breath again.

"I absolutely refuse to go blind," she said in a shaky whisper. Flipped open the cellphone. It trembled in her hand. She dialed Nat Colt's home number.

11

Roan learned that the patient who had received the cyber-optic implants was a retired captain of the United States Air Force. That intelligence would seem to be a critical piece of the puzzle, but she had just about given up trying to tease meaning out of the scraps of information she gathered from John. (Did he slip up now and then, or was he strategically leaking the news?) It was like delving into a set of Chinese boxes; each time she uncovered something significant, it exposed not an answer, but only the lid to another question.

She combed her hands through her thick hair, running out to arm's length on both sides. Why had her captors made such a spy drama out of a project to develop artificial vision? It meant offering sight to the blind—not some diabolical new weapon. So what's the big secret? What was there to hide?

Maybe spooks handled everything this way. Maybe they ordered Big Macs from MacDonald's by kidnapping the shift manager and torturing him until he revealed the recipe for the secret special sauce; then they made their own burgers. Government efficiency.

Roan ruminated on the riddle of the Air Force captain for a week. Then came the kicker: she found out that the patient had *not* been blind, but fully sighted. The son of a bitch was a veteran fighter pilot, could see like a hawk. The enigma had not just deepened, it had dropped into a chasm.

Why would anybody in his right mind want to replace perfectly functioning retinas? It was crazy. And here was an entire *team* of crazies laboring around the clock to make the nutty scheme work.

From what she had learned from lengthy consults with team scientists, their artificial vision system was not nearly as sophisticated as the design she and Nat had been developing. As just one example, the team had used peptide-coated implants, where Nat had been experimenting with fetal-cell coatings, a bolder approach with potentially much more dramatic results for the formation of neural nets. Contrasting Nat's system design to their design was like comparing a Lambhorgini Contouche to a riding lawnmower.

Roan didn't hand out any more information than was demanded of her, and if she were not a prisoner, she wouldn't care if the implants short-circuited the patient's brain and smoke belched from his ears. But her freedom was on the line. She had done her best to make sure their artificial vision system would function.

Which was no small challenge. Roan was only one-half of a duo that had been far more than the sum of its parts. The synergy she had come to expect in her research enterprises with Nat was spectacularly absent here. Husband and wife had worked together with a kind of rapport that was uncanny, seemingly telepathic at times. It was a special aspect of the love they shared as gifted scientists.

Nat's genius for biomedical engineering was amplified by Roan's acumen for physics and higher math. They helped each other translate Roan's equations into theoretical designs; the designs into experimental prototypes; and the prototypes into operational systems.

Here, it took a team of nine specialists—electronics engineers, eye surgeons, neurosurgeons, computer experts—to accomplish less than Roan and Nat Colt had accomplished as a pair. Roan took great pride in that fact. At times her pride in Nat, their achievements, were all that kept her from crumbling into despair.

On the other hand, it was those very achievements that got her into this frightful mess. Just goes to show, you can't trust the kind of trash who read papers in *Proceedings of the 5th World Symposium on NeuroVisual Sciences*. Roan was now convinced there had been spies scribbling notes in every lecture hall, a kidnapper lurking at every conference.

The eye and brain surgery had been performed three weeks ago. Two electronic retinas installed and two data cubes implanted; one in each visual cortex, right and left, of the twin occipital lobes. Stage One victory: the patient had not gone into convulsions and died on the operating table.

Eventually, Roan learned the test subject's name, Jack Wolfe. It didn't strike Roan as a time-honored Korean family name. And Wolfe was a combat-decorated Vietnam War hero. That tossed out her earlier suspicions about North Korean secret agents, but the revelation left her feeling more downhearted and afraid than ever.

Apparently her nation's government believed it had the right to kidnap its own citizens whenever circumstances justified. What the hell circumstances had justified stealing her from her home and using her as a mind-slave? Catch phrases like *national security* were no doubt emblazoned somewhere near the top of those secret orders.

Encrypted orders written in disappearing ink for use with the Captain Spook Decoder Ring—the kind of caper not even Congress or the president knows about, or if they've been informed, they "bear no recollection of that conversation."

I'm getting the hang of this, Roan thought, bitterly. *Now nobody can accuse me of not being a top-of-the-class paranoid.*

At two weeks post-surgery, Jack Wolfe reported he had begun to see smatterings of colored light. After three weeks; vague, spectral forms. Stage Two victory—War Hero had not died from brain infection or tissue rejection. Roan expected high-definition vision would kick in as soon as the neurons of the visual cortex grew into a richer living network with the data cubes.

Which made her dread her future.

If the system didn't work to the team's expectations, they would surely keep her here for more lonely months while she helped to improve the design. But what if the system worked well? Would they simply kill her on the spot? *Wham-Bam!* Thank you, ma'am.

110

Or would they really let her go home? To Nat and Jasmine and Seeker, to the parts of her heart they had torn out.

Roan had noticed that as the scientists grew more confident that their artificial vision system was going to be a winner, they had become more casual during their consultations with her. One physicist let slip that they were in the Dutch Antilles. Roan was not a geography junkie like Nat, but even she could place the Dutch Antilles somewhere in the Caribbean; a friend had gone to Aruba on her honeymoon and raved about the scuba diving. Roan couldn't recall the others islands, but she didn't think The Netherlands owned more than a half-dozen territories in the Caribbean.

Given the planet's surface area is about two-hundred-million square miles, the information had narrowed Roan's whereabouts by an order of magnitude. Would Loose-Lips get his paycheck docked—or did it not even matter anymore?

The veil of secrecy had slipped too far for her own good, she feared. Months ago, Roan had stopped pestering her handlers with questions and now tried her best to pretend she was deaf as well as blind.

"Curiosity killed the cat," Roan reminded herself daily. She figured the more they told her, the more she could expect to suffer that feline's fate. And above all, her goal was to survive.

Still, wasn't it marvelous how far a free democracy would go to offer its blind citizens hope for regained vision? Such commitment to a charitable cause! Of course, even if you're not blind, you may just want to graft electronic retinas onto your natural ones, drill out a couple holes in your skull and poke in a set of experimental supercomputers to link with your brain.

Right. Makes perfect sense—if you've been snacking on leaded paint chips.

Exactly what did this anonymous team of scientists—these ghosts with digitally distorted voices—have planned for the artificial vision system she had helped them to create?

Roan had a solid hunch, based on the line of questioning with which the team's physicists had drilled her. The data cubes held immense potential for information processing, and in fact, her equations pointed to a gaping unknown when it came to the upper limits of performance. Once the supercomputers were interfaced with a human brain—the most complex organization of matter in the known universe—who knows what visual powers they might produce? Theoretically, the cyber-optic system could enable extraordinary, superhuman sight perception. *Theoretically.* Who knew how such functions, symbolized by equations on a page, actually would operate in living brain tissue? Roan had not failed to warn the science team that another possibility, *theoretically,* was that sensory overload generated by the data cube vision system might fry higher brain function.

Nevertheless, Roan felt fairly convinced she now understood the purpose of the spook science project: to build the ultimate human spy. The team was willing to bet Jack Wolfe's life that he could be

112

turned into an advanced reconnaissance instrument like none other.

Ironically, Roan had spent little thought on the potential of the data cubes to deliver extra-normal vision, because, by her way of thinking, it didn't much matter. If the cubes enabled a formerly blind person to see infrared, say, or ultraviolet—or other frequencies beyond the scope of normal vision—well, so what? The person would naturally adapt. The expanded bandwidth of colors would, for that person, become completely normal.

Roan held up her hand before her own unseeing eyes. Slowly she brought the hand closer until her palm touched her nose.

Sight, even boosted to an unimaginably strange visual range, seemed to her infinitely more useful and worthwhile than blindness.

In spite of the terrible wrongness of her plight, Roan could not help feeling thrilled and proud that the artificial vision system she and Nat had spent more than a decade developing—indeed, a far *inferior* version of that system—appeared to be functioning perfectly.

All along, Project VISION had been meant to give *her* new eyes. Now Roan was dying to see for herself what Jack Wolfe could see.

Well, no. Not *dying* to...

"Curiosity killed the cat," she told herself again. Best say ciao to the meow.

12

Aria Rioverde awoke in a vault of total darkness. She gasped and opened her eyes wider, straining to see through the lightless void. She tried to shake her head, reach up to her blind eyes. But her arms and head wouldn't budge. Trapped. She struggled a moment in panic.

Gradually the veil of confusion lifted. She smelled Lysol and rubbing alcohol and her mouth tasted like the rubber mouthpiece of a scuba regulator. She remembered what had happened, where she was, who she was: experimental eye surgery; a recovery room at a private eye institute; Aria Rioverde, drummer, dancer, lover of storms. A restraining collar with a halo attached to her skull held her head still and wrist cuffs immobilized her—a precaution during the disoriented moments of rousing from anesthesia.

She whimpered and settled back. *It's done. The surgery is over.*

Complete blindness. Nat Colt had forewarned her, explaining a dozen times that the operation would render her sightless for several weeks. It would take that long for her optic nerves to grow into contact with the implanted artificial retinas. Then—if all went smoothly—her sight would be restored. It had worked for six blind chimpanzees.

Aria gulped. Even if those facts had been engraved with a tattoo needle on her forehead, waking up blind terrified her. She licked dry lips with a sticky tongue that felt like a size-eight sock. Cold water would be a splash from heaven. Maybe a strawberry daquiri. And a legion of miniature masseurs to knead her aching head. Through a dull haze of pain, two crochet needles stabbed her eyes, burrowing through her brain.

"Aria?" Nat's deep voice. "You awake now?"

"I'm awake." Her voice rasped.

"It's Nat Colt. Do you know where you are?"

"Yeah. The recovery room at INSIGHT. I'm blind, Nat. I can't see."

"Take it easy. Remember what we talked about? The blindness—"

"I know. It's temporary…and I'm scared to death."

He laid a warm hand on her bare shoulder. The contact of skin on skin sent a sensation to her brain, part shock, part pleasure.

"I'm sure it must be frightening," he said. "But you're going to be all right. The surgery went perfectly."

"It did?"

"Beautiful. Not a hitch. I'm really excited about this. I think you're going to be so happy with the results."

She sighed and relaxed a bit. Her head throbbed in a steady pulse with each heartbelt. Pain as metronome. She thought of the anole lizards on her balcony on Dogfish Key that puffed out their blood-red neckfolds in a regular rhythm: Puff. Puff. Puff. Puff.

115

"I'm taking off the cuffs now," Nat said. *Scritch.* Velcro strap unhooking. "Don't go scratching your nose with your left hand, okay? Got an IV line attached to that wrist. And whatever you do, don't rub your eyes—don't even touch them."

"I'll keep that in mind."

Scritch. "There. In a couple days the neck brace and halo can come off if you promise not to breakdance in bed."

"Great," she said. "It's giving me a god-awful headache."

"Sorry. But you know it's not that."

"That's what I was afraid you'd say."

"You've got a surgical wound in both eyes," he said, "and two postage-stamp-sized squares of bone removed and then replaced at the back of your skull. You've just got to grin and bear it for a few days, I'm afraid."

She made a ghastly grin and said through clenched teeth, "Like dis?"

Nat laughed. The confidence in his laughter signaled how well things had gone and reassured Aria more than any of the things he had carefully explained to her in the days before the surgery.

The artificial retina was as thin and flexible as a balloon skin, he had said. He described how the superconductive film would be tightly rolled into a tiny cylinder and then slipped through a narrow tube that punctured the cornea and lens at the pupil. Then, while monitoring the procedure with a magnifying videoscope, he would unfurl and manipulate the artificial retina with microsurgical instruments inserted through the same tube. The

116

artifical retina would be glued against the retinal wall using a paste of collagen, a protein that served as the body's natural glue. Lastly, the new retina's edges would be tacked down with miniscule gold tacks. In a separate procedure, two sugar-cube-sized supercomputers would be implanted, one in each brain hemisphere, at the back of the head at mid-ear level.

Nat had started the FDA application process a year earlier to get the experimental surgery approved for human trial, but he had finally had to pull every string he could grab and call in a lot of old debts to cut through the last tangles of red tape. Even so, Aria had needed to sign a half-dozen waiver forms, mostly stating that she understood the risks and the uncertainty of success.

The surgery had been performed at INSIGHT Vision Research Corporation with the help of a hired team of specialists. Aria would remain here for the next few days, with a hired nurse standing by round-the-clock to attend to her needs. Afterward, she had agreed to continue her recuperation at Nat's home until her vision returned.

"I could rub your temples, if you'd like," Nat said.

"Yes, please."

His warm fingertips touched her tenderly and soothingly. Aria liked feeling the contrast of the strength in his fingers and their gentleness. His touch was as intelligent as the rest of the man.

Aria dozed a bit and awoke with Nat still massaging her aching head. "Shall I increase your painkiller?"

"No thanks," she said. She tried to sing a line from Neal Young, "'I've seen the needle and the damage done,'" but it came out a croak.

"Well, you're well within safety margins on the Demerol. No problem."

"I think I can handle this."

"Have it your way. Here, got some ice water for you, take the straw."

"Ah. Just what I wanted." In spite of a trace flavor of chlorine, it was the best water she had ever tasted. She took her time emptying the glass, savoring each cold gulp.

"More?" he said.

She tried to shake her head, but the halo locked it in place.

"Sorry. That contraption will keep you from shaking your head for the next couple days. Then we'll remove it and you can be as contrary as you please."

She loved hearing his good mood. The surgery had gone perfectly, he had said.

"Sure you don't want more painkiller? I started you on the minimum dosage."

"Hmmm. Okay. Maybe just a notch or two."

"Good." She heard him fiddle with the IV drip. The narcotic reached her brain in seconds in a cooling rush like a blanket of menthol spreading over her senses. Aria realized she had no way of knowing how high Nat had increased the dosage.

118

She trusted him. But not being in charge felt crazy and scary.

Damn, never thought of myself as a control freak.

No, that wasn't fair, she realized. She was naturally easygoing and her personal style was to go with the flow. But it felt entirely different to be *forced* to go with the flow. To be dependent on others. Helplessness meant no choice.

"I definitely did the right thing," she said. "Being blind sucks big time." Again, she felt grateful for Nat's confident laughter. She hoped she would be dancing soon in a world made brightly visible.

"Can I get you anything else?" he said.

"No thanks. I'm really worn out." Her words slurred. "Think I'll just go back to sleep, if that's okay."

"Sure. Most healing thing you can do right now…Can you find this button?" He took her right hand and guided it to a nickel-sized button bulging from a bedside console. "Press it to call me or a nurse."

Aria felt too groggy to acknowledge him with words. She waved feebly as she felt herself slipping into deep narcotic sleep. Her eyes rolled up and she sank into an underwater cave where blind fish swam in utter darkness.

13

Jack Wolfe massaged his disfigured right hand. Beneath the thick scar tissue the bone stubs throbbed with a deep ache. Humidity made the hurt worse, so it didn't help that Isla Los Aves was beginning its brief rainy season, the only time of the year the arid climate turned muggy.

Wolfe sat at a steel desk in the semi-dark of the underground base's reconnaissance/surveillance office. Banks of radar, television and computer screens lined the far wall, forming a flickering patchwork of colorful electronic maps, sweeping arcs of yellow-green light, bright blips and computer-enhanced long-distance images. All else in the room appeared to be painted one hue: GSA Gray-11 "battleship gray." Several massive mainframe computers took up as much space as a parked bus. Four uniformed men wearing headphones were stationed at swivel chairs in front of blinking-bleeping electronic consoles, keeping their eyes and ears tuned to the lastest news from around the planet, brought to them via the U.S. spy satellite network.

Wolfe peered at a computer screen on his desk and re-read an intelligence report for the third time. It was hard to concentrate with his goddamn hand pumping out a rhythm of pain like boom box speakers rocking a car at a stoplight. He rubbed the gnarled flesh.

In a way, Jack Wolfe respected the dog that had done this to him. Loyal Soldier, Faithful

Defender—all that good shit. The heroic breed. Wolfe planned to carve out the mutt's heart as payback for mangling his gun hand and trigger finger—but even so, he respected the goddamn pooch. Wolfe had always preferred enemies that challenged him. It gave him cause to regard himself more highly when he managed to infiltrate their ranks, steal their secrets, use them, kill them.

The wound from the dog bite had healed raggedly, but Wolfe refused plastic surgery. He wanted the mean red scars to remind him that carelessness leads to mistakes, and mistakes are always costly. In this case, his carelessness had been in underestimating the defense installations guarding his target. He had paid for the error with two-and-a-half fingers of his right hand, plus a blight of rust on his ironclad reputation for swift precision in carrying out his duties.

Respect; an intangible that had taken him years to forge. During a thirty-year-career, first in the military, and then in covert intelligence operations, Jack Wolfe had never been made to look incompetent. Until now. Getting half his hand torn off by a house pet looked *way* fucking incompetent. As in, *How'd you let that happen, Stupid?*

Wolfe's squadron nickname as a combat pilot in 'Nam had been *Camo*, because his eyes featured one green iris and one brown iris—as if he had been born with military camouflage. The nose art spray-painted on his F4U Phantom jet fighter showed a grinning skull wearing an aviator's helmet, clutching an upraised fly-swatter in a skeletal hand. One green and one brown eye bulged from the skull's eye sockets. Eight red stars stenciled beneath the aircraft's bubble canopy stood for each Soviet-built MIG-21 fighter Wolfe had swatted out of the sky. Jack Wolfe: jet-ace, recipient of the Distinguished Flying Cross. Twice. That's how he had first earned respect.

Then he had been recruited by the National Reconnaissance Office, the top-secret arm of the U.S. Department of Defense that oversees spy planes, spy satellites, and covert ground operations. He had spent the next decade piloting the SR-71 Blackbird spy plane, snooping down on the enemy from the upper stratosphere at Mach Four-plus.

Later, Wolfe had been promoted to an elite espionage unit known only as The Shop, where he had been trained in solo and small-unit operations that included abductions and assassinations. Wolfe was skilled at his job; a natural. After all, he'd been born with camouflaged eyes. He rose fast.

Finally, he had been transferred to a small, ultra-secretive branch of the recon office, which he had heard about only in rumors. Like most of his colleagues, he had never been sure the branch existed: Psionic Clairvoyant Operations, or Psi-Clops. It exploited the bizarre powers of perception of personnel called "Talents." Wolfe's mission in the special task force was to learn how to develop the Talents, use them, control them.

Turned out, it wasn't hard to control them. He did it with stark fear: bad stuff and the threat of more bad stuff. Same way he controlled most operatives.

At first Wolfe worried he had been kicked upstairs, out of the real action. *Psionics*—the word meant *applied psychic phenomena.* Pure bullshit, right?

Then he had watched as a chubby 11-year-old, mentally-retarded girl, described an underground chemical weapons plant in Baghdad with the elaborate detail of a blueprint draftsman. She had inspected the facility from the inside, wandering its locked rooms and high-security labs freely. To the girl, the extrasensory feat was just a game, like hide-and-seek. Her friend, "Dr. Susan," had pointed to Baghdad on a 24-inch globe and told her to "Go there and sweep your 'feelers' below ground, find the hidden places."

Psionics wasn't outside the action; it was the radical future of espionage. And Jack Wolfe had been given command of America's ultimate intelligence service.

More respect. Earned by slow degrees while his military crewcut gradually faded from black to gray to white.

Then he had blown his standing within the military spy fraternity on a raid so simple and straightforward it could have been handed to a Tobacco and Firearms agent—the kind of guy who couldn't get into his own house with a front door key unless a flame-throwing tank smashed it down first.

The mission had seemed a joke: snatching a blind woman from her home—without getting seen. Hee hee.

Months before the nab, one of Wolfe's agents had staked out and bugged the target's home, but his report had failed to mention a guide-dog on the premises. That guy was now re-assigned to a NORAD listening post somewhere in the Aleutians.

Wolfe rubbed harder at the stubborn ache beneath the thick layer of scars. He remembered how he had entered the house undetected through a back door and had smoothly drugged Dr. McKenzie, almost without a stir.

But then the freaking dog had shot out of nowhere, like a surface-to-air missile. Wolfe had killed half a dozen attack dogs in his time, often by strangulation, and this dog had been a mid-sized house mutt, not some huge, spike-collared T-Rex trained to tear out throats. But the goddamn dog had caught him by surprise. It locked its fangs through his gloved hand and twisted and yanked its jaws savagely. Wolfe had struggled to reach left-handed to his knife in a sheath on his right thigh. He could still vividly see the bloodlust in the dog's crackled blue eyes. Wolfe had finally managed to grab the knife just as the flesh tore away from his hand, fingers and all. He'd got in one good slash as the frenzied dog retreated, and it hobbled off with Wolfe's leather-wrapped fingers clenched in its jaws.

Blood everywhere. A simple grab-and-go had turned into the sloppiest goddamn mission since the hostage-rescue fiasco in the desert near Tehran. Planting the counterfeit corpse, installing the incendiary device in the surge protector, rolling the unconscious scientist to the car in a wheelchair—all the while ripped arteries squirting blood like a fountain pen squirts ink—and Rin-Tin-Fucking-Tin in the backyard howling to wake up the cavalry. Wolfe saw lights wink on in the neighboring ranch house as he drove away with his right hand tucked tightly under his left armpit to prevent fainting from pain and traumatic shock.

Within a few months, his hand had healed as much as it was going to. But his reputation was still ragged, at least as far as he was concerned. And to Jack Wolfe, his own regard for himself was the only thing that mattered.

That's why he had volunteered for Operation Argus. The artificial vision system held the potential—in theory, at least—to boost normal human perception to clairvoyant levels.

"Trouble with the Talents," Colonel Trager had explained, "their performance is unreliable. When they're *on*, they can close their eyes and count the girls with IUDs in a sorority house. But when they're off, they couldn't find a pair of golden arches if they were sitting in the parking lot at MacDonald's.

"The idea is, the computer vision system will make remote viewing dependable," Col. Trager had said. "But we can't guarantee the system is even going to work, Jack." He paused to puff a Perfecto cigar, straight from Havana. "It could leave you blind as a rock—or worse. Might drive you mad, kill you."

"I understand the risks, sir. I'm willing to try."

Wolfe remembered the colonel had seemed to frown and smile at the same time. "That's what we were hoping to hear," he had said. "You've made quite a name for yourself, and it's well-deserved. We need you. And nobody is going to soon forget your loyalty to your country."

"Thank you, sir."

Wolfe's surgery had gone off without a hitch. And already, after the first few scary weeks of seeing only blobs of moving lights, he was beginning to see clearly. The scientists assured him his vision would keep gaining power and acuteness as more and more neurons linked to the data-cubes, enriching the net. According to their best predictions, the gadgets implanted in his eyes and brain would eventually grant him far more reliable abilities than the Talents in Psi-Clops. Wolfe would become the most gifted remote viewer on the planet.

Then the real experiment would begin. Wolfe's computer-boosted perception would make the high-tech information-gathering of his spy plane days seem like peeking through a keyhole in the dark.

Yet for the first time in his intelligence career, Wolfe's mission had nothing to do with spying on enemies.

Fewer than fifty Americans knew Wolfe's actual goal. The number included physicists, electronic and biomedical engineers, the project's ophthalmic and brain surgeons, military officers, upper-ranking members of the National Security Agency, and exactly three senators; but it did not include the United States President and Vice-President.

The obsessive security that cloaked the project was tighter than the secrecy surrounding the Manhattan Project at Los Alamos in the 1940s. Everything connected to the mission—right down to the lunch menu—was on a need-to-know basis. And most of the team members on Isla Los Aves simply did not need to know the real purpose of the artificial vision project. Neither did the Commander-in-Chief need to know.

"North Korea is onto this," Col. Trager had said. "How the hell they discovered it…maybe a security leak, maybe they stumbled upon it same way we did. But they know. Whether they know of Operation Argus itself is not clear. In any case, the goddamn race is on. They're going to try to beat us to it, exploit it before we do."

"Yes sir."

"I don't have to tell you that the nation that taps in first is likely to emerge with a vast technological superiority—perhaps of an unimaginable kind."

"Yes sir. That's a 'No shit,' sir."

"We're counting on you, Jack. You're America's best hope."

"Thank you, Colonel." Wolfe rose from his chair and saluted stiffly and the old man honored him by standing to return the salute.

Now, weeks after receiving the computer implants, Wolfe set his jaw as he massaged his mangled hand. Operation Argus. Named after the hundred-eyed sentinel of Greek myth. The urgency and secrecy of his mission sang of renewed respect. And respect equals *power*. Jack Wolfe knew the song by heart.

Today he felt good in spite of the humming pain in his scar. The pendulum was swinging back his way. The report on the computer screen before him revealed that somebody else had received cyber-optic implants. A woman: Aria Rioverde. Dr. Nat Colt had performed the surgery ten days ago.

Wolfe would soon pay a visit to the woman with the witchcraft eyes. And the dog that mangled his hand. Poor girl. Poor pooch.

He grinned. Power was his personal anthem; revenge would be his greatest hit.

14

Jasmine Colt sat at the kitchen table of the ranch house drawing a unicorn and thinking about their houseguest. She liked Aria Rioverde from the get-go. Aria was hip. Cool. And very pretty. Best of all, she came from a mix of races, just like Jasmine.

Jasmine's friends at school never mentioned her mixed-race heritage, but some of the other kids treated her like an outcast. She was too white for certain groups of black kids and too black for some cliques of white kids. She had toughened up on the surface to guard her heart, but hardly a day went by that her feelings weren't hurt by some dumb comment like when Lysandra said, "How come your hair isn't kinky like it's supposed to be?" or Tobias said, "You don't dance too good, must be the white in you."

Black, white. Boy, how she hated those categories.

But somehow even she got stuck on them at times. Like when she looked at herself in the mirror, she wasn't sure she looked *right*. She looked sort of *in-between* the way pretty was supposed to look for one race or the other.

At least that's the way she had always felt about it, until she met Aria. Jasmine had no doubt that Aria was pretty. *Really* pretty. And Aria had light cocoa-colored skin *plus* freckles, just like Jasmine. And Aria's hair wasn't wooly, but she had big, full lips. So what's that? Black or white? And Aria's bold nose, it was kind of broad and hooked,

Mexican-looking—what were those Indians called? Mayans—her nose looked Mayan. And her eyes were really cool, kind of Kung-Fu, the color of honey. And, wow, could she smile! Like an ad for teeth brighteners. Dazzling.

Aria was a drummer. That was way cool, too. She had listened to a couple tapes Aria had made, one with an Afro-Cuban drum and dance troupe and the other, a Brazilian jazz ensemble. Aria had taught Jasmine how to play a drummer's exercise called a *paradiddle*. The hand pattern was right-left-right-right, left-right-left-left. The beat repeated the sound of its name, pa-ra-di-dle, pa-ra-di-dle. You started slow and went faster and faster: R-L-R-R, L-R-L-L, R-L-R-R, L-R-L-L...Aria had said Jasmine had a knack for it. *Who says I don't have rhythm, Tobias?* And Aria had promised to teach Jasmine how to hold drumsticks as soon as Aria could see again.

Sure hope Daddy's and Mommy's science works.

If the experiment worked, Jasmine would feel happy for Aria, but sad it wasn't her mother who got to see again. She felt kind of guilty about the opposite of that: If it didn't work, she would feel sad for Aria, but glad it wasn't her Mommy.

Jasmine had drawn a unicorn that looked remarkably like her pony, Balderdash. She added a picture of herself riding him bareback, but kind of messed up on the girl's head; looked like an alien. Oh well, she could draw horses better than people. She drew a fairly good picture of Aria and her daddy standing in the pasture holding hands. She

130

gave Aria long red hair to see what that would look like. Aria was "petite." At nine, Jasmine was almost as tall.

Jasmine got up and stuck her drawing to the refrigerator with a magnet shaped like a lady-bug. Stepped back to admire her masterpiece. Then she grabbed a crimson crayon and added three hearts floating in the sky like valentine balloons.

That was one more thing she liked about their houseguest: the way Daddy cared for his patient. Yeah, kids were supposed to be blind to grown-up feelings, man-and-woman-stuff, ignorant about what goes on. But, *duh*! Jasmine knew Daddy liked Aria. And Aria liked him back. He watched over Aria in that strong, kind way he was so good at, that made you feel safe and warm, and he often talked or read to her, and Jasmine could tell Aria liked it a lot. And sometimes her Daddy just plain looked at Aria in a real nice way, and although Aria couldn't see him watching her, Jasmine could tell Aria could *feel* it.

Jasmine was in the fourth grade but could read at college level and she had read *Cosmopolitan* and *Glamour Girl* a bunch of times and she wasn't dumb. She knew grown-ups needed grown-ups. For sex. And not just sex. Stuff. All kinds of stuff. Most of all, she knew her Daddy was lonely and she wanted him to be happy again.

Jasmine missed her mom terribly. Huger and deeper and skyscraper-higher than words. Always would. But she had already decided Aria should move into their home for keeps and be her stepmother.

131

She's so perfect. Her nose stud. Her colorful tattoo. And I'm not even jealous of her. Not much. Well...kind of. Sometimes. But Seeker can sleep on my bed, so I won't be alone.

Jasmine found Aria in the living room reclining on a leather couch listening to one of her dad's jazz CDs. A royal guy named Basie—a count, or something. Or maybe it was the other royalty, the duke. Seeker sat resting his head on the edge of the couch, allowing himself to be petted into oblivion. He looked up with crackled blue eyes as Jasmine stepped down into the sunken room.

Aria sat up. "Halt," she said. "Who goes there?"

Jasmine giggled. "It's me. Can I get you anything?"

Aria shook her head. "Check it out—doesn't hurt me to shake my head anymore."

Jasmine sat near the couch on the beige Berber carpet. "Starting to see anything yet?"

"No. But you'll be the first to know if I do."

"I'll be the second to know."

Aria smiled. "Right, smart-butt, knew you were gonna say that," she said. "Have you been practicing paradiddles?"

"Yeah. I'm getting pretty good. Wanna hear?" Without waiting for a reply, Jasmine began tapping the rhythm with her hands on the couch.

"Great," Aria said. "But you don't need to try to go so fast. For now, just concentrate on getting the *feel* of the rhythm, speed will come later. Tell you what—scoot a little closer, give me your shoulders to play on."

Jasmine shifted toward the couch and Aria found her with her hands, then tapped a paradiddle on her shoulders, slowly repeating the accented downbeats.

"Neat," Jasmine said. "Let me try. She reached up and played a paradiddle on Aria's muscled shoulders. Then they both broke into giggles at the fun of drumming on bodies.

"Listen to this," Aria said. She started making percussion music on her own body. Jasmine sat back, amazed at what she was seeing and hearing. By tapping, thudding, slapping her chest and belly and knees with her fingertips, palms and fists, Aria played a wide variety of notes and sounds. She stamped the floor for a bass-drum beat and made assorted noises from her throat and mouth. She finished the virtuoso performance by tapping out on her cheeks the same melody she had once played for Jasmine on a Ghanian talking-drum—changing pitch by changing the shape of her open mouth.

Jasmine laughed and clapped her hands. "Bravo! That's so great. Can you teach me that?"

Aria smiled. "You want to be a drummer?"

"Man, do I ever. That'd be so cool."

"You'd be patient enough to start out slow and practice hard?"

"I would."

"Well, it would be fun to teach you. But there's a lot more to it than just drums," she said. "I've always maintained you can't trust any drummer who can't dance."

"Dance?" Jasmine thought again of what Tobias had said. She didn't have enough soul to dance.

"I'd be willing to teach you to play drums," Aria said, "all kinds of drums from all around the world—if you'd be willing to study dance with me. Interested?"

Jasmine stared at her bare feet. Her toes dug into the thick carpet piling. "I'd like to, but...trouble is...I can't dance."

"Impossible. Who says?"

"A kid named Tobias. He's in eighth grade and he can dance just like Michael Sorenson. He does all the moves from the videos."

"So what did he tell you?"

"Told me I'm too white to dance good."

Aria frowned. "Hoo boy. That old crap. You believe it?"

Jasmine shrugged. "I can't do Michael Sorenson stuff."

"So what? Imitating another dancer is only useful at the very beginning—*maybe*. I bet if you studied dance techniques and learned to move freely you could end up dancing like Jasmine Colt. Ever heard of *her*? She's terrific."

"Ha."

"No, really. You'll surprise yourself with moves you've never seen *anybody* do before—not even you."

"Guess so." Jasmine shrugged. "I'm willing to try."

"Just remember, anything worth doing is worth doing poorly."

"Huh?"

"Until you can do it well."

"Oh."

"In other words, it's okay to be a beginner. It takes time to develop into an artist in any field. It's *experts* like Tobias who risk getting stuck in their ways early. They hit a plateau because they're know-it-alls. Beginners stay wide open."

"But you're no beginner. Said you've been playing drums and dancing since you were my age."

"Sure, but even so, I'm a beginner," Aria said. "It's an attitude. See, I'm still hungry, still curious. I learn something new about dancing and drumming not just every time I study a video of Katherine Dunham dancing the *cumbia* or hear Billy Cobham pound the skins, but every time I watch the ocean, listen to the birds, feel the wind shake the treetops. I pay attention to my art wherever and however it shows up. Do that, and the whole world becomes your teacher."

Jasmine smiled broadly. Aria's words reverberated through her mind like a gong. "That's such a great way of looking at life."

"Got it from my grandmother," Aria said. "She gave me that advice when I was ten and I've never forgotten it. Always thought that if I had kids I'd try to pass that attitude along."

Jasmine was silent a moment, wondering if Aria had meant she thought of Jasmine as sort of a daughter. *I hope she meant it that way.*

"Where's your dad?" Aria said.

"Sleeping upstairs. I think he's kind of worn-out."

135

Cancer. Jasmine despised it. Cancer sucked more than anything. It scared her more than anything. She wanted Daddy to get well, but he kept losing weight. She baked him pumpkin pies and brownies, and tried to get him to eat more, but he looked skinnier all the time.

Yet ever since he met Aria, he seemed better somehow. Brighter. That's the thing about grown-ups needing grown-ups. Daddy needed Aria, Jasmine thought.

Maybe Aria could make him well somehow.

Aria seemed to read her mind. She touched Jasmine's face with graceful fingers. Even her hands were dancers.

"Are you in the mood to talk about something heavy?" Aria said.

Jasmine shrugged, but felt her throat tighten into a lump.

"Have you ever thought of what you're going to do if your dad dies?"

"He's not going to."

"Your dad and I had a long talk last night while you were asleep next to us on the couch. He said he needed to find someone to watch over you."

"He's not going to die."

"I know, sweetie. That's what we'd all like to believe. But, realistically, with his type of cancer..." Tears shone in Aria's dark honey eyes. The woman traced her fingers down the girl's arm, took one of Jasmine's small hands and cupped it in both of hers. "Jasmine, your dad probably won't make it. That's the truth of things."

136

The lump in Jasmine's throat tightened painfully. She wanted to slug Aria. Then Aria bent forward and kissed her tenderly on the forehead, and suddenly, Jasmine longed to hug her.

"Your daddy told me that at first he thought I was too hip for the job," Aria said, "You know—who ever thought of having a drummer for a mommy?"

"What's he say now?"

"Still thinks I'm too hip. But since you want to learn to play drums anyway—well—he asked me to marry him."

"Wow." Jasmine felt stunned, but in a good way for a change. "Means you had sex, right?"

Aria laughed. "No. Nothing that nice. Your daddy really has been quite sick lately."

"If you don't have sex, why get married?"

"So I can be your step-mommy, take care of you. Legal stuff—makes it much easier."

"You told him yes?"

Aria shook her head. "I told him I'd think about it—soon as I'm able to see again." Her smile turned down at the corners. "Don't think I'd be much good to you if I'm blind."

"It'd be okay. We could take care of each other. Mommy was blind. I know how to love blind people."

Tears brimmed again in Aria's eyes. "You're an angel," she said softly. "C'mere. Can I give you a hug?"

Jasmine climbed into Aria's lap to be enfolded in a warm squeeze. She hadn't expected to cry, but tears leaked out on their own. Lots of them.

137

She couldn't stop the cloudburst. Her shoulders shook against Aria's warm bosom; Jasmine tried to cry more quietly, but her sobs turned into loud wails.

"Sweetie," Aria whispered in her ear. "That's it, let it out...it's okay...let it flow, let it go."

Aria's body seemed miniature contrasted with her mother's tall frame. But in Aria's strong arms Jasmine felt as safe.

The royal count or duke played jazz piano with a big, fine orchestra and the music painted the living room with the sounds of brass and drums and stringed bass. Aria gently rocked Jasmine, and the girl clung to the woman as if to a life raft rocking upon the deep.

15

Aria was in the middle of a ballet stretch when the miracle occurred. Like dawn, her vision came on swiftly, an overturning of darkness by light.

It happened at the end of the third week following surgery. Aria stood on the back porch of the Colt ranch house which perched atop a knob overlooking green and rolling horse pastures.

For days, Aria had been seeing a dimly glowing fog streaked with moving bands of light and ghostly blobs, with an occasional confetti of colored sparks sprinkled through the haze. Nat had cautioned her to expect a very gradual transition to full sight, like a camera lens slowly resolving to sharp focus, or theater lights creeping up to full brightness. And, indeed, over the past week, she had noticed the fog by degrees becoming more enriched with hints of form and detail. But the return of vision struck with the bold suddenness of the original day.

She had placed her left ankle at chest-height upon the porch railing and touched her forehead to that knee. The morning sun daubed her face with warmth as she glanced up, and instantly—like throwing a switch—the warmth burst into light. Golden light, streaked with pink clouds stretched over the green land like WELCOME HOME banners. Rays from the new sun zoomed a billion miles-an-hour from eight light-minutes away to flood her electronic retinas and illuminate her brain.

And the experience was beyond lovely, beyond riches; like being reborn.

A small stream at the base of the hill flowed east toward a neighboring subdivision called Forest Oaks—Nat had joked sourly that the place's name was chosen in memory of the oak grove that had been cut down to make room for the two-level brick homes and screened swimming pools. Aria could clearly see the tiled rooftops and the stream snaking across verdant backyards, reflecting like a ribbon of chrome. Pink clouds turned orange and swam in the bowl of sky like fat goldfish. A black-dappled appaloosa colt, glorious as a young god, romped and pranced in the tall bluegrass with Seeker and another dog-pal.

Colors kept on rising with the sun, adding tint to each shape and texture of the first morning of the world. The goldfish clouds morphed into a turreted Moorish castle carved of soft red sandstone.

Aria spilled down the stairs of the porch, knelt in the grass, and wept. Gratitude soaked her cheeks. It had rained during the night and when the sun backlit the moisture steaming up from the lawn, a small rainbow formed before her eyes. Aria cried out in ecstasy and wept harder, knowing the rainbow had formed for her.

"*Fiat lux*," she whispered, recalling a Latin phrase from Catholic Sunday school. "Let there be light."

Then, remembering something her Hindu great-grandmother had taught her, she placed her

140

hands together and bowed, saying in Sanskrit, "*Surya namaskar*," meaning, "I bow to the Sun."

Many-splendored things entered in through her new eyes into her new mind. Cells in the visual cortex of her brain had grown an interface with the data-cubes, and the universe had formed a fresh set of eyes through which to behold itself.

Seeing was believing. Aria believed in Nat Colt. She believed in hope. She believed in grace. With another gush of tears, Aria dashed up the stairs to Nat's bedroom to tell him his artificial vision system was online.

Nat was asleep beneath a big framed sepia-toned photo of the past-century black cowboy, Nat Love, after whom his father had named him. He had been weak and ill yesterday, and Aria debated with herself if she should wait for him to awaken on his own. She paced the bedroom for a moment and realized *Ain't no way* she could wait.

She shook his arm. "Nat, wake up—it's working! It really works! I can see!"

16

Aria knew she had fallen in love with the scientist with the Wild Western name, Nat Winchester Colt. But after a month of basking in his care at his ranch house it had taken exactly one night spent away from him at her beach bungalow for the depth of that love to sink in, and then it dropped to the bottom of her heart. She had found the love of her life in a man who was dying.

"Jasmine is crazy about you," he had said, when he asked her again to marry him. "I'd be so grateful if you'd raise her when I'm gone."

In her heart she had blurted *"Yes!"*—but she did not answer aloud, and asked him for a little more time to think. "Let me sleep on it."

But she had not slept. Sighs of shore break, sighs of heartbreak had washed the room. The crescent-moon crabbed sideways up over the dark sea and then glided, like a gondola with its high prow and stern, down to the western horizon as the sun made its comeback over the eastern edge of the world.

Now Aria stood on the balcony of her island bungalow gazing across dunes thatched with sea oats, green waves breaking lacy-white against straw-colored sand, cottony clouds sailing over the broad lap of the gulf.

In asking her to marry him, Nat had never mentioned love. Was it because he did not expect her to love him? Or because he did not love her?

Aria felt she knew the answer, and though it saddened her, it added to her respect for him.

"He's still in love with Roan," she told herself. "It's not that he loves me. He's doing this for Jasmine."

Seagulls wheeled overhead crying *KEE-eer KEE-eer KEE-eer*. Aria did not look up. She knew they were crying for Roan. For Nat. For Jasmine. And for her.

Before meeting Nat, Aria had felt self-complete, or nearly so, and in her past relationships she had asserted a fierce personal freedom. Perhaps it was the dancer in her that demanded plenty of room to move. Occasional bouts with loneliness over the years had seemed an affordable price to pay for the power of her individuality. And if her will-to-independence faltered, she could always browse her bathroom-reading copy of Emerson's *Self-Reliance*. And while her sexual appetite often felt unsatisfied, she found that dressing in a black mini-dress and hitting any college nightclub in the two-university town made it easy enough to prevent starvation.

But since meeting Nat Winchester Colt, Aria's life lacked vital necessities. Lying awake in her loft on her futon all last night, in a house that did not contain a brilliant, sweet-hearted man and his adorable little girl, plus their heroic three-legged pooch, Aria had concluded the house no longer seemed like home.

Aria remembered Nat's haggard face the day they met in his laboratory office. It had not been love at first sight. More like love at restored sight.

Now she swigged the ocean by the eye-full and felt deep gratitude and affection for the man who had made it possible for her to see again. As far as she was concerned, Nat had earned the right to possess a big ego, having built an artificial vision system that was surely going to rock the medical world and offer renewed lives to the blind. But unlike other geniuses it had been her fate to know— she had once been married to one—Nat never flaunted his high intelligence as personal property; he seemed to understand that his gift was dispensed to him for sharing.

Nat was indeed lovable. But falling in love with him was maybe the dumbest thing she had ever done. The man was busily dying of brain cancer.

Nat did not deny his doom, though sometimes he got angry at the universe for not creating a better design, "considering it had billions of years of evolution to work out the bugs."

She had asked him, "So how would you have improved the package?"

With the confident blasphemy of a scientist, Nat had described his Better Universal Plan: "From an engineering viewpoint, it'd be far more efficient for people to age until, say, forty years old," he had said, "then start growing younger again. That way youth wouldn't be wasted on the young."

She had laughed. "Yeah, right."

"Really. Think about it," he had said. "After middle-age, when a person has finally figured out who he is and what he wants to do with his one precious life, he would start getting younger, stronger, more flexible, more energetic—the glory and vitality of youth would return.

"Then, after the rejuvenation phase—ages forty through eighty—having achieved personal milestones in music, art, science, athletics, the person would rapidly regress to the stage of an egoless infant and fearlessly die—a pink, naked, ninety-year-old—perhaps in the arms of his own great-grandchildren."

Now tears brimmed over and swam down her cheeks. Falling in love with a man midway through the Third Act did not leave much script before the final curtain.

Then again, it had not exactly been a *decision*. She couldn't help loving him. Nat fulfilled an ideal Aria had been searching for since she was old enough to envision her perfect mate—which happened to be when she was nineteen and first rode a Honda 1100 sport-tourer motorcycle. Great concept: blend a high-torque, agile, sport bike with a comfortable, smooth-cruising touring bike; the hybrid gives you a motorcycle that's lean-into-the-curves fast on snaking canyon roads but doesn't jellify your kidneys on long rides.

Hybrid motorcycles—so why not hybrid men? Instead of *either* cute, hard-bodied surfer boys who can skillfully ride a wave and a woman, but can't produce an original thought; *or* owlish, artsy sophisticates who can't dance, including in bed—why not a *hybrid*? The blend would yield a handsome, athletic man with sex appeal *and* intellectual, creative drive. Someone *interesting*.

Aria's late husband, the gifted choreographer, had met those requirements. But mostly she had to settle for men who lived on either bank of the body/mind rift. She had greedily made love with the first variety, in the he's-warm-and-smells-good-and-doesn't-need-batteries-for-a-weekend-of-sex mode. And with the tweed breed, she had drunk bottomless cups of coffee and yakked till dawn about Gustav Klimt, Thelonius Monk, Twyla Tharpe, Carl Sagan and all the great Bringers of Light.

Then along came Nat Winchester Colt, the genius who gave her back the visible world.

Was Nat good in bed?

"Yes," she said aloud, and laughed at her certainty, for she had not made love with him and did not expect to. In the past two weeks Nat had been very weak and sleeping most of each day.

But there were clues.

He had The Touch. She could tell from the way he had cared for her, fed her, read to her, when she was blind.

God, yes, Nat was a great lover. And if he were physically well, by now she would have thanked him with her whole body for his gift to her.

Today she would give Nat her answer.

"Yes," she would tell him, "I'll marry you." Not just to repay him for his blessing, though she would feel indebted to him for life. But because it would be an honor to raise Jasmine as her own daughter.

And Aria would say yes because—however briefly—she now wanted more than anything to be the wife of the man she loved.

17

At six weeks post-surgery Aria's eyesight had become as clear as the crystalline coves of her girlhood in Curacao. She lounged on the cedar deck of Nat's ranch house in an Adirondack-style birch rocking chair, bronze bare legs poking from flannel pajamas, ankles propped on the railing. On a silver pennywhistle Aria played a refrain from a Spanish lullaby, then paused and listened. A bluejay in a nearby live-oak tree tweeted the melody back to her. Aria had been sharing music with the jay every morning for a week. As soon as the bird learned a new line, Aria moved on to another stanza of the tune. At this rate, they'd soon be able to whistle a duet.

The morning sun burned the fog off the hollows and the fall foliage in the apple and peach orchards began to glow like a black-light poster. This effect, caused by seeing in the ultraviolet range, had been going on for about a week. Aria also had begun to see infrared light. As the day brightened, she slipped on pair of wrap-around sunglasses to cut down on the reddish heat glare from the sun-gilded pasture; at night, she could scan the dark woods and watch small, moving shapes of red light that radiated from the warm bodies of foraging rabbits and raccoons.

Before the surgery Nat had prepared her for the possibility of extra-normal vision. He had said that people see the same bandwidth of light as apes, but with computer-enhanced vision, Aria might wind up being able to see infrared, like snakes, and ultraviolet, like bumblebees.

"To be on the safe side, let's presume that you're going to be able to see frequencies the rest of us can't," Nat had told her. "Roan thought it was likely, and didn't judge that to be a serious problem for her. What about for you? Will you be able to handle it?"

Aria had believed that she could adjust to anything more easily than blindness. But when the augmented vision had actually kicked in, she had told Nat, "Too psychedelic for my tastes."

"I know it must be hard to get used to," he had said. "Give it time."

"I'm not complaining. Not much," she had said. "It's a lot more interesting than utter blackness."

Then he had smiled. "Now you're like my hero, Geordi LaForge."

"Who?"

"I forgot. You never watched *Star Trek*. LaForge is a character on the show—the ship's engineer. His picture hangs above the clock in my lab."

"The guy with the visor."

"Right. LaForge is blind but the high-tech visor enables him to see."

"Ah, no wonder you love the character."

"Geordi's my man. His enhanced vision can even detect metal fatigue and magnetic fields and so forth. But to him, it's just his ordinary eyesight. Roan and I figured whoever received the artificial vision system would gradually adjust to the

149

expanded visual range until it would become completely normal."

Sitting on the deck trilling a call-and-response with pennywhistle and blue jay, Aria worried about her ability to cope with the latest developments in her eyesight.

For the first several weeks after her new vision 'awoke', her developing perceptions pulled her into a wonderful sharing with nature. Each day had brought new artistry to Aria's eyes, a two-way communion, like the musical rapport with the blue jay: The world provided beauty to be seen and loved, and Aria gratefully played the willing lover, taking in every form and detail.

But lately, her enhanced eyesight had often led her to view extraordinary scenes that were disorienting and frightening. She needed to talk with Nat. She stood and strolled into the house.

Nat was sitting up in bed eating oatmeal—the same meal he ate for breakfast, lunch and dinner these days—and playing a game of chess with Jasmine. They both looked up and smiled. Jasmine's face shone with the life-force of a sun-blushed peach; but the skin on Nat's face appeared like dull plastic, a thin mask stretched tautly over a skull.

"Good morning, songbird," Nat said. "How's the duet coming?"

"Great. It's fun." Aria sat at the foot of the bed, careful not to jiggle the chess board. Jasmine tilted her head toward the chess pieces she had captured and flashed her dark red eyebrows.

150

"I see your protégé is beating you," Aria said.

Nat winked at Jasmine. "Thrashing me is a better descriptive," he said. "How are you doing today? Headache gone?"

Aria nodded. "Vanished. By the way, I've made the connection that each time after I go through one of those awful migraines, my visual acuity takes a giant leap forward."

"That so?" he said. "What about the synesthesia? Still tapering off?"

Nat referred to a condition that had appeared soon after Aria regained her sight. Her visual sense had blended with her other senses, producing an unbidden fusion of colors flavors, fragrances, sounds and textures. For Aria, the experiences had mostly been amusing, not scary. Even so, she was often startled, even overwhelmed.

When Aria had listened to, say, a Gerry Mulligan sax solo, she might see brassy flashes of yellow light while getting a strong burst of butterscotch flavor and the sensation of smooth satin sheets touching her everywhere. In contrast, a Miles Davis trumpet riff might elicit blue laser jolts in her mind along with the taste of bitter almonds and the sudden sensation of dragging her bare feet across warm, rough bricks.

She had made an experiment: Working in reverse, she had tried to elicit the experience of a Miles Davis trumpet groove by squirting almond extract on her tongue, but the semi-bitter burst had caused a color blast of duck-egg green and the stench of burning tires.

151

At the peak of her synesthesia, Aria's senses had melded so completely she was able to sit on the porch and listen to and taste the harmonics that arose in her head as she watched the sunset; or simply close her eyes and 'finger paint' on the keys of Nat's piano.

Synesthesia was rare in the normal population, Nat had said. It showed up in about one in every five-hundred-thousand people; most often among artists. Aria felt relieved that for her it had mostly faded away. But she had come away from the condition with a unique and unusually *intimate* appreciation of Van Gogh: staring at *Night Over Toledo* for a half-hour had actually brought her to an orgasm—by its swirling golden violin music, the flavors of rum and whiskey, and the erotic tickling of feathers from her crown to her soles.

"I still get a synesthetic reaction when I eat coffee ice cream," she told Nat. "Tastes high-pitched, like a piccolo above high-C, kind of Arctic black and sharp-edged. Funny thing is, it only happens with *coffee* ice cream. Anyway, the effects are nearly gone now."

"Good," Nat said. "As the circuitry in your visual cortex is enriched with more connections, your eyesight should continue to differentiate from your other senses. Your vision will keep improving."

She shot him a worried look. "I'd rather it stopped 'improving'. If you ask me, it's already gone past where I wanted to stop."

He frowned. "The ultraviolet effect?"

Aria shook her head. "No, no, I think I'll get used to that," she said. "But my vision just keeps on *expanding*. Yesterday, I had the migraine, and today—wow..."

"What?" Nat sat up taller in bed. "Tell me."

"When I was going blind," Aria said, "the leaves on trees looked to me like one blurry cloud of green. Then, a few weeks back, after the first headache, I started to see individual leaves again."

"I remember. You told me."

"Yeah, but what I'm saying—now, if I shift my focus, I actually can see the *veins* on each leaf."

Nat cocked his head as if he hadn't heard her right.

"No, really," she said. "I never imagined the world was so detailed."

"Cool," Jasmine said, "I wish *I* could see each little vein."

"I'm happy for you," Nat said, beaming. "I'm happy for me. The system is a fantastic success." He reached out and squeezed Aria's bare foot, causing the chessboard to capsize and spill its armies. "Oops. Sorry, Jazz."

"I was ahead," Jasmine said, "so I won."

Nat laughed, showing his teeth in his skull in a ghastly way. "With your help, Aria, thanks to your courage, I've accomplished my life's purpose. You can't imagine the peace and satisfaction that gives me."

Aria matched his tearful smile with her own. "Nat, I'm not ungrateful, believe me," she said. "But keep listening."

He nodded.

153

"Last night I wandered in the pasture gazing up at stars," she said. "It reminded me of camping in the Andes. Stars, constellations, meteorites, like a blizzard of fireflies—I wondered why I'd never noticed them all before. Then I suddenly realized I was doing the same thing with the stars as with the trees—you know—seeing with telescopic vision."

Nat leaned forward studying Aria's expression. "My god, you *are* serious," he said. "I thought you were speaking figuratively. Can you really make out the veins on the leaves?"

"Nat, I can see the veins on the wings of honeybees crawling on those leaves."

Nat looked stunned. "This is...this is startling. You're telling me you can shift your vision to higher magnification. How do you do that?"

Aria shook her head. "I'm not sure I *know* how. I just...*do it. I focus*, some way, like tuning a radio in my head—and suddenly I can see the big red stallion on top of Belle Hill over at Buckley's."

Nat's mouth dropped. "Get real!"

"I kid you not."

"That's—what?—twenty miles away, at least."

"I can just barely make out Belle Hill from here," Jasmine said, "a little bump."

"I saw the red stallion standing on the hilltop this morning," Aria said.

Nat furrowed his brow. "But, at that distance, how could you be sure it was the stallion—or even a horse?"

154

"Kosmo," Jasmine said. "The stallion's name is Kosmo."

Aria pointed to her forehead. "Because Kosmo has got that gorgeous white star on his forelock."

Now Nat bolted upright, scattering chesspieces from the bedspread to the floor. "You can see the freaking star on his forelock?"

Aria nodded, nervous and excited. "Each of its four points."

"Geez-Louise," Nat said, and fell back into propped-up pillows.

"Daddy, can I use your telescope to look at Kosmo?" Jasmine said.

Nat didn't answer for a long moment. "No, honey," he finally said, "My telescope isn't powerful enough for that."

"Nat, you're scaring me," Aria said. "Is this a bad thing, or what?"

"No, no...I don't think it's a bad thing...not a bad thing...just...unexpected. It's truly amazing. Terrific, really." He looked at her with a worried frown on his tight-skinned face. "So long as you feel comfortable with it."

Aria felt her guts get shaky. "And what if I'm not comfortable with it?"

Nat's mouth tightened and he didn't answer.

"I mean, if this keeps up," Aria said, "A few more headaches and I'll be watching fishermen poling rafts down the Yangtse River."

Nat kept quiet, buried in his own thoughts.

"Something's happening, Nat. I don't have a clue. But something tells me you do."

155

He nodded, chewing his lower lip.

"Okay. Time's up," she said. "You're scaring the crap out of me. Start talking now or I start running in circles screaming."

"Sorry. Sorry," he said. "I'm just...getting my bearings. I think I know what's going on. I was reviewing in my head an advanced-geometry theory Roan published a paper on."

"Theory about what?"

"About something called hyperspace, about the possibility of extra-dimensional vision."

"Oh-oh. Is this going to take a doctorate in math to understand?"

"Not for someone who can see the veins on honeybee wings," he said. "I think you'll catch the drift right away."

18

Aria and Nat needed to talk in private. They sent Jasmine outdoors with a wicker basket half her size to pick wildflowers and herbs that were scattered in patches along the split-rail fences.

"Fill the basket and we'll dry them and you can help me make an autumn wreath," Aria said. "Be sure to get an armful of goldenrod, and some lavender and bee balm."

Jasmine beamed at the assignment. "And lady's mantle and purple coneflower and foxglove..."

Aria chuckled. "Sure. Fill your basket, sweetie."

When Aria and Nat were alone he surprised her by suggesting they go for a walk. "Great," she said. "You must be feeling stronger."

He nodded. "I feel more energetic this morning than I have for weeks." He glanced out the bedroom window at the sunny October day; a reprieve of mild weather in late fall before the cold plunge of winter. "Must be I'm entering my own Indian Summer."

Aria let the comment pass. Nat rolled out of bed, navy silk boxer shorts drooping at his thin waist, and padded off to the bathroom to take a shower.

Indian Summer. He's probably right, Aria thought. She had heard about terminally ill people getting to feel better, almost normal, just before their deaths. Sometimes the burst of strength and energy lasted only minutes, sometimes weeks or longer. She deeply hoped she would get a few happy weeks with Nat before the bittersweet chariot swung low.

She and Nat had been married the week before in a private ceremony. A notary public came to the house, and a neighbor couple, the Armstrongs, served as witnesses. But Aria and Nat continued to sleep in separate bedrooms. Aria told herself it didn't matter, theirs was a union of mutual respect and goodwill, but at times she ached to bestow bodily pleasure and comfort on the man she loved, and receive his intimate blessings in return. Before she met Nat, she had been a globe-trotting gypsy; a dancer who loved to move freely to her own spontaneous music. But these days, she yearned to give herself away to the soulful music only two can make.

Standing in front of her bedroom closet, stripping off her pajamas, Aria became aware she was singing a line from a Marvin Gaye tune: *When I get that feeling, I need a sexual healing.* She laughed. "Don't I know it, bro'!"

After a time, a fresh-shaved Nat showed up at Aria's bedroom door, dressed in a purple corduroy shirt, denim blue jeans and moccasins. Despite his gauntness, he looked more handsome to Aria than ever. She saw past the emaciated flesh to a beautiful spirit, her husband, whose science would change the world forever—as surely as he had changed hers.

Nat laughed as his gaze fell over Aria.

158

Aria felt suddenly shy. *Maybe I overdid it with this outfit.* She had traded her pajamas for a black linen rodeo shirt and matching split skirt with a nubby, silk tweed, rust-colored vest. She wore Spanish riding boots and, at her waist, a hand-braided leather belt with a hammered-silver-and-turquoise Navaho buckle, an antique sterling pin at her collar, and topping off the *Señora del Ranchero* look, a black wool Mexican hat with rounded crown, slung back on her shoulders.

"Too much?" she asked.

Nat's brown face shone. "Richard Burton once said that when he first met Elizabeth Taylor she was so beautiful he laughed out loud." Nat laughed again. "That's how you look to me—more beautiful than can be necessary for any purpose in this world. Yes, it's too much—you're *unreasonably* lovely."

Aria felt her body gush warm all over. In the reflection of Nat's eyes she felt exorbitantly pretty. She drew him into her arms and held on for a timeless moment.

How did the saying go? All the good ones are either married, gay, or dying of brain cancer. Something like that.

After a while, Nat stepped back and offered his arm. Aria took it, and they stepped outdoors into the bright autumn morning at Hilltop Ranch. The front lawn spilled down a slope to rolling pasture that stretched for dozens of fenced-in acres. A breeze ruffled Aria's hair and combed the tall rye grass in broad strokes that flashed silver-green.

159

Nat and Aria held hands and strolled in silence, listening to the landscape. A trio of palomino horses grazed at the eastern fence line. Aria noticed they had begun to grow shaggy winter coats. A year-old colt named Derringer chased Seeker toward the split-rail fence. When the playmates reached the fence, Seeker spun around on his three legs to chase Derringer in the opposite direction. The plucky dog tripped and hit hard and jumped right back up and bolted after the colt.

After a time Nat began the conversation. "These visual abilities you're developing—they're far beyond anything I expected. I'm stunned."

"That makes two of us," she said. "Nat, let me know the truth. What's happening to me? I'll be living with this long after you're not around to help me to understand."

He stopped walking and faced her, eyes like dark suns. His angular face softened and his body language whispered deep caring.

Is that love I'm seeing? Aria wondered and hoped. She resigned herself that if it wasn't love, it was the next best thing.

"I'll do my best to explain," Nat said, "and I won't hold anything back—"

"Thank you."

"—but I don't have all the answers." He sighed. "If Roan were here, she could help us to grasp this, know where it's heading."

Aria felt a pang of jealousy but quickly sidestepped the emotion.

"To begin," he said, "the human eye contains well over a hundred-million photosensitive

160

receptors, which give a data output of more than a billion bits per second. Now, the fact is that much data exceeds the carrying capacity of the optic nerve and the data processing rate of the brain's vision center."

"Okay."

"So the retina is like a sophisticated computer that somehow *reduces* the data to a manageable load before it feeds the signal through the optic nerve to the brain. In other words, the retina is selective, like a tuner, filtering out the 'noise'—the extra frequencies."

She nodded. "I know about tuners."

"Good. In the early years, Roan and I tried to figure out how the retina reduces such a huge gush of data to a manageable stream. But we were stumped. Mother Nature's engineering outsmarted us. So we switched to a new strategy: design a system to process the whole information flood at once."

His eyes remained locked on hers. "Shortly before Roan's...death...we had a breakthrough that got us around the problem of data reduction," he said. "I'll skip the technical details—"

"Smart choice."

"The bottom line is: The computer implants in your eyes and brain enable you to process a signal that is extraordinarily enhanced—extremely broadband. That's why you can see beyond normal human vision."

"*Way* beyond," she said, and searched his eyes. "Do you understand? I wonder if angels could handle some of the visions I see. It scares me, Nat.

161

It's hard to describe. I shift my focus and the most solid-seeming thing—my hand, a stone wall, the ground—turns into transparency. Nothing hidden. Open space everywhere. The world is a wide-open window..."

"You familiar with the word *synergy*?"

She nodded. "When the whole is greater than the sum of its parts."

"Yes. Well, you've boosted that definition to a new level. Your neural nets are being stimulated by the energy-input of the new retinas and their interaction with the computers. The synergistic effect is nothing less than awesome."

"'Terrifying' is the word that comes to mind."

Nat squeezed her hand. "You've probably heard that a person typically uses only a small portion of her brain, ten-percent or so."

"Right. We're ninety-percent asleep."

"Asleep—that's a good analogy," he said. "The brain has units that lie dormant or underused, and other portions that are redundantly engineered as back-up protection against damage, and various other parts in which we have no idea of their function. I believe that all these areas are coming 'online' for you. Your entire brain is waking up."

"But what's that mean?"

Nat let out a sigh and shook his head. "I don't know. Roan created a mathematical model of the vision system. She ran the numbers through a computer but she was unable to pinpoint the system's visual limits."

"Oh boy."

162

"In theory—"

"Let me guess," she said. "In theory, the system has no visual limits."

"Well...that's right...or virtually none. But..."

Anger ignited in her like a red flare. "*Now* you tell me! How dare you keep this to yourself Nat Colt! I trusted you; you *made* me trust in you."

He shrugged lamely. "We didn't believe the numbers. They were too far-out. And the chimpanzees I implanted all behave normally. They climb their gym set and groom each other and handle all the things in their environment routinely."

"And when you interviewed them, they said, 'Nothing unusual, here, Doc.'"

His face looked pained. "We expected the system to perform within the ballpark of ordinary vision. We predicted there would simply be a broadening to the scope of visible light—which I cautioned you about."

"Sure. Expanded color band. Sounded tolerable. I tried to think of it as getting extra paints on my palette," she said. "But you never said a word about my vision tunneling down into the spaces between the cells of my hand."

His mouth tightened.

"Yeah," she said. "I did that this morning just by gazing at my palm."

"Honestly, Roan and I went over and over the numbers and finally concluded the math model was flawed in some way—some little bump in her equations had been magnified into Mt. Everest," he said. "We decided that a vast perceptual range, while *possible*, was about as damn likely as getting hit by lightning every day for a month."

"Guess I must be a lightning rod." Aria dropped his hand and turned away, crossing her arms over her chest.

Nat put his hands on the backs of her shoulders. "I understand your anger," he said. "I feel that I've betrayed you. But, Aria, you gotta remember—Roan was next up to receive the implants."

"Your point?"

"What I'm saying is I didn't ask you to test a system we didn't fully believe in. I never could have done that."

"I know that," Aria said in a small voice.

"If the chimps could talk, if they'd told me they were staring at the molecules in their food dish, I would've gone back to the computer model...well, no. No, I would have simply quit. I don't have enough lifespan left for a major redesign."

Aria turned back to him and forced a smile. "Nat, I was going blind. My whole world would have been lightless. Now I can see stars beyond stars," she said. "You did the right thing. We both did the right thing."

She gave Nat her hand. "Now go on, I've got to hear the rest. Just tell me what's coming next."

He squeezed her hand and gave her a soulful look. *Yes, that is definitely the look of love.*

They began to walk again, this time crossing a long hollow in the main pasture, heading toward a half-dozen round bales of alfalfa hay perched at the far rim.

Nat took a deep breath. "Extreme magnification, amplified distance vision—Aria, that's not the end of it—it's only the beginning."

Aria felt a chill lodge itself beneath her ribcage.

"Seeing the markings on a stallion from twenty miles away…Aria, spy satellites have such cameras, but now you're starting to see beyond the range of optic wavelengths. I didn't realize it until just this morning."

Nat stopped walking and met her gaze. Fear cramped Aria's chest. "Keep talking to me. You're freaking me out, but I need to hear all of it."

"Aria, it's clear to me you're now able to see into higher dimensions."

She felt suddenly dizzy. "Gotta sit down." She sank down in the silver-green rye grass. Any other day she would have savored the sun-heated fragrance of the clay soil, hay, rye and scattered horse muffins. But now she wanted to close her senses to the expanding universe that threatened to overwhelm her shrinking self.

Nat sat next to her. "When I was in the house getting dressed, I was trying to sort out how to explain this to you in words. The concepts are much more assessable through mathematics."

"Good grief." Aria gave a weak laugh. "And I was just thinking, 'Higher dimensions? Why *me*? I don't even like math.'"

Nat pulled up a handful of rye grass, held it in the sunlight. "Aria, this world we tend to think of as real—grassy meadow, pine trees, clouds—it would be far more accurate to regard it as a *portrait* of reality. A human-specific portrait. After all, there's far more to this world than the narrow slice of features our limited human senses perceive."

"Ha. So I'm learning."

"Through the synergy of brain and computer, you've developed a new order of perception. You now can see into a higher level of this world—beyond the three spatial dimensions we're used to. Mathematicians call it *superspace* or *hyperspace*—referring to four-space and higher."

"Sounds weird." Aria shuddered. "Not that I know what the hell you're talking about. Hyperspace?—isn't that some kind of techno-babble out of science fiction?"

"No. I mean, yeah. But the writers didn't make it up. Hyperspace is a very old concept in geometry—at least as old as Plato."

"Must've taught it on the days I skipped class to go surfing."

He shook his head. "This is well beyond Euclidean geometry taught in high-school."

She gave a shaky sigh. "And now I'm getting a crash course."

"Picture the three spatial dimensions we're familiar with—three-space—as only the surface of a deep and vast, many-dimensional sea: hyperspace."

She gulped. "I'd rather not."

"Everything we look upon in this familiar realm," he said, and patted the ground beside him, "can be located and described using three points of spatial reference."

166

Aria wrinkled her mouth as she concentrated on Nat's words. "Explain."

"Say you had an *Etch-A-Sketch* ...you know, the drawing toys?"

She nodded.

"They've got two knobs for drawing lines and curves in a flat plane," he said. "But let's pretend you had a special *Etch-A-Sketch*, and in addition to its two knobs for etching up-and-down and side-to-side, your super *Etch-A-Sketch* had a *third* knob for etching in-and-out. Follow me?"

"So far."

"Etching in those three directions—width, length and depth—you could sketch a figure of anything you see here, right?"

She shrugged. "Guess so."

"Well, look around: You could draw that stand of oaks there, the fencing, the pile of stumps—any of it. Using those three knobs, you could trace the shape of any object in three dimensions."

"Okay. Our ordinary spatial experience is three-dimensional," she said, nodding, "so we can draw any part of it by sketching in three directions."

He nodded. "Exactly. Three mutually perpendicular directions, three axes, three spaces, three dimensions—they each mean the same," he said. "It's also called three degrees of freedom, because...*look!*"

He pointed up at a black sparrow chasing a red-shouldered hawk out of its territory. The little bird zoomed and strafed like a fighter-interceptor attacking an enemy bomber.

167

"There you see it," Nat said. "Three degrees of freedom. You, or a bird or a fish, are free to *move* in any complex pattern within the realm of three-space."

"I can't fly, last time I checked."

"No, but dive into a swimming pool and you can do underwater ballet, right?"

She nodded.

"But if you were a raindrop on a windshield, you could only snake about within the bounds of *two* dimensions—the windshield's surface."

"So that would be two degrees of freedom," Aria said, "and we've got three degrees of freedom. I follow you."

"Good. Now that we've considered three dimensions, let's go beyond them," he said, "because, in fact, the *total* world is more than all that appears in three dimensions." Nat waved his hand in a sweeping arc that took in the pasture and sky.

"You're saying we can see three of the world's dimensions," Aria said, "but they are just its...surface."

Nat smiled. "Who said you aren't good at this stuff?"

"You said the cosmos is vast, multi-dimensional..."

He nodded. "You'd need an *Etch-A-Sketch* with at least four knobs to show the true complexity of the space-time continuum that we're already certain of: three of space and one of time." He paused. "But most physicists say you'd need four knobs just to show the *spatial* dimensions." He

168

hesitated again. "And some theoreticians insist you'd need infinite knobs."

Aria moaned, feeling dizzy. "Infinite dimensions."

"Sorry. I know this is scary for you."

"No, keep going, this is actually sinking in a bit."

"All right. Now think of how you would direct someone to meet you at your office in a city. You'd tell them to find you by traveling so many blocks East-West and so many blocks North-South—that's two dimensions, that gets them to your building. You'd also tell them to take the elevator to a certain floor."

"That's the third dimension."

"Right. But then they might arrive at the meeting place and still not find you, unless you include one more dimension."

"What?"

"You tell me."

Aria frowned. "The street address, the height above the street...*Oh*—the time...what time they should meet you."

"Exactly. Time has to be included in the directions of how to locate anything in space-time."

"Okay."

"So clearly our world is at least four-dimensional," he said. "Three spatial and one temporal dimension. Most of us don't observe any spatial dimension higher than three. Apparently, however, rare individuals can glimpse life from a 'higher vantage,' so to speak, can witness events from across the continent or planet—even the solar system. An urban legend has been going around for years that the CIA uses them—'remote viewers'—for long-distance spying. I thought it was nonsense."

She managed a little laugh. "New Age Nat! Clairvoyants, ESP... What about your favorite mag, *The Skeptical Inquirer*? They'll kick you out of the club."

He smiled wryly, touched his sunken cheeks. "I have no need to save face. With my life running out, I'm finding it easy to dump old opinions—once the truth has smashed me over the head. When you told me you saw the star on Kosmo's forelock, it dawned on me you were seeing beyond three spatial dimensions. There's no other explanation. That got me to accept that others may have managed various degrees of your ability without the advantage of bionics."

"Born with the talent—a gift."

"Let me tell you more about hyperspace, help you to understand what's happening."

"Yes. Please."

"Imagine that we're two-dimensional beings, 'flatfolk,' living on the surface of what appears to us to be a flat, two-dimensional space. We call our home Flatworld. But Flatworld is actually a globe."

"And we don't know it?"

"We don't realize we're on a globe because we're as thin as a film of oil on the surface of a puddle. Our eyes are slits at the front edge of our heads. We cling to the globe's surface with no means of looking *up* into higher space."

170

"Hmm. Okay."

"Then one day, a flat-man has a powerful insight—"

"Nat Flat?"

He laughed. "Let's call him Scientist Flat. He's a theoretical physicist, albeit a very flat one. One day he says, 'Hey, you guys! Reality is more than North-South-East-West. According to my advanced mathematics, this world we're dwelling on extends into *another* dimension beyond flat space! The surface of our world is *curved* through a third space, which I've named, *Up-Down*."

"And all the other flatties groan in confusion," she said.

"Sure they do. They can't picture a shape curved in three-space. So Scientist Flat sets out on a journey to demonstrate the truth of the third dimension, beyond flatfolk's everyday awareness. He slides non-stop in one direction, northward, and eventually reaches the point he started from. Then he repeats his experiment traveling due east, same result. Thereby, the scientist proves that flatfolk dwell on the two-dimensional surface of a higher-dimensional world. He proclaims to his fellow citizens that Flatland is a *globe*."

"I'm still with you," Aria said. "And now for the analogy..."

"Well, just as the two-dimensional surface of a globe requires a higher dimension—a higher *space*—to provide room through which the surface can be curved, our three-dimensional universe requires at least one higher *spatial* dimension—

four-space—in order for the three-dimensional space of our universe to be curved."

Aria furrowed her brow. "How do we know our universe *is* curved?"

"Because, like the surface of a globe, the universe has no end, no edge, no boundary, no center."

"Says who?"

"Einstein, in his special theory of relativity," he said. "You can travel through space in the same direction *forever* without reaching the end, or hitting a wall, or falling off a ledge."

"Who's tried it?"

"No one, of course. But the equations—"

Aria rolled her eyes.

"You'll just have to grasp this intuitively. An ant can walk around and around the two-dimensional surface of a beach ball, right? The ant will never get to an edge. No end. See that?"

"Sure."

"Well, the math says that we can't reach the edge of our three-dimensional cosmos, because three-space is actually the surface of a four-dimensional *hypersphere*."

"Gee, of course. A hypersphere. Which is...?"

"Well, we can't easily envision it. It's a four-dimensional sphere, and we tend to picture everything in three dimensions. But mathematically, four-dimensional curvature is no more strange or difficult to compute than a curved line or surface."

"Nat, if only I were a math-whiz..."

"Think of it this way: if a spaceship traveled far enough in one direction, it would arrive back where it started from," he said. "Einstein said if you could peer out from any point in the cosmos with an unlimited, unobstructed view, you'd be gazing at the back of your head."

Aria nodded slowly, taking in the cosmic view. It reminded her of a verse from the *Tao Teh Ching*, the ancient Chinese "Book of the Way." Composed of just eighty-three short verses written by Lao Tzu, "Old Man," it was the only scripture Aria took to heart. "'The Tao is never-ending,'" she quoted. "'Never-ending, it is far-reaching. Far-reaching, it is returning. Returning to source, it is never-ending.'"

"Lao Tzu had the right idea—and without the math," Nat said.

She shook her head. "You amaze me, Nat. Should've figured you'd know Lao Tzu."

"Oh, physicists love the *Tao Teh Ching*. Niels Bohr placed the yin-yang symbol on his coat-of-arms."

"Bohr?"

"Father of quantum mechanics. Nobel laureate. Einstein's best friend."

"Help, I'm surrounded by geniuses."

"Aria, you're a genius, too. I've seen you dance."

She looked up at his face. "You watched me?"

"I saw you from the top of the stairs. It was very late. You were dancing without music. Pure genius. Poetry in motion."

173

"I was *nude*, Dr. Colt," she said, trying to sound outraged but unable to suppress a smile. "I was your surgical patient. We weren't yet married."

"That's when I fell in love with you, Aria."

There. He said the magic words. *Pass Go! Collect a zillion dollars!*

She cupped his face in her hands and tilted her chin up to meet his plump lips in a first kiss that felt, oh, so fine. *Maybe I can fly, after all.*

Nat leaned into the kiss with real hunger, but then she felt him hesitate. He pulled back and his face struggled between desire and some hard-to-read inward expression.

"Oh, Nat, let's save our talk for later. Let's hurry home and toss off our clothes and spend the morning making love."

He did not say anything. He was thinking about it too much. *Not good.*

"Aria, I do desire you—terribly. How could any man not want you?"

Oh hell. Here it comes.

"But...I know I've only got a short time left on Earth—"

"So why not *live*? Make love with me, darling."

"Because..." He broke off their embrace. "I want to die while still loyal to Roan."

"You mean loyal to her *memory*."

"All right, then; faithful to her memory." His eyes turned downward. "Look, I'm sorry. When I asked you to marry me I explained it was to give you my wealth so that you could raise Jasmine. You said you'd be honored to be her stepmother."

174

"Yes, of course. She's absolutely precious to me. I love her to death and I'll never, ever abandon her. But, sweetheart, I long to be intimate with *you*. Today. Not just 'faithful to your memory,' long after you're gone."

His face grew sadder still, and Aria thought it would make her cry.

"I'm a dancer," she said. "I commune with the world through my whole body. I want to love you, Nat, with my whole body."

He looked up with hope. "Then dance with me, Aria. Now! Here in the pasture. Please, let's dance together."

He's trying so hard. And I can't dislike him for being a hopeless romantic.

He bowed elegantly and then held out his hand. "Strauss: *The Blue Danube*. What a gorgeous waltz! And what a beautiful woman you are! May I have this dance?"

She fell into his arms and instantly he swept her away, in swirls around the pasture, quietly humming the famous waltz in her ear. Round and round they whirled in 3/4 time. And Aria gave herself to him, whole-bodily; she surrendered to the sweetest, saddest, most intimate *pas de deus* of her years in dance. And then, suddenly, they were both laughing giddily as the world turned and turned like the Milky Way.

They were soaring! The horses gazed in rapt witness at the two joyful fliers.

Aria did not know how long their waltzing lasted; but at some point they slowed to a stop and held each other tightly in the middle of the grassy field, the deep stillness of their peace punctuated by their beating hearts.

Aria felt no doubt that she and Nat had made love, and she recognized their fulfilling embrace for what it was: the afterglow.

*   *   *

Nat and Aria walked hand in hand back to the ranch house. "I need to finish telling you about hyperspace," he began.

"Yes, do. I want to understand."

"Let's return to the Flatfolk Saga," he said. "Thanks to Scientist Flat, the scientific flatfolk have come to conceive the third dimension, though it's beyond the mental capacity of most flatfolk to fathom."

"I can empathize."

And then along comes a very unusual flatman, or rather, a flat*woman*: Mystic Flat." He chuckled at the name. "Mystic Flat not only conceptualizes the third dimension, she can actually *see* into three-space. With enhanced vision she watches the flatfolk sliding about in their flat cities, as thin as a layer of paint. But gazing up into the height of three-space, she beholds other globes inhabited by wondrously-shaped beings who scale mountains, fly in balloons, dive under seas—three-dimensional creatures whose forms and movements can exist only in higher space. Mystic Flat tries to describe to her fellow flatfolk her visions of these marvelous higher-dimensional creatures and landscapes—"

176

"And they lock her up in the funny farm," Aria said. "They try to shut her visions down."

"You bet they do," Nat said. "But that's where she gets spooky on them. Turns out, they can't stop her from seeing into higher space, because their two-dimensional padded cell is just a square printed on the skin of the globe—its four 'walls' are only surface lines."

"Oh. So the walls can only block the view of an inmate who's limited to two-dimensional vision," Aria said. "Anyone who can see freely in three dimensions simply has to look *up*. Flatfolks don't know about *up*."

Nat smiled. "I say again: Who told you you're not good at math?"

Aria returned his smile, grateful and proud that Nat respected her mind. "Thanks."

"Now," he said, "here's your analogy: A *three*-dimensional windowless room cannot prevent anyone whose vision extends into the *fourth* spatial dimension from freely seeing beyond the walls, floor and ceiling."

"That person can look right through the walls?"

Nat shook his head. "Not even necessary," he said. "Go back to our heroine, Mystic Flat: she can see into the third dimension; now does she have to look *through* the lines printed on the globe's surface in order to see beyond two dimensions?"

"Oh," Aria said. "She just looks *up* into three-space, into height. There is no ceiling to peer through."

177

"Neither does a person who can see freely in four dimensions have to peer through walls or ceilings that exist only in three dimensions."

She frowned. "Hmm."

"Keep in mind: four-space is not a direction you can point to with these 3-D fingers." He shifted his pointing finger along three axes. "We're talking about a *higher* direction—a completely new and other space. One who can see into hyperspace does not have to look *through* three dimensional …anything. She simply can look *beyond*. It would be absolutely easy and natural—as easy as it is for Mystic Flat to look upward into height, where the two-dimensional lines of the cell walls do not extend," he said. "By analogy, someone like you, trapped in a three-dimensional windowless room could easily peer *beyond* the floor, walls and ceiling into a higher space where the room simply does not reach."

"You're spooking me, Nat. Are you saying I really can do that?"

"Yes. I'm quite certain you're doing it already."

"Holy shit." A jolt of fear shocked her nerves. She felt as if she were balancing on tiptoe at the sheer edge of a cliff overlooking a bottomless deep.

"Eventually I think, you'll learn how to focus your vision anywhere in four-dimensions," he said. "In any case, your line about watching Chinese fishermen poling down the Yangtze was not farfetched after all."

"Explain."

178

"Nothing anywhere in three-space is hidden to you, because hyperspace is the *matrix* or container of three-space—it includes and touches every point of three-dimensional space, always."

"Hoo-boy." Aria pressed her hand to her tightening belly.

"Theoretically, there's nothing stopping you from not only seeing the fishermen, but—by adjusting your focal length—looking *inside* the fishermen, observing their viscera, what they ate for lunch."

"I think I'm going to be car-sick."

"You should be able to snoop within the secret catacombs beneath the Vatican. Seek from room to room inside underground missile silos. Watch sailors playing poker in a nuclear sub cruising beneath polar ice—and find who holds the best hand, or even detect which guy's lungs are most irritated by the cigarette smoke."

"My god. I'd make the perfect spy."

"That's putting it mildly," he said. "The surveillance powers of the most high-tech spy satellites are so inferior to your powers it's like comparing reading glasses to the Hubble Space Telescope." He thought a moment. "No...even that comparison understates it. The reading glasses and the telescope both amplify light wavelengths in the same realm; one is merely tremendously stronger than the other. But you can gaze into an entirely *other* realm. Aria, you own the eyes of a god or goddess."

Aria shivered, rubbed her shoulders. An abyss of freedom loomed before her.

"And from here it gets even more fascinating—"

"Nat, I don't think I can handle any more fascination."

He gestured with his hands. "I predict you'll learn how to *move* through four-space. Then you'll literally possess four degrees of freedom."

They had arrived at the front steps leading up to the wrap-around porch. Aria froze in her tracks and held her breath. She felt the urge to sprawl face down and anchor her fingers and toes in the red clay soil.

Nat waved a hand at her reaction. "No, I don't mean you'll be able to move *bodily* through higher space."

"Move what, then?"

"Move your control. Your influence. Direct your energy anywhere in the world," he said. "Once you get the knack of how to focus your vision on any point in four-space, you may find there's a way to focus your energy there as well, to manipulate objects at a distance. It's called telekinesis."

"I've heard of it," she said. "Sliding a paperclip across a desktop without touching it. Stuff like that."

He nodded. "I believe you'll learn how to do it. Then distance will no longer limit your power to change your world."

She took a deep breath and blew out forcefully. "The little life I had been living has been blown to smithereens."

Nat gave her shoulders a squeeze. "I know all this must be frightening for you. And I know it would be for me, too. But still, I envy you."

She shot him a frown.

"No, really. I swear it," he said. "On the one hand, I apologize for not anticipating the synergistic effect, not enabling you to make an informed decision. But on the other hand, how I wish I could be around to be a part of your adventure."

A wave of vertigo passed. She managed a nervous laugh. "Spare me the pep talk and hand me a Valium."

"Aria, think about what I'm saying. This is enormous. Epoch-making. World-changing. Imagine: you could be the perfect scientist. Artist. Mystic. The possibilities for discovery and understanding—"

"Know something, Nat? For a genius, you sure can be full of shit."

That shut him up.

Aria felt an almost unbearable mix of euphoria and terror. To her surprise, she learned that freedom and fear are cousins. She knew she could not balance on the ledge: she must learn to soar, or plummet.

"I think I know what a fledgling eagle goes through, just before it gets booted out of its nest." Tears started down her cheeks. "Just don't forget there's a person behind these miraculous eyes, and right now, this girl is feeling scared."

Nat drew her into a warm embrace. It comforted her more than she could say and she clung to him. After a moment, he said, "Let's go in.

I'll draw for you a hot bath and you can soak in the tub and listen to Chopin while I rub your shoulders."

"Now that's a genius talking."

19

Aria called them *awake dreams*: altered states of awareness that occurred while she was fully awake, but exhibited a freedom of view usually found only in REM sleep. Or madness.

Sometimes these experiences happened without warning, triggered by some mundane act like opening her front door and looking out—but with the radical difference that she would suddenly find her vision not roaming the ranchland in North Florida, but gazing down at the snow-flurried peaks of the Himalayas, or peering up through a tangle of purple kelp at sea otters swimming beneath sun-streaked Monterey Bay.

More often, her awake dreams were preceded by a brief psychedelic overture: Her attention would abruptly be drawn inward toward a brilliant point—like a blazing star—in the deep center of her brain between her eyes. The instant she focused on that locus of light she would find her awareness floating somewhere above her head, gazing down at her own body. If she then turned her attention toward the "fourth degree of freedom"— her term for the unique "direction" of four-space— there followed a rush of expansion into a radiant void that seemed infinitely beyond, yet all-inclusive of her body and world.

The shining realm completely swallowed her sense of a separated self, so that Aria's body was reduced to only one of infinite possible points of reference contained within the bright space.

While in this enlarged state of consciousness, it seemed as easy and natural to contact any of the other points as it was to reach up with her hand to scratch her nose. But she had noticed an important difference: Touching her nose required physical movement and took a second for her hand to cross the distance to her face. But, once she had made the conscious transition into hyperspace, "traveling" to any point then required no motion at all and was instantaneous. "Distance" had no meaning, for as soon as she focused her attention on where she wanted to be, she found herself *already* there.

She put it to Nat in these words: "I *am* the 'where' of everywhere."

On Tuesday morning, Aria munched a croissant and remembered a rainy summer in France on tour with her ex-husband's dance company. Later in the day, after she shifted her attention into hyperspace, she thought again of Paris and instantly found herself examining at close-up range a mottled crust of pigeon droppings atop the Arc de Triumphe. She scanned along the avenues that radiated like spokes from the central monument. Her view zoomed past the Eiffel Tower where she spotted a used condom on a steel girder eighty feet above the observatory deck and she wondered at the lusty escapade that had left behind such evidence. She focused in for a closer peek at a sidewalk café and found she could read a menu; a *folded* menu. With her liberated vision she scoped through subways as easily as she toured the Louvre.

On Wednesday, a swig of strong Arabica coffee sent Aria off on a tour of the desert near

184

Cairo, where she hovered above the Sphinx, reddish-gold in the rays of Ra. She watched for a half-hour as Egyptian laborers and an international team of archeologists sweated away at their project of restoring the crumbling memorial, more ancient than the pyramids. Aria pondered if she should send them an e-mail from Tallahassee, Florida, revealing the location of the treasure-filled burial chamber they were overlooking, sixteen meters below their sandals.

No way, she decided; who would believe her?

*   *   *

Aria felt afraid.

She rocked on a birch Adirondack chair on the cedar porch, looking down at the pond in the lap of the hollow. In the soft lunar light the waters shimmered like a moon jewel embedded in Earth's navel. But Aria was not enjoying her computer-enhanced vision of the lake, or the infrared-lit raccoons hunting for frogs.

Nat Love sat in a rocker next to hers. Crickets and two barred owls gave sound texture to the quiet night. Jasmine was indoors, asleep on her bed with Seeker.

Power corrupts, Aria worried. It can even corrupt a dancer from the islands who had never thought of herself as ambitious. Such awesome power. She did not doubt it carried the potential to destroy her, or others. How could she be sure to wield her power safely without harming herself or anyone else? How could she learn to use her abilities for the good of human society and the planet?

"What an ego trip," Aria said. "I'm actually sitting here sorting through the kinds of moral dilemmas only comic book superheroes go through. Maybe I should design a costume with a cape. If it wasn't so scary it'd be absurdly funny."

"I've been thinking," Nat said. "What you could use is a kind of guidebook."

She laughed. *"Fodor's Vacation Tour of Hyperspace*? Why didn't I think of that?"

"Seriously. Others before you who have ventured into higher dimensions. We should get on the Internet and see what others have had to say about it, historically."

"So what do we use for a search term? Science-fiction-fantasy, or schizophrenia?"

"I think we should find out what mystics have had to say. Clairvoyants. Yogis. Read everything we can on remote viewing and related subjects."

"But, see that's exactly what worries me," Aria said. "I'm just an ordinary woman. I wasn't born a clairvoyant and I'm certainly not a yogi or saint. I haven't *earned* this power. It's not my own born-talent and it's not a skill developed by fifty years of meditation training in a Tibetan cave. It's just bits of silicon hardware in my eyes and brain—Instant Lama."

"That's not so," Nat said. "Yes, the computer implants were the catalyst. But the vision

186

system has awakened the latent faculties of your own brain. It *is* you, Aria. *You* are doing it."

"Maybe so. But I don't feel ready for it. I'm a twenty-first century woman who suddenly can see like some goddess out of ancient mythology—"

Nat snapped his fingers. "The Oracle at Delphi. We should do a web-search for that."

Aria frowned. "Oh forget it, you're not even listening."

"I'm sorry," he said. "I was listening."

Aria folded her arms across her chest and rocked harder.

"Really, Aria. I was listening. It's just...I read somewhere that men and women handle problems differently. Women want to explore their emotions about the problem and have those feelings acknowledged. Men tend to jump right onto the fast track of how to fix the problem, solve the puzzle. So men may end up seeming calloused—"

"According to the latest studies, 'jerks' is a term that's frequently used."

"—but in fact, men just have a different approach to coping with the problem."

He touched her hand. "You were telling me how you feel. I'm listening with my heart, this time."

She rocked slower and smiled. "You're forgiven."

Aria told Nat her anxiety reminded her of the several dozen times she had skydived.

"I know skydivers who love to jump from above the clouds but wouldn't leap from a swimming pool high dive unless at gunpoint," she

187

said. "Because when you're standing on a diving platform and you peer down at the water you feel a definite sense of that height, but from 10,000 feet up in the sky, the feeling is entirely different. You're way too far up to judge the height above ground using your everyday bodily senses. The height just doesn't compute. Instead, when I skydived I was always aware of the vast *space* on all sides. Unobstructed openness. It always felt to me that when I leapt from the plane, I wouldn't fall, but *disappear*—dissolve into boundless space."

"And that's how I feel about my powers of perception," she said. "I can expand into hyperspace, a sky without boundaries. But I'm scared I'll vanish in the vastness; won't be able to find my way back to this comfortable little rocking chair."

Nat stood and crossed to Aria, bent low and hugged her tight. A tear started down her cheek. "Ahhh. That's what I needed."

"I'm learning," he said.

After a while Nat asked, "Is it okay if I tell you something from my head?"

She smiled and nodded. He turned his chair to face her and sat down.

"Just remember that the rocking chair and this entire world are already contained in higher space. Hyperspace is the matrix that enfolds three-space. It's omnipresent—it contacts every point here. From a purely mathematical point of view, I can assure you that it's impossible to venture anywhere in hyperspace where you would lose touch with this little rocking chair. Or, as you're implying, lose touch with yourself."

"Thanks," she said. "It's true, that has been my experience so far. No matter what I'm viewing, I'm still aware of this place, in the here-and-now. But it's reassuring to hear that the contact can never be broken, no matter what. I'll keep that in mind next time I'm watching the Shuttle crewmembers floating around in their cabin."

Nat stood and guided her up from the chair by her hands. "Come on, Mystic Flat. Let's go in and do some Internet research," he said. "See what we can learn from your fellow seers."

20

Despite a glut of idiotic homepages ("Here's a pic of my psychic pet iguana, Farley."), several hours of electronic legwork produced a stack of invaluable articles on clairvoyance, astral projection, and out-of-body experiences, as well as "navigational charts" offered by mystics from diverse traditions: yogis, Taoist sages, Mexican brujos, Amazonian shamans, Tibetan lamas and various other Magellans of the psychic sea.

Aria felt put off by all the foreign-language and religious terms for her various experiences so she made up her own vocabulary. For example, Nat called the higher-dimensional realm *superspace* or *hyperspace*, Hindus called it *Akasha*, Buddhists called it *dharmakaya*, Alchemists called it *ether*—but Aria named it *EveryHere*, because at that level of awareness, all locations became a singularity: each point of Everywhere was always only Here. Focusing through higher space to a chosen point she called *locating*, since it was instantaneous, involving no travel time.

From her Internet downloads, Aria reviewed a number of time-honored training programs for gaining mastery of her power. She intuitively chose one basic method—a simple breathing-concentration exercise from the Dzogchen sect of Tibetan Buddhism—and began practicing it daily in earnest. To her relief, by week's end, she had gained a far better understanding of her power and had formed the beginnings of a mental map of the vast territory she was now free to explore. Best of all, she was gaining control over her visionary expeditions.

Monday afternoon Aria was alone in the ranch house for the first time. Jasmine was at school. Nat had felt well enough to drive to the lab to check on the chimpanzees in the care of a biology grad.

Aria sat soaking in the bathtub, practicing the breathing exercise that helped her to control her attention in higher space. And yes, according to the mystics a seer *could* project energy and create effects "at a distance"—because, truly, distance did not pertain within EveryHere. But she had not yet tested that ability; one superpower at a time for our new superhero.

For today's drill, she planned to visit a little isle off the coast of Curacao named Islas Los Aves. The United States had bought the islet from The Netherlands in the '50s to develop as a remote tracking station for space missions, but had never followed through.

The islet was a volcanic remnant a few miles in diameter, jutting up from the green sea in a single craggy peak of granite and pumice. A huge population of terns, albatrosses and frigate birds made rookeries on its rocky, cave-pocked slopes. Twice a year, a fleet of guano harvesters motored over from Curacao to fill their cargo holds with bird shit, which they sold for fertilizer in Venezuela. It was said the stuff could grow tomatoes the size of cabbages.

On the western shore of the islet consistent Pacific swells wrapped around a rocky thumb called Punta Guana and broke long and true to the right in flashing liquid tubes. For the intrepid surfer, willing to wade ankle-deep in guano to reach the water, Punta Guana was the best point-break in the Caribbean. Very few Americans knew about it, which kept the waves uncrowded, even on cover-photo perfect days that occurred almost daily in the winter months.

Surfers camped some distance from Punta Guana on the islet's only beach, a quarter-mile long crescent of shiny black sand named Playa Negro. Nice place. No bird shit. But no waves either. It was somewhere in the fine black grit of Playa Negro that sixteen-year-old Aria had lost a favorite silver bracelet while losing her virginity to a twenty-year-old Rasta surfer-god from Kingston.

The winter after Aria lost her bracelet, the U.S. Public Health Administration banned surfers and guano harvesters from returning to the islet because of a series of surfer deaths the officials had linked to a mysterious viral infection caused by exposure to the bird crap. Montego Montenegro, the Jamaican Rasta and Aria's first love, was among eight surfers who had become ill and quickly died.

Isla Los Aves went back to being a habitat where a hundred-thousand seabirds watched perfect riderless waves tubing to the right off the rocky point. But local fishermen claimed the island was now haunted; they'd spotted strange moving lights and heard mysterious noises coming from the lava cliffs and caves.

Aria decided that "arriving" at the islet via hyperspace and searching for her bracelet under the black sand would make an excellent test of her much-improved control.

While remaining aware of her body soaking in the bathtub, she turned her mind inward and shifted her attention into higher space. Her mind floated freely, now conscious of her body as only one of infinite viewpoints within EveryHere. She controlled her extended vision by focusing the "lens" of her attention. Meanwhile, the breathing exercise kept her oriented to her physical body, anchored in the three-dimensional world.

Aria focused her mind-lens on the black shore of an islet in the Caribbean, three-thousand miles from where her breath linked her to her body soaking in a bathtub in Tallahassee. At the speed of now, she found herself already at the crescent of black sand that hugged the crashing breakers. By shifting her focus, she would have been able to examine it from a hundred miles above in space, or from miles deep in the bedrock of the sea-floor mountain. She chose to zoom-in and scan a flat plane a few inches under the surface of the sand in hopes of spotting her long-lost bracelet.

Her control was inexact. Her vision drifted a few hundred yards to the east, scanning inside the mountain. Cinderblock walls and a roomful of computer equipment swung into view.

She flinched in the tub. *What the hell?*

She was in some kind of underground complex. A couple dozen personnel, most in white lab coats, moved about—busy at whatever the hell people *do* inside a mountain on an islet in the middle of the sea. Aria drew her body into a ball, breathless with the irrational fear that the people she was spying on could see *her*.

No, impossible. I'm invisible to them. Like a person looking down from the sky is invisible to the flatfolk.

Even so, she noticed she had automatically slowed her breathing to calm her thumping heartbeat, lest the noise betray her unseen presence.

What is this place?

She scoped through the vault-like rooms connected by round tunnels. Solid objects did not block her view; she simply adjusted her focal length to bring clear vision at a new position, interior to walls and doors.

The personnel wore name tags, which struck Aria as a ridiculous formality: how could only a couple dozen employees not know each other's names? But when she zoomed in to examine the tags more closely, she saw they were electronic badges with printed circuit boards, evidently some sort of ID in a deadly serious security system.

On the lowest level, several stories down inside the mountain, Aria saw what looked like dorm rooms, and in one such room a lone woman in gym clothes pedaled an exercise bike. She was strikingly tall, with emerald eyes, long red hair and fair skin, and she stood out like a lovely white swan against a gray pond.

Aria didn't need an ID tag to recognize her. She was staring at Julia Roan McKenzie.

194

Aria heaved her body straight up out of the bathtub, sloshing water onto the floor tiles.

"Nat!" she screamed. "Jasmine!"

Roan was very much alive.

21

The hands of the clock creeped forward as Jasmine Colt waited for the final bell to ring. Today after school she would get to play with Mojo, Bobo and the other bonobo chimps at her dad's lab. She hadn't seen the animals for a month and she missed them. *Bet they miss me, too. Especially Mojo.*

Jasmine was supposed to go to Red Ridge Stables for riding lessons with Taneesha and her mom after school, but she'd already told Taneesha that she was going to skip today's lesson. She could always ride horses, but her daddy wasn't feeling good lately, so to keep him company was more important. He always liked it when she played with the chimps, which he said was good for the animals. *Daddy will be surprised to see me.*

Her father's office was only two blocks from the school and when at last the bell rang, Jasmine shot up from her seat and ran toward the door.

Ms. Murray snapped her fingers. "Jasmine, *walk.*"

Jasmine walked until she got out the door, then she raced down the corridor and out past the parking lot and the school's front gate. The crossing guard said, "Slow down, honey." At last she was on the sidewalk that led two blocks to her father's office and lab. She sprinted the whole way.

The red brick structure that bore the sign INSIGHT Vision Research Corporation was similar to the other buildings in the block of small industries. Jasmine had the front door key to the lab, but found the door already open. *Daddy's here already.* She shoved through the door and froze at first glimpse of the chaos inside.

Her father's office looked as if a cyclone had churned through it. His computer perched on the desktop, smashed open, exposing circuit boards and wiring. The desk drawers and six metal file cabinets had been gutted, their contents dumped on the floor in heaps. Charts and diagrams papered the carpet along with pages of handwritten notes, X-ray and MRI graphs, color photos of surgical procedures, and crazy ribbons of videotape snatched out of their cartridges.

Jasmine's heartbeat galloped. She stepped back and reached for the door behind her. Just as she turned to flee, she thought of Mojo. The three-year-old male was her favorite; she had played with him since he was a two-pound fur ball. Mojo had been born blind, but with her daddy's implants he now could see. He was real smart—the world's greatest strategist in games of tag—and he lived to be tickled and cuddled. She loved him.

I can't just leave him. He might be hurt, need my help.

In spite of her fear, she forced her feet to shuffle forward into the office. At the rear of the room a sliding glass door led outside to the screened-in enclosure for the chimps. The door stood wide open, derailed from its track. Jasmine stepped toward it cautiously, listening. Her heart drummed, tom-tom loud. She paused and held her breath, straining to hear beyond the doorway.

Birds twittered, a dog barked somewhere down the block, traffic slushed and droned, she even made out the faint squeaking of the tree swing in the breeze. But she heard no chimps. No excited chatter and screeches of play, no yips and hoots of arguing. Just dead quiet. Jasmine realized she would rather hear loud barks of fright than the unnatural silence.

She inched her body out into the overcast afternoon. She spotted Spatz first, sprawled near his tricycle. Jasmine recognized Spatz by the white fur on his ankles that looked like leggings. A gruesome stump appeared above his shoulders. His head was gone.

Jasmine screamed and covered her eyes with her hands. But not before she glimpsed the headless bodies of four other chimps crumpled near the swing set and jungle gym.

A discord blared so loudly in Jasmine's head she thought an alarm had been tripped in the lab. Then she understood it was the jangling buzz of her own horror.

She wanted to spin around and dash back through the lab and office and out the front door. But she couldn't catch her breath. Terror paralyzed her legs.

"Mojo!" her voiced choked on her sobs. Instead of fleeing, she forced herself to step further into the screened enclosure. Mojo's body was not there.

Hope flashed in her heart. Could it be? Mojo had seen the killer coming and he had hid. But where could he have hidden himself?

Inside the lab behind her human footsteps sounded.

22

Something was screwy. Nat Colt had sensed it as soon as he turned the Volvo into the driveway of INSIGHT Vision Research Corporation. Now he stared, blinking, at the entrance door of his lab standing ajar.

First his home, now his office. Some asshole was breaking into his lab in broad daylight.

Nat turned off the engine and waited. The prudent thing to do would be to dial 911 on his car phone. But he felt pissed, not prudent. Just under his skin, grief and rage were still bloody raw. The last intruder to invade his territory had killed his wife.

Bile rose in the back of his throat at the physical memory of the terrible phone call that found him in Sydney. *Why the hell had he traveled so far from home?*

He reached into the Volvo's dash compartment, unzipped a canvas handgun case, pulled out a Beretta Bobcat. Its blue-black steel smelled faintly of gun oil. The .25 caliber semi-automatic was no Dirty-Harry-style cannon; Nat's big hand wrapped the slender grip and made the small gun seem like a toy. But its magazine held eight rounds of expanding-point ammo with a ninth round seated in the chamber. It could fire as fast as he could squeeze the trigger and each slug was designed to flatten on impact to the diameter of a dime, bouncing off bones and shredding blood vessels as it zig-zagged through flesh. All of which made the pocket pistol sufficiently deadly at close range—The Little Gun That Could.

After Roan's murder, Nat had taken a handgun shooting and safety class and was licensed to carry a concealed weapon. Before he became ill, he had trained with the gun twice a week and had impressed his shooting coach with his natural marksmanship. Nat had taken grim pleasure in shooting holes through the hearts of cardboard silhouettes that sprang up, threatening, on the target range. He had hit the kill zones again and again until the bullets had torn open holes the size of his fist. Nat had promised himself that if Jasmine was threatened, he would be there to keep her safe—not in freaking Australia—and he would protect her to his dying breath.

Nat flicked off the gun's safety with his thumb. A blood-red dot appeared. The little weapon was ready to kill, and so was he.

He hurried toward the front door of the office, his pulse hammering. *Whoever you are, you lousy punk, you sure as hell picked the wrong guy to rob.*

Inside the front door he saw the mess. The lab's office had been ransacked, everything in sight trashed and smashed. Manila folders and white papers carpeted the floor; framed artwork had been yanked down from the walls.

The cover on his computer had been removed and set aside on the desk, and then the innards had been savaged with an axe or similar tool. *What the hell? This is no ordinary burglary. They were looking for the hard-drive.* From the evidence of the wreckage, Nat guessed that someone had gotten mightily pissed when he discovered that the hard-drive, the unit that contains the computer's memory, was gone. Nat used a removable hard-drive, so he could easily transfer his work between office and home. Right now, the hard-drive with all the computer files pertaining to Project V.I.S.I.O.N. happened to be sitting in a plastic carrying case in the Volvo's dash compartment.

Someone is trying to steal my life's work.

Nat stepped into the lab. At its far end the sliding glass door leading to the animal pen stood open and cocked sideways, off its rail. He followed the rules according to Florida gun laws and announced his armed presence. "You're trespassing on my private property," he called out in the most commanding voice he could muster. "I'm armed. I've phoned the police."

Running footsteps sounded from inside the backyard enclosure, heading his way. Nat ducked behind the corner of the hallway leading to the surgical suite. He crouched in a shooter's stance, left wrist bracing his pistol hand, finger hovering on the trigger.

He aimed at chest-height, waiting.

Jasmine burst around the edge of the sliding door, green eyes huge with fright like cat-eyes caught in a camera flash.

23

Nat recognized his daughter at the last instant between life and death.

"Jasmine!" He lowered his gun, flicking on the safety.

"Daddy!" She burst into sobs and ran to his arms. She smelled of shampoo and blackboard chalk and nervous sweat.

"Holy shit, girl," he said, hugging his daughter and shuddering. "Almost blew your head off." He felt sick and dizzy at the thought of what had nearly happened. "You're supposed to be at the stables."

"I wanted to help feed the chimps," Jasmine said, crying harder. "I'm so sorry, so sorry. Oh, Daddy, I'm so sorry."

"Shhhh. It's okay. You didn't do any—"

She pulled back and shook her head furiously. "They're *dead*!"

Nat gulped. "What are you talking about?"

"Spatz and Sally, Bobo, Pee-Wee, Frodo— someone cut off their heads." She clung to him again and wailed so loud it hurt his ear.

Curse words exploded from Nat's mouth like a string of firecrackers. After he caught his breath, he said, "Let's get out of here and call the cops."

Jasmine looked at him pleadingly, face streaked with tears. "Mojo!" she bawled. "He's alive!"

Nat glanced over her head to the crooked sliding door. "Where is he?"

She shook her head. "Dunno. He hid from the bad guys. We can't leave him." Her eyes burned bright. "We gotta find him!"

Bravery blazed in her eyes like flames trapped in fire opals. She was scared, but willing to risk her life to save a friend. Nat had never loved his little girl more fiercely.

"I'll come back for him, honey. I promise." He grabbed Jasmine around her waist and hauled her out the front of the office into the parking space. "Quick, jump in the car."

As they hit the seats he cranked the engine and stamped the gas pedal. A bluish puff of rubber shot from the tires as he whipped the Volvo station wagon backward into the street. With a squealing take-off, the car raced toward the school two blocks away. Nat veered into the school bus semi-circle and screeched to a halt in front of the BUSES ONLY sign. A bony woman with silver-blue hair scurried over to the car fluttering her arms like a flight deck officer waving off a pilot on a bad approach.

Nat interrupted her and shoved his cellular phone into her hands. "Ms. Peters, there's a break-in at my office. Call the police." The woman's mouth fell open like a satchel. Jasmine leapt from the car. "Please watch my daughter," Nat said. "Be sure to tell the police that I'm on the premises. I'll be back. Thanks."

He gunned the Volvo out of the bus loop and slung a U-turn back toward his lab. His thumb again flipped off the safety on the Beretta Bobcat.

25

Nat stared at the headless bodies of five chimpanzees. Mojo was not among them. His eyes carefully combed the enclosure and its trees. He threw aside a tarp.

"Mojo?" he called. "Where are you? It's safe now, little buddy."

Nat tried to think of where he would hide from killers. In the office, the lab. Where was there to hide?

Oh shit. The lab's walk-in freezer.

Nat spun and raced back into the lab. The four-year-old chimpanzee was smart, but not smart enough to figure out that the freezer had an interior safety release so that one could not get trapped inside. *Please be okay, little guy.*

He threw open the freezer door and found Mojo curled on the floor, his dark fur frosted white, hugging himself and shivering violently, his breath puffing out in clouds.

"Mojo! I'm here." Nat scooped up the chimp and it clung to him like his own child.

"Police!" a female voice shouted at his back. "My weapon is out. Get your hands in the air, and turn around slowly, step out of that freezer."

"It's okay," Nat said. "I'm Dr. Nat Colt, this is my lab. I can't put my hands in the air, take a look. I'm holding a chimpanzee. See?" He made his voice sound much calmer than he felt. "Now I'm slowing turning around."

"Mister, put that monkey down and step out of there with your hands in the air."

"I can't let go of this animal. He was hiding in the freezer and now he's hypothermic. He's got to have my body heat."

Back inside the office, more law enforcement personnel had shown up and three of them spilled into the lab with handguns drawn.

"Bettie, he's the real McCoy," one cop said. "I recognize him from TV."

The police lowered their weapons.

"Thank all of you for doing your jobs," Nat said. "I'm glad the good guys are here."

"How we can help?" Bettie said.

Nat nodded toward a storage cabinet. "Grab a couple surgical drapes from that cabinet. They're blue. Second shelf. Wrap them around the chimp like blankets."

Bettie moved quickly.

"Someone else, please call the vet for me: Roger Smith at Apalachee Animal Hospital. Tell him Mojo has hypothermia and ask him to get here ASAP. Tell him it's an emergency."

Nat walked into his office clutching the still-shivering chimpanzee. The small room had grown as crowded as a cocktail party. With one hand on his cellphone Nat managed to dial the school to check on Jasmine. The school principal, Dr. Hornsby, said the school nurse had given Jasmine a mild sedative and the girl had just fallen asleep on the cot in the infirmary.

"We'll be glad to keep her for a few more hours," she said. "I understand you've had a burglary at your office? Jasmine was very upset."

"If she wakes up, tell her the police are here and let her know I'm okay and Mojo is safe. Everything's going to be fine."

"She said you went back to rescue Mojo. That's one of the monkeys?"

"Uh, yes," Nat said, glancing down at the chimpanzee peeking up at him from under the makeshift blanket. Mojo had stopped shaking and was breathing more deeply. "Mojo is going to be fine."

After Nat hung up the phone, a police officer with a nametag that read Lt. McMann approached him with an open notepad. "Dr. Colt, can you lead us on a walk-through, tell us what's missing?" He jotted in the notepad and a Sgt. Kazinski appeared at his side with a digital video camera.

"Yeah, sure," Nat said. "We can start right here in my office. Follow me."

Nat guided the police through his office and laboratory; trying to inventory the extent of the damage. Pilfered videos, scavenged file cabinets and emptied drawers. The computer hard drive was safe in his car, but back-up disks and paper copies of his research data had been stolen along with working models of the artificial retinas and data cubes.

Now that the adrenaline rush had faded, a numbing fog of exhaustion and resignation descended over Nat like a narcotic. He noticed his hands trembled, which is how his guts felt inside.

Dr. Smith, the veterinarian, arrived with an assistant named Sheila Duncan, both of whom Mojo knew and liked. Even so, he seemed reluctant to let go of Nat's warm embrace.

Sheila spread her arms, "Come here, sweetie. Bet I'm as warm as Doctor Nat—plus I've got your favorite food." She held up a soft pretzel studded with chunks of salt. Mojo went to her, but did not take the pretzel. He wanted to cling to her comforting body with both hands.

Dr. Smith returned from viewing the carnage and he looked on the verge of tears. "I'm so sorry, Nat." He petted Mojo's head under the wrapping. "I'll take good care of him."

"I'm certain of it," Nat said. As the three went out the door, he shouted after them, "Call me."

Nat resumed leading Lt. McMann around the premises.

Industrial espionage and sabotage. The police wouldn't be able to handle this kind of case; Lt. McMann already had said as much. They'd have to turn it over to the FBI. It might prove to be a case of international spying. Nat kept thinking of the obnoxiously persistent South Korean businessman who'd had a hard time accepting the refusal of his lucrative offers.

Clearly, someone wanted to scoop up all the available data and every working model of Nat and Roan's Project V.I.S.I.O.N. system, even if it meant butchering the chimpanzees that held the technology in their eyes and brains.

But if the purpose was to steal the technology, how could the culprits expect to get away with it? Nat and Roan's INSIGHT Research Corporation had been light-years ahead of other research teams in the field of artificial vision. After Roan's first journal paper, dozens of scientists from around the world had applied to join the INSIGHT team—some applicants even volunteered to work without pay. Serious bait had been dangled, from major funding to prestigious faculty positions. But Nat and Roan were strictly a duo, in tune with each other and on a roll. It was clear to anyone who followed the technical literature that INSIGHT's lead was ever-widening.

Therefore, the first company to market a commercial model of the artificial vision system might as well advertise in *The Wall Street Journal*: "Look! We're the guilty ones. We didn't develop this technology, we stole it."

But what if this wasn't about commerce? What if his life's work had been clawed through by military agents?

Nat chewed his lower lip. Was it possible some spook scientists had read Roan's paper on her theory of extra-dimensional vision? That paper had ended up being published internationally. In it, Roan had suggested the possibility of extraordinary visual enhancement, and although she had discounted its likelihood, Nat now suspected Roan's scientific judgment was clouded by her own intense desire to see again. Had some government scientist—perhaps a mathematical theorist, like

210

Roan—decided Roan's equations on super-vision were well worth testing?

Even worth killing for?

Nat thought of Aria's powers and remembered her comment: "I'd make the perfect spy, wouldn't I?"

He clenched his jaw. What if those powers fell into the wrong hands? If the technology had been stolen to be used by a foreign military—say, China or North Korea? Iran? Israel?

Foreign, hell! The U.S. government was not innocent of committing crimes against its own citizens in order to expedite military and national security projects.

How could I have been so naïve? The place should have had twenty times the security measures he had installed. Spatz and the other chimps had paid for his laxity. He swallowed hard. *Thank god Jasmine didn't arrive earlier.* The thought made Nat shiver and then a jolt of hot rage shot through his nerves.

Bastards! They'd robbed him and Roan of their scientific legacy. Made it impossible for anyone else to resurrect their work after his death—which, obviously, was exactly what they were intending. More than half the creative input had come straight from Roan's brilliant mind. Not even if Nat could expect to live a full, healthy life, would he be able to make up for the missing half of the design team. Not without his research notes and collected data.

Suddenly a thought slammed Nat like a sucker-punch in the gut. He halted in his tracks and

Lt. McMann, jotting in a notepad, collided with him.

These could be the same thugs who killed Roan.

"Find something else, Doc?"

"Holy Christ," Nat said aloud. "They'll stop at nothing to get their hands on this technology."

"What's that, sir?" Lt. McMann said.

Nat's mind swept to the only two working models of the artificial vision system that remained: the set implanted in Mojo and the set in Aria. The killers had decapitated every chimp they found. Nat had to assume they knew about Aria.

"Oh my God," he shouted. "Aria! They'll be coming for *you* now."

"Is there a problem, Dr. Colt?"

Nat fumbled with his cellphone. As he flipped it open, it rang, caller ID: Aria.

"Nat," she began, not waiting for a hello. "I *found* her! She's alive!" Aria choked on her tears.

"Aria! Get out of there, now!" Nat shouted into the phone. "Your life's in danger. You've got to move fast."

"What's going on?" Aria said.

"I'll explain later. Just leave. *Now*! Meet me at the school. Jasmine's there."

"Shit. Someone's at the door."

"*No*! Don't answer it. Get out the back. They're after you, Aria. Go, go, go!"

Aria dropped the phone. Nat heard the loud splintering of wood, male voices shouting.

"Aria!" Nat screamed. "Aria!"

They were going to murder Aria and mutilate her for the prize he had placed inside her head, and Nat could do nothing to stop it.

26

Jack Wolfe sprang from the white utility van before it stopped. Large red script on the side panel read *HIS WORD Karpet Kleeners* and featured a Christian fish-motif woven into the logo. Wolfe strode toward the ranch house. From his gray jumpsuit he drew out a plastic Glock pistol with a sound suppresser threaded into its barrel. He clipped in a fresh 13-round magazine, cocked the slide to load a 9-mm. cartridge into the chamber.

A silvery shepherd dog was curled up asleep in a rectangle of sunlight on the front porch. Perfect, Wolfe thought, and a half-smile creased his hard face. This mutt was the very reason he carried the Glock in his *left* hand.

Suddenly the dog pricked up its ears and hopped up in a crouch, snarling. Wolfe held up his mangled hand as he approached the porch.

"Remember me, Fido?"

The dog laid its ears flat and unleashed a deeper growl from down in its belly. Wolfe was glad the dog recognized him. "That's right, it's your ol' buddy," he said. "Come to pay you back."

Not taking its eyes off the intruder, the dog backed up against the front door to guard the entrance to the house. Wolfe climbed the first two porch steps, paused and aimed. The gunshot made a sound like ripping silk. The bullet pierced the dog's throat at the level of its vocal chords, spraying bright crimson specks on the sunlit cedar boards.

Wolfe unsheathed a commando knife with a blued-steel blade. While the muted dog kicked its legs, struggling to breathe, Wolfe reached down and with a heavy hand slit the dog's chest, exposing yellow fat, red muscle, white bone. A punching stab broke through the sternum. Purplish-gray lungs strained inside the ribcage like bellows. A few seconds of gouging freed the beating heart from its tissue moorings. The rusted-iron odor of fresh blood wet the air.

A blond man dressed in gray coveralls came up the steps behind Wolfe. The second man was nearly a foot taller, thirty years younger and more powerfully built than his senior. "Jesus, God, sir," he said. "Why'd you do that?"

Wolfe skewered the dog's heart on the end of his blade and spun to face his associate, thrusting the grotesque meat in the man's face. "Maybe you got a fucking problem with it, Sorenson?"

A shadow fell over Sorenson's eyes. "Uh, no sir. No problem."

"What I thought." Wolfe felt a huge letdown. He slung the dripping organ over the porch railing onto the grassy lawn. He had not enjoyed killing the dog as much as he had anticipated. For more than a year Wolfe had looked forward to carving out its heart, and now it was already *over*, in less than a minute. Done. No replay. *Shit. Revenge never tastes as sweet as you hope it will.*

Wolfe wiped the slick blood from his knife and hands on the dog's thick coat. He turned toward the front door. Locked.

215

The blond man said, "Thames is in position around back, sir."

Wolfe held the gun in his left hand behind his waist and rang the doorbell with his mangled hand.

No one answered the door.

Wolfe double-checked the silencer on the Glock barrel, twisting it to the right; it was already tight. *Maybe the next part will be more fun.*

He nodded to Sorenson. "Break it down."

27

Aria dropped the phone and raced from the kitchen through the utility room and flung open the back door. She dashed out onto the porch and nearly fell into the arms of a dark-haired man in a gray jumpsuit. He grabbed Aria, spun her around and locked her torso in a bear hug from behind.

Aria screamed and stomped his instep with the heel of her Spanish riding boot. The man howled. She smashed down again and ground her heel into his foot. He loosened his grip enough for her to twist away, spin and launch her best chorus-line snap-kick straight into his groin. His air wheezed out and his face sagged to the height of a ballet-bar. Aria snap-kicked again, like a Rockette. Her pointed boot nailed his mouth and two front teeth hopped out like Chiclets. He crashed down with a grunt as Aria sprinted toward the barn.

Ping! Ping! Ping! A metallic popping sound. Bullets sliced the air. Plumes of clay and grass spouted around her feet.

"Hold it right there," a gravelly male voice called out behind her. "Unless you don't believe I'm missing you on purpose."

Aria stopped in her tracks. Her heart pounded so hard her small breasts bounced with each beat.

"Ms. Rioverde," said the voice. "Please turn around, slowly."

She turned to find a short, solidly-built man with a silvery white crew cut aiming a silencer-equipped pistol at her chest. Behind him a huge blond Viking stepped out of the house pointing a similar weapon. Both men wore the same gray coveralls as the dark-haired man who now hunched on his side on the porch, groaning.

The white-haired man stepped over to him. "Thames?"

"I'll be okay, sir." His bloodied lips had already swollen grotesquely. "She caught me off-guard."

In a blur of motion the white-haired man kicked Thames square in the mouth again. The man cried out in pain and threw up his hands to protect his lips and teeth.

"Never," the older man said, and kicked hard again. "Be." *Kick*. "Caught." *Kick*. "Off." *Kick*. "Guard." *Kick*.

Thames lay unconscious, hands splayed loosely near his ruined mouth.

"Sorenson, get this incompetent piece of shit back into the van."

The Viking pocketed his gun. "Yes sir." He seemed relieved to have something to do. He grabbed the limp body under the armpits and dragged it down the porch steps onto the grass. Sorenson disappeared around the side of the house lugging his comrade.

The white-haired man did not shift his piercing gaze from Aria. Unmatched irises, brown and green, colored eyes deep-set beneath a bony brow. Their unblinking coldness reminded Aria of something reptilian. The man shoved his pistol into a pocket, but Aria thought she would rather have the gun aimed at her than those chilling eyes.

She remembered Nat's warning over the phone. *What's happened at the lab? How did Nat know I was in danger? Is he staring at a gun in his face, too?*

"Ms. Rioverde. You and I need to chat."

Aria forced in a deep, full breath, trying to calm her panic. Brownish-red splotches stained the man's coveralls like the apron of a butcher. For the first time she noticed the logo, *HIS WORD Karpet Kleeners* with the Christian fish-motif, over the nametag on his chest: RANDY.

"So you want me to join your church, Randy?" She tried to sound unfazed. "Jehovah's Witnesses have got nothing on you guys."

He laughed in an ugly way.

"Who are you?" she said. "How do you know my name?"

"Who I am is not relevant. But what I'm here to do is critically important."

"What do you want? Who do you work for?"

"I'm assigned to protect the national security of the United States. You don't need to know more than that. "

"Where's Seeker?"

"Seeker. That would be the watchdog?"

"The dog. Where is he?"

The man held up his wounded right hand. "Seeker did this to me a year ago. I've thought about him every day since. Today I paid him back.

219

Call it a matter of honor—it was between us two old dogs."

Aria swayed with sudden vertigo. The bastard had kidnapped Roan, killed Seeker. "What do you want with me?"

"I'm concerned about the gadgets inside your eyes and brain." A smirk creased his face. "It's something you and I have in common."

Aria shifted her vision to paranormal range. Switching visual modes was beginning to seem natural, automatic, though she couldn't explain *how* she did it. Then again, neither could she explain how she did other mental tasks, like remembering multiplication tables or conjuring fantasies. She just *did* it.

The experience was akin to opening the iris of an optical instrument to let in more light. Suddenly a higher dimension of sight poured in. Aria scanned inside the man's skull and saw electronic retinas and data cubes implanted in his eyes and brain.

Aria gasped. "Then can you...can you *see*?"

The smirk flashed across his face again. "Let's just say I like your lace panties. Black's my favorite color in lingerie."

Aria was at once afraid and angry. "This is a military thing, isn't it?" she said. "You're a soldier. They've built the perfect spy."

"As I told you before, I represent the national security interests of the U.S.—and that's all you need to know. You are a threat to our nation's security."

She forced a nervous laugh. "I'm no threat to anybody. I'm a dancer, a surfer. I believe in Bob Marley and mango smoothies. Sound like a threat to national security?"

"More than you know." He waved a hand toward the kitchen window. "Get inside. We can talk in there. Go. Lead the way."

In the kitchen, the man gestured toward a round mahogany dining table. "Take a seat." Aria sat in a wicker chair. The intruder stood with his back to the black refrigerator.

"I've been directed to do one of two things with you," he said. "Kill you. Or take you with me into protective custody."

Aria snorted. "*Protection*? If you're the good guys, who the hell are the bad guys?"

"Enemies of the United States."

"That's pretty damn abstract."

"Foreign agents who would go to a great deal of trouble to chop off your head, pack it in dry-ice and ship it to their home labs so they can retro-engineer the gizmos in your brain. Concrete enough for you?"

Aria licked dry lips. "Why is everyone after this technology? To build their own spies?"

He shook his head. "This has nothing to do with spying, at least not in the sense you're thinking of—stealing military and industrial secrets, surveillance, sabotage." He smiled strangely. "It's beyond anything you might easily imagine."

"Try me."

"Let's just say it concerns mankind as a species—it's about who comes out far ahead and who gets left far behind."

She waited. He only stared at her coldly. "That's all you're gonna tell me?"

"'Nuff said."

"But I still don't have a clue what—"

"You don't know, and that's why you're still alive." He glanced at his watch. "We're running out of time. You can go with me in one piece, or I can take back just your head. That's the deal. I couldn't care less which way it goes down."

But when he licked his thin lips Aria knew he preferred the violent outcome; he hungered for cruelty and he hoped she would force him to kill her.

Since the conversation had begun, Aria had been thinking hard about escape. Her attention kept returning to a large black steel flashlight—the long, heavy kind cops use—perched atop the refrigerator. A week ago, Nat had suggested she might be able to move objects with her mind. Now she desperately wished she could call forth the flashlight to hop off the ledge and bomb the man's skull. It might provide enough distraction for her to flee. But if psychokinetic ability existed in her, she had not discovered how to harness it. Despite practicing daily over the past week, trying with willpower alone to force a train of paperclips to slide across a glass desktop, she had not managed to budge even one paperclip.

She needed to stall for time.

"Let me work this out," she said. "Some kind of government intrigue has got something to do with the artificial vision system inside me. Inside both of us. And it goes far beyond ordinary spy stuff. But the secret leaked like a condom, and now international agents are on a mission to hunt me down and grope through my brain to learn what makes me see. Because with this technology they, too, can...what? If it's not spying…"

He held up his right wrist and glanced at the non-reflective glass of a military watch. He tapped the face. "I'll give you exactly one minute. *Decide*."

"You, my nameless rescuer, are offering to whisk me away to some secret prison where I'll be safe, a slave of my special abilities. Or you'll spare me the hassle and kill me now."

"Forty-five seconds." He casually bent down and drew from its ankle sheath a knife with a serrated razor edge of ten inches of blue-black steel.

The heavy flashlight with its six D-cell batteries hovered in Aria's peripheral vision just above the man's head. A trickle of sweat ran down her spine as she strained invisibly to make the flashlight move. It sat as motionless as a rock, like the paperclips had done.

The callused hand gripped the knife with an intimacy that told Aria this man had killed with this weapon many times. A dark red paste had dried along the knife's blood groove and Aria winced to realize it was Seeker's blood.

The man stroked the flat edge of the blade obscenely and said, "Thirty seconds."

Aria's heart pounded in her ribs like fists beating on the bars of a jail. She recalled the methods she had tested in her experiments with the paperclips. She had tried shoving them across the tabletop by the force of her will. No effect. She tried vividly picturing the paperclips slipping along the smooth tabletop. No effect. She had peered deep into the molecular and atomic levels of the steel wire, looking for some force field to attract or repel. No effect. She had even tried getting angry, cursing at the stupid things, firing hot mental darts at the paperclips to goose them along. It had all been futile.

"Twenty seconds." His mouth squeezed tight to form a tight smile like a slit in his granite face.

Concentrating—without staring—at the utility flashlight, frantic and sweating from silent exertion, Aria suddenly realized the one thing she had not yet tried was simply *to ask*.

She allowed her emotions to flow toward the flashlight on top of the refrigerator—as if befriending it—and she asked it to move. Summoned it prayerfully. *As a favor. Please. Move for me.* She thought she noticed a vibration in the heavy flashlight. *Please. For me. I need your help. Move now.*

Yes! The flashlight wobbled!

Aria felt abrupt surprise at sentient contact—not the presence of another thinking mind, but a kind of sympathetic space that linked her feelings with the energy of the flashlight. It was as if the energy field that included her and the flashlight could sense her great need. *Please. I need your help. Move for me.*

"Ten seconds."

The flashlight shifted an inch or two toward the edge of the fridge. Aria extended her heartfelt supplication toward the flashlight, beseeching more deeply, fervently, for it to move. Her eyes closed as her entreaty took on the pitch of intensely personal prayer. Her plea became pure feeling, without words. Suddenly she broke through to an experience of total connection, as if the flashlight had become an extension of her own body-mind.

"Seven seconds...six...five ...four ..." He slowly moved toward her, brandishing the knife.

A burst of pure hope leapt from Aria's chest to the energy of the flashlight, the whole refrigerator. Their atoms danced in felt synchrony with her mind and Aria could not help but open her mouth in wonder. She understood clearly now: The flashlight had not become an extension of *her*, but rather, she and the flashlight were both extensions of the same all-encompassing field—one unifying matrix that enfolded everything. And the thrilling revelation: it was a matrix of *mind*.

The man stopped, wary. The flashlight shot from its perch and missed his head by inches, ricocheting off the far wall with a loud clang. "What the fuck?" He spun around, whipped the pistol from his pocket.

The refrigerator leapt four feet off the floor as if it were a killer whale exploding upward from the sea. It rammed a square dent in the ceiling and plaster rained down as the leviathan crashed on top

225

of the gunman, pinning him to the floor tiles under its bulk.

Aria turned and fled the house.

As she ran, she still felt the atoms of the refrigerator resonating, vibrating, harmonizing with her being, like the proverbial rocks singing in the desert. And in the midst of her flight from evil she laughed with unexpected joy.

28

Aria dashed out the back door and raced to the barn, hopped on her Yamaha off-road motorcycle, turned the ignition key and kick started it with one savage swipe. A blue cloud spat out the pipe and the 250-CC four-stroke engine whined like a hornet. She cranked hard on the throttle and blasted out the open barn doors, gunning the engine through second and third gears as she rocketed down the dirt road that led past the ranch house.

The linebacker-sized agent, Sorenson, had just finished shoving his unconscious comrade into the utility van, rear doors still open. He glanced up as Aria flew around the corner of the house. He grabbed for the gun in his coveralls pocket. Her only hope was to reach him before he reached the gun. She jammed the throttle to the grip stop and popped a wheelie in third gear, aiming straight at the man. Just as the gun barrel swung up the motorcycle rammed the man full-on. He flew backward and slammed against the van. Something snapped loud as a wishbone. The impact knocked Aria off the bike. The big man crumpled to the ground like a bean-bag dummy. A crater the size of his head dented the steel side panel.

Aria shakily picked herself up. Her nose trickled blood and she had bit deep into her tongue. But she was far better off than the guy sprawled in the red clay driveway, whose neck couldn't have twisted at that angle even if he were a yogi. She grunted as she stood the dirt bike up. The clutch handle had broken off.

Better to take their wheels anyway, she realized. Then they couldn't give chase.

The van's engine was running, keys in the ignition. She jumped in, shoved the gearshift into first and scratched off at a furious clip. She watched in the rearview mirror as the sudden acceleration dumped the limp body out the back door. Then she hit the brakes and the door slammed shut. She lurched off again.

The cargo area of the van was stuffed floor to ceiling with electronic surveillance gear, and a sweet smell of fiberglass resin and the ozone-whiff of transistor boards filled the cab. She pinched her dripping nostrils, tasted on her tongue the coppery flavor of blood.

Aria sucked in a lungful of air and let out a scream that started from the soles of her feet and blew out through the top of her head. Then she screamed again. She needed to go on screaming and screaming, to let loose her pent-up fear and anger, her sense of having been violated.

Ruddy clouds billowed behind in a long vortex, the wake of her escape. Cinders and pebbles skipped and bounced, clanging loud as gunshots on the undercarriage of the van.

The rocks themselves will sing.

She screamed from her belly one last time. This time the emotional mix included a new ingredient—exhilaration.

She side-slipped off the red clay road onto a two-lane blacktop and punched the gas pedal, heading at high speed toward the elementary school in town to rejoin Nat and Jasmine.

Roan was alive. Nat's wife and Jasmine's mother—*alive.*

Aria rolled down the window to let the chill October air gush into the cab, ruffling her hair. The van flew down Old St. Augustine Road beneath a dark green canopy of live oak trees draped with silvery Spanish moss.

Roan lived! That truth made Aria very happy.

And more than a little lonely.

29

In a helpless fury Nat bellowed a string of impotent curses at his cellphone. Then he slugged a file cabinet over and over with all his might, leaving dents in the thin steel.

"What the hell's going on?" Lt. McMann said, grabbing his arm to stop the rampage. "Is it a police matter?"

Nat turned and examined the frowning police officer. McMann's wrestler-physique seemed too bulky for the black TPD uniform into which it was stuffed. A dozen other cops milled around the rooms of the lab. All had weapons, radios. Nat had never met Lt. McMann or any of them before. How did he know who the hell they were, or who they really served?

Nat realized with sudden anguish he could trust no one. The paranoia brought with it a sickening rush of energy, as if a hypodermic had stabbed his chest and a syringe-load of adrenaline shot straight into his heart. His mouth went dry and his gut cramped. Never until this moment—not even when Roan had been murdered—had he felt such fundamental distrust of every human stranger. Now he was forced into war with the whole world.

"No, no, it's okay," Nat said. "Thank you, lieutenant. Just stress. I'm...I'm very upset." He glanced down meekly. "Sorry, I lost my temper."

"Understandable, Doc. Been an awful day. You'd better take care of your hand."

Nat noticed all his knuckles were skinned and bleeding. His hand was beginning to swell.

"I'll go grab a first-aid kit," McMann said, "Got one in my squad car."

"Yeah. Thanks."

The policeman left the building and returned in a moment with a blue plastic box with a red cross on its side. Nat applied antibiotic ointment and bandaged his own palm. All the while, he felt himself sinking into an ugly gloom, and could not stop the descent.

First he had failed to protect Roan and she had been murdered in their home. Then his daughter had strolled in on the gore and butchery at the lab—and Nat knew if Jasmine had arrived minutes earlier she would have collided with the killers and ended up among the carnage.

Now someone had invaded his home *again* and attacked Aria. Had she been murdered? Even if Nat had trusted the lawmen and had screamed for their help, they could not have raced to his ranch in time to prevent whatever already happened.

Aria. Please be okay. Please. Have mercy on my heart.

Nat told Lt. McMann he needed to pick up his daughter from school.

"All right, Doc. Stop by the police station tomorrow morning." He handed Nat a business card. "My phone number is on there if you need anything in the meantime. Tomorrow we'll get a more detailed statement from you."

They exchanged business cards and Nat turned to leave. At the front door the cop called after him, "Take it easy, sir. Have a glass of wine. Get some rest."

Nat drove away in the white Volvo station wagon. The rearview mirror reflected his painfully thin face, shoulders hunched beneath their invisible burden. By the time he parked near the elementary school office, his spirit had plunged down and down, as in a bathyscaph; down into an inky abyss of despair.

To marry Nat Colt was to wind up murdered. He felt he was a hideous failure at being a good husband, a protector. And, for the first time, he realized how much he loved Aria. Not just for the mothering she could provide Jasmine after he was gone, but for herself.

Why did I never tell her that? The answer, he knew, was his loyalty to Roan's memory. *But Aria gave her love to me in so many ways. I should have confessed my feelings.*

Fifteen months ago, when Roan was murdered, Nat had decided he owed it to their daughter to master his emotions, keep his bow pointed into the heavy seas and ride out the storm without sinking. He had done a decent job of toughing it out. Except for the morning he had sobbed while he and Jasmine scattered Roan's ashes, Nat had made sure he was alone before allowing his feelings to erupt and sweep him away. Even when cancer hit, he did not buckle. He wept and raged in solitude. Jasmine needed a strong and supportive father, not an emotional wreck, and Nat had vowed to hang on in one piece for his daughter till the end.

But as he dragged his feet toward the infirmary in the school office at Greenwood Elementary, Nat felt his ship floundering in the gale, listing in the waves, sinking. Tears streamed down his brown cheeks. He couldn't hold them in, couldn't deflect the overwhelming sense of hopelessness and defeat.

Jasmine took one look at his face and the light drained from her eyes. "Daddy, what happened?"

He shook his head numbly, unable to speak. Jasmine ran to him and pressed herself into his arms, sobbing. "Daddy," she blubbered, "I'm so scared."

"I know baby. It's okay. It's okay." He patted the cornrows of soft red hair and fumbled for adequate words. He tried to shove his terrible anguish back inside the vault and lock it tight again.

Abruptly, a distant explosion rocked the school building. Jasmine moaned and cried harder, clutching him tighter. Acoustic tiles dropped from the ceiling and slapped a desktop and the floor. Nat stared out a window of the infirmary. A roiling ball of black smoke expanded into the late afternoon sky in the direction from which he had driven. A dozen security alarms from cars in the parking lot whooped and shrieked; set off by the shock wave. People dashed out of the school building, pointing and shouting in horror. As Nat watched, the black smoke formed a fat column and shot upward into the orange sky on the wings of its own heat.

In his gut he had already known it was his lab that had exploded, and now the tower of smoke

233

marked the site beyond doubt. Nat stared at the tendrils of orange fire snaking in and out of the black fumes. He grieved for the cops who were inside the building when the bomb went off. So they had not themselves been the enemy, but victims of his enemy.

In another minute, approaching sirens could be heard.

Jasmine abruptly left her father's arms and darted toward the door. "Jazz, wait!" Nat spun to follow and saw Aria standing in the doorway.

He gasped. "My god, you're safe!" In two strides he grabbed Aria and swept her off her feet in a crushing embrace. "I'm so grateful to see you," he said hoarsely. "I love you, Aria. I never told you how much you mean to me."

Aria squeezed him back till it was hard to breathe. "Oh Nat, I've been longing to hear you say those words," she whispered, and her tears wet his neck. "Now when you finally say them, it's too late for us."

"Too late?" He held her at arm's length, fear in his black eyes. "What's wrong? What do you mean?"

"I have great news. But everything has changed. I'll have to explain later. Right now, we've got to get out of here, far away. All three of us are in danger."

"I know, I know," he said, "but I can't figure what the hell is going on."

"Let's get on the highway fast and drive. Give us time to talk and think."

They both grabbed Jasmine's hands and the trio walked out the door. "Which way we heading?" Nat said.

"I figure South. Miami or the Keys."

"Okay. We'll need cash. We'll have to stop at my bank." They walked at a brisk pace toward the white station wagon. The air smelled scorched and sooty.

"I'll drive," Aria said, "but wait for me, I need to do something first."

Nat opened the rear door of the Volvo for Jasmine to climb in. He watched over the car's roof as Aria hurried over to a parked and empty yellow school bus. *What's she up to?* Aria opened the rear emergency door of the bus and grabbed a fire ax affixed inside. Then she ran to a white utility van with *HIS WORD Karpet Kleeners* painted along its side panel in red script. She climbed in through the rear doors and in the next instant Nat heard a clanging and crunching of metal and shattering of glass as the white van rocked on its tires.

Aria hopped down out of the van, ran back to the bus and replaced the ax in the exit door, then scurried over to the car, jumped in the driver's seat and started the engine.

A small crowd of teachers, parents and students had their backs to Aria, their attention glued a few blocks away to the roaring fire that shot flames fifty feet high. But Ms. Peters, the Parking Lot Monitor, had watched Aria's act of demolition and now stood in speechless shock, both hands pressed against her bosom, mouth gaping like a goldfish.

Nat rolled down his window. "It's alright, Ms. Peters. Serves them right—they weren't parked in a valid spot." The Volvo screeched out of the school parking lot, trailing a bluish haze of tire rubber.

"Equipment for electronic eavesdropping," Aria said. "That was a citizen's protest against the way my tax dollars are spent."

"Remind me never to disagree with you on politics," Nat said.

A quarter-hour later, Nat was arguing with a bank officer. "Ma'am, I have more than $35,000 in my checking account, and ten times that much in savings. And you're trying to tell me I have *no* money deposited at this bank?"

"Sorry sir," she said, staring at a computer screen. "We have no records of any money accounts in your name. Now or ever." She swiveled the monitor so he could see for himself the plain digital facts.

Nat realized his computer bank records had been hacked into and deleted. "Are you going to believe me or that machine?" As soon as he asked, he saw the question was futile. The bank officer eyed him as if he were crazy. Clearly her trust lay with the printed circuit boards, not his wetware.

A tall, skinny, rent-a-cop appeared at her side, squinted at Nat. The sleeves of his blue polyester shirt didn't quite reach to his hands. "Is there a problem?"

"No," Nat said. "No problem—a misunderstanding. Okay, look, Ms. Combes," he said to the bank officer, "You said no money accounts. See if you still have a safety deposit box registered in my father's name, James Samuel Colt."

In a flurry of keystrokes she produced an account number for the valuables box. "Got it. Uh, fees paid in full to date, no balance. You're listed as co-owner of the account." She looked up, hopeful the news would appease him.

"Great. I'll need to get into the box immediately."

"That we can do. Follow me, Dr. Colt."

The bank officer opened the safety-deposit vault. Nat stepped in and unlocked a steel cabinet with his personal key. As he opened the twin doors, the smells of gun oil and moth balls spilled free. He pulled out an antique wooden pistol case that held two vintage Colt revolvers that had belonged to the black American cowboy, Nat Love. The rest of the collectibles included an early model Winchester repeating rifle and several racks of vintage clothing from the American West of the 1870s, plus a hammered-coin necklace that had belonged to Asi Hadjo, an escaped African slave who became the wife of Chief Osceola of the Seminoles. Nat planned to sell the items to a wealthy South Florida collector, a federal judge, who for years had badgered Nat to part with his Black Cowboy and Black Indian artifacts. Nat figured the sale would bring fifty thousand dollars or more; enough to live on while they regrouped and came up with a plan.

Nat hurried out to the Volvo and returned with an Army surplus canvas duffle bag to carry the stuff. He packed the bag and loaded it into the rear of the station wagon.

Aria drove, heading due south on I-75 to Miami. Nat sat in the front beside her. Jasmine lay across the back seat asleep with Nat's nylon windbreaker as a blanket.

The setting sun swelled into a fat red ember as it neared the horizon. Red light swamped the wide pastures that ran along the highway, painting cattle and pine trees with a ruddy aura of fire. Vehicle headlights came on as the tableau darkened.

Aria turned her head to check that Jasmine was sound asleep.

"Nat, listen to me." She took his hand and met his eyes. "Roan is alive."

His eyes shot open and his heart skipped a beat. "*What*?"

"Roan is alive. She wasn't murdered. It was a hoax, some other woman's corpse."

If it were not anatomically impossible, Nat would swear his heart had leapt into his throat. *Roan is alive!*

He finally managed to stammer, "But...she was charcoal, burnt beyond recognition..."

"Exactly: 'beyond recognition'—because it *wasn't* Roan, it was faked. They kidnapped Roan. One of the men today, the leader, he was the one who abducted Roan."

Nat was not aware of his tears until they splashed on his hand that clutched his chest. *Roan is alive!* "Who? Who are they? Where'd they take her?"

"U.S. government agents, talking some national security bullshit. The creep with white hair was in charge. He killed Seeker."

"My god…" Nat wiped at his tears, glanced back at his sleeping daughter.

"Roan is on an island."

"He told you?"

She shook her head. "I *saw* her. I was practicing to gain more control of my vision and I accidentally found her. The island is called Isla Los Aves. I know the place, it's near Curacao. I surfed and camped there a hundred times as a teenager. It was just birds and empty lime rock caves. But now it's some kind of secret military spy base."

"But why Roan?" Even as he asked, he knew the answer. "The data-cube?"

Aria nodded. "They've been using her to build their own vision system. The white-haired son of a bitch, their leader, he can *see*, Nat, he can see like me. He's got implants."

"Oh no! Goddamn it. What are they up to? Is Roan safe for now?"

"I don't know. The bastard said my choice was to go with him in one piece—or from the neck up."

Nat glowered. "That's what they did to the chimps. It was brutal."

"I know, I used my vision, scanned the lab looking for you. I saw the slaughter. But I don't believe it was the same team that assaulted me."

"Who, then?"

"I don't know. The leader said agents from other countries are onto this. North Koreans, for one. It's a freaking international race. Every country is trying to copy the technology that gives me special vision. They'll stop at nothing."

"For what purpose? Why the urgency? I don't understand."

She shrugged. "I don't get it either."

"For special warfare operations?" He dreaded the answer.

She shook her head. "The guy said it's not for espionage, not for reconnaissance, sabotage, things like that. He made it sound much more...*ultimate*."

"Like what? What's that leave?"

"He wouldn't tell me. But obviously something very major is going on here. Something critical enough to trigger an international dash to grab this technology fast, by any means. These agents are being pretty goddamn bold, wouldn't you say? I'd guess that they're desperate—but I don't know what's at stake."

Thoughts careened around Nat's head like a pinball machine with ten steel balls in play at once. Nothing made sense to him. But *Roan is alive!*

"And there's something else," Aria said. "I can *move* things now."

"The paperclips?"

She giggled nervously and swept fingers through her bangs. "The refrigerator."

He shot her a look.

"I made it leap into the air. It came down and flattened the son-of-a-bitch. That's how I escaped."

He shook his head slowly. "I'm in awe."

"Me too. As in *aw*fully scared."

"Aria, maybe you can tap Roan on the shoulder, move something around in her room. Let her know we know she's alive."

"Been thinking along those lines myself, but I'm not confident I've got that much control. I try to tap her shoulder, might dislocate it."

"Hmm."

"She's in the Carribean. We're heading to Miami. At least that's the right direction. By the time we arrive we might have formed a plan."

Nat blew out his breath forcefully. "A plan. To invade an island military base and rescue a blind woman." He twisted his mouth in an ironic grin. "We've got you, me and a nine-year-old girl. Hell, what we need is a battalion of Navy SEALS commandos."

"Don't forget, I can move refrigerators with my mind. How many SEALS can do that?"

"True." He grabbed her hand. "You're our secret weapon. We've got to use your power somehow. We've got to think this through."

The news of Roan's survival recharged Nat's energy to the fullest it had been in months. He had felt physically exhausted and spiritually beaten from the afternoon's ordeal, but now his heart pumped the elixir of hope to all his bodily parts and revitalized his sagging will. *Jasmine, your mommy is alive!*

But the wonderful revelation also added to his burden. Roan was in danger. All his loved ones were in danger.

241

Nat had never felt more responsible for the safety of his family. Because of his obsession with creating artificial vision, he had ignored the potential military applications of his research. He had not been paranoid enough. He should have figured the techno-freaks in the spy shops would want to seize the project in order to build a better spook, a stealthier assassin. Espionage and death were their crafts and they were damn serious about staying on the cutting edge.

An international race was on to steal the artificial vision technology, but for what purpose? What goal had launched the deadly hunt?

He had been so naïve. Never saw the threat coming, left his family defenseless. *And I was supposed to be helping the blind to see!*

Now he had a second chance to protect his loved ones, to save them from harm.

Roan, Jasmine, Aria: the only universe that mattered.

This time, I can't fail them.

How he wished he could trust himself to not blow it.

30

The starry heaven, hilly pastures and the stream of family wagons rolling down Interstate-75 South provided a backdrop of normalcy. After four hours riding in the car Nat wished he could convince himself they were going to be safe and relax his aching shoulders.

But he didn't like the sinister looks of a charcoal gray Mercedes SUV with dark-tinted windows that flashed in and out of view behind them in the silvery wash of halogen headlights. Nat had first noticed the vehicle a half-hour ago, and it gave him an increasingly bad gut feeling. It continued to slip in and out of the frame of the Volvo's side mirror. It seemed the Mercedes was keeping pace at a distance, stalking them like a predator.

Nat told himself he was only suffering a bad case of nerves. The green Volkswagen Beetle, the rusty silver Ford Pinto, and the Greyhound bus were also trailing them. After all, *every* vehicle on I-75 South was a fish in the same asphalt river, speeding in the same direction as the Volvo. So why picture the other vehicles as harmless guppies and the dark Mercedes as a killer shark?

Aria read his mind. "Dark gray Mercedes?"

"Right."

"Take the steering wheel." She half-closed her eyes and an instant later said, "Hell. Six men inside. At least three handguns, one automatic rifle. And a knife. Two knives."

Nat's heart banged away. He glanced back at his sleeping daughter. A tiny streak of mustard and ketchup decorated one edge of her mouth. An hour ago, they had turned off the highway to grab dinner: burgers and fries to go at a Wendy's. Jasmine had eaten and immediately crashed into sleep again. The trauma of seeing the mutilated chimpanzees had drained her. Nat had not told her about Seeker, but the dog was not with them and Jazz was no dummy.

He looked back at the Mercedes, three car lengths behind. *Think!*

"Hang on," Aria said. Without signaling she whipped the Volvo into the passing lane and punched the gas pedal. The station wagon lurched into passing gear and sped past a long caravan of recreation vehicles the size of barges. The speedometer needle pointed to 80, 85, 90 miles an hour. The other drivers glanced at them in disgust as the Volvo zoomed by. Beyond the train of Winnebagos, Aria slowed to 80 for a few miles, then slid back to the right lane at the proper speed limit, 70 miles an hour.

They drove in silence a few minutes and Nat lamely hoped that maybe the Mercedes was not stalking them after all. Maybe it's just six guys heading to a gun-and-knife show. Maybe the Tooth Fairy is real.

The charcoal gray Mercedes popped out from behind an 18-wheeler and shot forward until it was tailgating the Volvo. At close range, the dark sedan seemed even more shark-like and the station wagon felt no safer than a thin rubber life raft.

"Shit," Nat said, frowning. "Are they just supposed to tail us, keep an eye on us, or are they planning to do us in?"

"Don't know," Aria said, "but they're not trying to be subtle; seems like a bad sign."

"Look daddy!" Jasmine had been awakened by the quick maneuvers. Now she pointed at a billboard for Wild West Territories that featured a crash dummy dressed in cowboy garb clinging to a mechanical bucking bronco. The bold lettering blared, *LIVE THE ADVENTURE OF THE WILD, WILD WEST: YOU DRESS THE PART! YOU PLAY THE ROLE!*

"Cool. That's the place where you get to dress up like a cowgirl," Jasmine said.

Nat eyed the side view mirror trying to devise a way to escape their hunters. The halogen headlights kept pace less than a car length behind. "What's that, Jazz?" he said, trying to keep his voice calm.

"Wild West Territories. It's a role-playing park where you dress up in costumes like the olden days. I told you about it, remember? You said we'd go someday. And here we are! Can we go, Daddy? The sign said only five miles to the exit."

Nat was hardly listening, his mind obsessed with the menace off the Volvo's rear bumper.

"Most people just stand around with cameras," Jasmine said, "but if you dress up to play a role, you get to walk through all the sets and the actors interact with you. Sounds really fun."

"That does sound fun, baby."

245

In a moment, the Volvo passed another billboard advertising the theme park. In rodeo-style typeface the words *WILD WEST TERRITORIES* blazed across the top. Reviews ran along the bottom of a stagecoach robbery scene: "Top-notch participatory theater!" (*New York Times*); "Unrelentingly authentic!" (Western Writers of America); "Western fans, grab your ten-gallon hats! Don't miss this!" (*San Francisco Chronicle*).

Nat suddenly thought of the set of antique handguns and the rifle gathered from his safety deposit vault now stashed in a canvas duffle bag at the rear of the station wagon. The pair of 1870s Colt six-shooters in a close-up fight could punch a nickel-sized hole through a bad guy as well as any modern .45 caliber handgun.

"Look, now there's a second car," Aria said.

Behind the Mercedes SUV, another Mercedes—this one a sedan, light gray instead of charcoal, but with identical opaque windows—had appeared out of the black night. Hair stood up on Nat's neck as he imagined the grills of both cars as rows of shark teeth.

"Shit times two," he said, and took the steering wheel.

The focus of Aria's eyes turned inward. "Four men," she said. "Four automatic rifles."

"Oh, lord," Nat said.

The SUV sped up and moved into the passing lane, while the Mercedes sedan took over its place, tailgating their station wagon. The dark SUV pulled alongside. Its tinted windows prevented Nat from seeing inside.

"They're going to try something now?" Nat said, "In the middle of I-75?"

"Who's to stop them?"

Nat saw the umpteenth billboard advertising Wild West Territories. The sign read THIS EXIT. He pointed. "Take the exit, take the exit."

Aria waited until the last second, then hit the brakes and swerved the Volvo onto the off-ramp at twice the posted exit speed. The Mercedes SUV in the passing lane jammed its brakes with a squeal and a cloud of rubber smoke and veered across two lanes and over the shoulder to make the exit. The trailing Mercedes sedan hit its brakes and swerved too. The SUV sideswiped the sedan and metal crumpled and in the next instant the heavier vehicle shoved the sedan off the paved curve of the exit ramp.

The sedan hugged the grassy embankment at a steep angle for a couple seconds, then launched high into the air and rolled twice—perfect mid-air snap-rolls as if performed by a wingless stunt plane—before a concrete light tower tore the car in two with a screech of steel and shattering glass. Gasoline exploded and a yellow-orange fireball blossomed in the night.

Jasmine screamed an instant before the noise and concussion rocked the Volvo.

Now the charcoal Mercedes SUV, its right headlight gone, hugged the Volvo's rear bumper.

Aria shot a glance at Nat. "Four men down; Six to go. Now what?"

"Got a plan," Nat said. Turning back to Jasmine, he smiled. "We're gonna be okay, Jazz.

247

Trust your daddy. We're going to Wild West Territories."

Jasmine nodded without a word. Her eyes were big, bright emerald globes.

31

Male voices and laughter echoed through a dressing room as men and boys donned rented costumes for their roles as citizens of a turn-of-the-century western town. The customers of Wild West Territories theme park—accountants and car dealers, lawyers and dentists, truck drivers and computer programmers—were transformed by the period clothing into gunslingers and undertakers, livery stable owners and bartenders, preachers and ranch bosses.

A banker wearing a pin-striped black suit and silk top hat chatted with a stage coach driver dressed in a fringed deerskin jacket and high-crowned Stetson. Each character bantered with the other in his best version of 1800's Western dialogue—tinged, in this case, by heavy Japanese accents.

Nat sat on a bench and tugged on stove-pipe cowboy boots with underslung heels and silver rowel spurs. He wore a blue-and-white-broadstriped cotton shirt and a red bandana beneath a calfskin vest. A pair of leather batwing chaps with tooled-silver conchas covered a vintage pair of Levi denim bluejeans. He stood and checked his outfit in a full-length mirror, topped it off with a broad-rimmed plainsman's hat of brown felt.

The other role-playing customers of Wild West Territories had selected their costumes from huge wardrobe racks, but Nat's clothing was authentic, more than a century old. The other men

249

strapped on fake six-guns that fired caps; Nat's pistols were genuine antiques, their cylinders loaded with real ammo. The other customers dressed their parts to create a drama with professional actors for the fun of it. But Nat had fled to the theme park with Aria and Jasmine to escape real killers; his purpose was survival for himself and his family.

Twenty minutes ago, Aria had managed to get away from the shark-gray sedan by zipping the Volvo around a shuttle bus just before the bus made a scheduled stop, blocking the narrow lane that led to the main parking lot. Tourists spilled off the bus onto a railroad platform to catch a ride on a restored locomotive, steam and smoke panting from its stack. The horn of the Mercedes blared, but the car couldn't squeeze past the wide bus.

Aria and Jasmine had rushed to the women's dressing room and Nat had carried the duffle bag filled with antique clothing and guns into the men's dressing room.

Glancing around the locker room at the other men now, Nat saw that the two most popular costumes were those of outlaw and sheriff. He wasn't the only one who noticed.

"Gents, I can't help but detect a preponderance of gunslingers in this room," said a teen-ager with bad acne. He wore the stark black cloth of an undertaker and grinned beneath a fake black handlebar mustache. "If I do say so myself, the situation looks right promisin' for my line of work."

"Well, pilgrim," said a sheriff-costumed man in a credible imitation of John Wayne's

250

Western drawl, "I'm gonna do my best to provide you with a steady clientele."

Nat looked at the teen-age undertaker and cursed himself. His chest knotted like an overwound spring. He couldn't believe what was happening, what he had caused. He had led a team of hit men *here*, to a family vacation park. What the fuck had he been thinking? This was insane.

He had reacted on impulse; had not known what else to do. On the open highway he and his family were shark bait. Here, at least, there might be some chance of hiding, blending with the crowds until they could shake off their killers, steal a car, catch a bus—*whatever*—just get the hell away from the predators in one piece.

But now, by his flight from danger, all these innocent people were exposed to it. He hoped beyond hope that none of them would get hurt or killed just because they got in the path of Nat Colt's terrible karma.

Nat strapped on a wide gun belt of basket weave horsehide with twin low-rider holsters. An 1873 Colt .45 Peacemaker, the six-shooter revolver that killed more people in the untamed West than any other weapon, fit snugly in the right hand holster. An 1878 Colt .44 Frontier revolver rode his left hip. The ammunition for the .44 also fit the Winchester 1873 Model lever-action repeating rifle Nat toted in his left hand; its 16-round rapid-fire capability made it the most formidable hand-carried weapon of its day. In an ankle sheath rode a Bowie knife crafted in 1826 by Colonel James Bowie himself; the 9-inch tempered steel blade affixed to a carved bone handle, balanced perfectly for throwing.

The loaded six-guns slung low on his hips felt to Nat like lead dive weights. Around his thighs he tied leather straps to keep the heavy holsters from bouncing. He strode out the dressing room door, spurs jingling, the loaded Winchester rifle resting in the crook of his arm. Nat heard a man tell his son, "He's one of the professional actors."

"Wow, cool," the boy said, "he looks totally *real!*"

As planned, Nat met Aria and Jasmine in front of the women's dressing room. Unlike Nat, each was dressed in rented outfits, but the costumes fit them surprisingly well. Jasmine wore the faded blue dungarees and brass-buttoned shirt of a Union Army drummer boy; her red braids tucked up inside a faded blue wool cap.

Aria's ensemble was tailor-made to show off her feminine curves: a deep-purple satin décolletage dress with a wasp-waisted corset and a wide hoop skirt; a floppy hat with fat white plumes and a matching purple parasol.

In spite of the tension of their situation, Nat found himself tipping his hat and saying, "Ma'am, you have got to be the prettiest dance hall queen on either side of the Mississippi."

She curtsied and offered her arm. "Thank you kindly, cowboy. You look mighty fine your own self."

"Smells kinda bad, though," Jasmine said.

"That's the smell of history, gal," Nat said. In the threads and skins of his rugged wardrobe Nat could smell horses and gunpowder and hard-earned sweat from the era of Nat Love and the fabled wranglers of the American West.

"I'm a *boy*," Jasmine said.

"Yep. So you are, boy. I can see that now, plain as can be."

A sign above a printed ruler at the dressing room entrance said: GUESTS MUST BE AT LEAST THIS TALL TO DRESS IN COSTUME; the minimum height was 4-foot-10-inches.

Lucky thing Jazz is tall for her age, Nat thought. Which brought to mind Roan, Jasmine's statuesque mother, and the giddy fact that Roan was still alive. How the hell were he and Jazz and Roan going to live long enough to see each other again?

And where does Aria fit in now, with Roan alive? He gazed at Aria with unconcealed respect and admiration. He wished he had never gotten her entangled in the nightmare his life had become. But then, without Aria's miraculous vision, he would never have discovered Roan had survived.

Aria met Nat's eyes and seemed to read his mind. "We can sort it out later," she said. "Come on. Let's blend with the crowd, look for a safe exit and the right moment to get out of here."

The three merged with a stream of people walking through a covered corridor from the costume-rental area toward a gate leading to the theme park's main stage. A mural on the gate depicted a bloody shoot-out. Nat's glimpsed the artwork and his guts went cold. The taut spring in his chest cranked an impossible extra turn tighter. His fingers brushed the butts of his guns.

A large digital clock above the gate displayed the countdown before the start of the next live theater. Nat saw with dismay it would be another ten minutes before the gates opened. The hit men from the Mercedes might be among the throngs of tourists who did not dress in costumes, searching each face in the crowd for the three of them.

"Stand in the center of the mob," he said, "stay away from the fringes." They moved into the hub of the herd in front of the gate.

A sandy-blond woman with a sun-burned nose, wearing the fringed white vest and white Stetson of the Wild West Territories staff, began reciting a series of rote announcements through a bullhorn. After a memorized welcome and an announcement about insurance non-liability, the host said, "Our purpose is to have fun and our rules are simple. Those in costume, please try to stay in character. Professional actors will engage you in dramatic dialogue and situations. You are not just observers in the scenes, but participants. Feel free to improvise. No two enactments are ever the same. You are about to step out of the Twentieth Century back into the 1800s of the Wild West Territories!

"Those not in costume, please keep behind the dotted yellow lines which you will see at the borders of every staging area. Camcorders and cameras are welcomed, but flashes and spotlighting are not allowed. Feel free to talk and laugh with each other and to boo and cheer and applaud. We want you to have a great time. However, please *don't* talk to the actors in the scenes, or try to get

254

their attention, or attempt to pose your subjects. If the actors are doing their jobs, they'll ignore you. Keep in mind that to the professional cast and guest-characters of Wild West Territories, you and your video cameras won't even exist for another hundred years!"

The crowd buzzed with excitement. Nat saw an adolescent Hispanic girl dressed in black boots, black jeans and a black leather vest over a black cotton rodeo shirt with faux-pearl buttons, a black felt sombrero and black leather eye-patch. She was deep into the overblown role of mean-teen *bandita*, sizzling to make trouble. She slung wavy brown hair over one shoulder, shot Nat a challenging look and thrust out the hip that held her fake gun.

Nat swallowed, wishing this whole event was only for fun and the muscles in his neck would stop twitching. He licked dry lips and nervously twiddled his thumbs over the hammers on both his revolvers. The teen's eyes flashed at the perceived challenge and she thumbed the hammer on her gun, cocking it back. Her thumb slipped off the hammer and the firing pin struck the black powder cap with a loud *POW!*

The crowd jumped as one body. Ripples of excited laughter followed.

Only the gaunt black gunslinger, the sensual dancehall queen and the red-headed drummer boy seemed not amused. They huddled closer in the center of the horde.

Nat scoped the sea of unfamiliar faces. He had to assume the killers from the Mercedes were here, somewhere in the crowd, but he had no way to identify them.

What clues to look for? Would the killers have had time to get dressed in Old Western costume? Or were they in street clothes concealed among the camera-toting tourists? What telltale signs instantly reveal a secret agent on a mission of murder?

"I'm scanning," Aria whispered, her eyelids half-closed, "but there are too many guns…"

Guns, guns everywhere. Every pudgy kid and his sunburned uncle carried at least one six-shooter. A modern weapon, say, a 9-millimeter semi-automatic pistol, would be a giveaway. Nat had noticed several men and women who had forgotten or declined to take off wristwatches, modern eyeglasses, casual shoes, but he didn't spot any anachronistic firearms. Plenty of room to conceal a modern weapon though, under the many vests and longcoats and jackets all around him.

Paranoia pressed in on Nat. He knew in his gut the killers hadn't just given up. Every stranger posed a threat. And because he had led the assassins to this park, he himself was a threat to every one of these strangers.

32

At last the entrance gate opened. Nat and Aria and Jasmine ambled onto the wagon-wheel rutted Main Street of Wild West Territories and tried to blend among the intermingling streams of cowpokes, settlers, ranch bosses, townsfolk and gunfighters.

At first glance Nat understood why the theme park had earned an international reputation as a role-playing attraction. Its large main street ran through the fictional western town of Silverton, Colorado. Everything about the place and the costumes had been rendered in authentic detail. Except for the lack of snow-capped peaks on the horizon and a tropical humidity that would drown a true Colorado mountain town, the saloons and casinos, dry-goods store and bank, livery stables and blacksmith shop were strikingly true-to-life.

Nat couldn't spare time to feel impressed. Under normal circumstances, he might be having the time of his life, but tonight nervous sweat ran in rivulets down his ribs. He kept imagining the hammer-shock of a bullet's impact. And the worst torment of all was to know that his loved ones were just as afraid. He would gladly trade his life to keep them safe from harm. But how could he protect them?

"I feel like we're Day-Glo targets parading around out here," Nat whispered to Aria.

"Me too, let's get inside a building."

"The saloon," he said, and steered her and Jasmine toward a clapboard building with a Western-style facade painted with the name of the establishment, The Watering Hole. Rinky-dink ragtime piano leaked into the street through its swinging doors.

Nat immediately discovered that the back wall of the saloon was missing, so that the camera crowd behind the yellow line could film the interior scenes. Red monitor lights glowed on dozens of camcorders. *So buildings offer no protection.* Nat eyed the camera crowd warily, as if the monitor lights were red eyes in a nest of vipers.

Professional actors seated at a round poker table in the center of the saloon entered into a heated argument. A card player in a denim shirt stood up fast, knocking his chair backward to the floor. "You cheatin' scum! You had that ace up your sleeve."

The man he accused of cheating was a dandy in tailored formal evening attire, white shirt with ruffled sleeves, and a black felt derby. "My hapless friend," he said in an Eastern accent, "subterfuge is not required to defeat a player who lacks all skill."

"You callin' me a liar?"

"I would label you an uncultured lout whose own cheating was so crude and obvious it didn't enable you to win a single hand. You, sir, are the deceiver. And you would fail to beat me in a poker game if I were sound asleep."

"Why you—!" The denim-shirted man went for his six-gun.

In a flash the dandy pointed his right hand at his accuser. A sharp *BANG! BANG!* A woman in a flame-red ruffled skirt screamed. The six-gun had only made it halfway out of the holster when its owner slumped to the floor, squirting fake blood from small packets taped to his chest. Then Nat saw the stubby, double-barreled over-under pistol—a Remington .41 caliber "Derringer" model— concealed in a sleeve holster and mounted on a spring, it had flicked into the dandy's palm when he snapped his wrist outward.

Camcorders whirred. A smattering of laughter, applause and cheers drifted from the audience beyond the yellow line.

Only then did Nat notice he had drawn his own Colt .45 revolver, fully cocked, and was aiming it at the man with the phony Derringer.

"Take it easy," Aria said, and gently pulled down Nat's gun arm. "They're actors."

Nat realized how close he had come to shooting the actor out of his automatic fear reaction. He began to shake badly. It took two swipes to reseat his revolver in its holster.

Aria squeezed his shoulder. "Nat, take a deep breath. You're hyperventilating."

He nodded, took a slow, full breath from the bottom of his lungs. Held it for a count of three. Let it out in a ragged sigh. *Relax, man.*

The piano player resumed plinking the keys. Nat's hands had nearly stopped trembling when the gates of hell tore off their hinges.

33

A man in a black leather jacket lunged from the crowd of tourists behind the yellow line and barged into the saloon scene pointing a black handgun at Nat and then at Aria.

"Both come with me," the gunman shouted in heavily accented English, "Both come now." The man's flushed and sweaty face was moon-round with Oriental eyes. He stood no taller than Nat, but he was thick-necked, built like a bull.

"Hurry! You come now."

Nat bet his life that the attacker would not realize the vintage weapons he carried were real firearms, not fakes. The element of surprise could work only the first time.

Nat whipped the Winchester rifle up to chest height and squeezed off one shot. *WHAM!* The man flew backward against the poker table, flipped the table on end, catapulting beer glasses, cards and poker chips into the air. A wisp of bluish gun smoke curled up from the rifle barrel wafting the smell of burnt black powder.

The crowd applauded and cheered at the graphic live action.

Jasmine screamed. Nat spun around. A second attacker had backed Aria against the bar with a blade. In a graceful blur of motion Aria smashed a whiskey bottle against the side of his skull and leaped away. His legs folded and he sagged to his knees. Nat levered a fresh round into

260

the rifle's chamber, squeezed the trigger. The back of the man's head smashed open like a watermelon.

"Aria, Jazz," Nat shouted, "Let's go!" Aria grabbed Jasmine's hand and the three raced out of the saloon.

As they stepped down off the saloon porch onto the dirt street, another Asian man leapt out of the crowd across the way. The man strode into the center of Main Street and opened fire with a black pistol. Splinters flew off the porch of the saloon behind Nat's head. Nat hit the dirt and rolled, coming up on one knee, pumping the firing lever on the Winchester. A hunk of skull-and-scalp blasted off the man's head like a wedge of turf flung up from a bad golf swing. The man's face registered dull surprise at the fact that the crown of his head had just been blown a dozen feet behind. Without crying out he pitched forward and landed in a sprawl.

"Aria! Take it! Use it!" Nat shouted, and pressed the Winchester rifle into her hands. "Get Jasmine out of here! Run to the car! Go!"

Loud footsteps above and behind. Nat spun to face the saloon's porch. Up on the tin roof a man was reaching for a gun in a shoulder holster beneath his jacket. Nat drew the Colt Peacemaker and fired. A slug from the six-gun caught the man in the left shoulder. He fell, bounced on the corrugated tin, rolled to the edge, flopped down to the dirt street, hit with a *whump* and instantly rolled backed onto his feet with the skill of a martial artist. A second bullet slammed into the same shoulder, spinning the man in a complete circle. Still he staggered toward

261

Nat, lifting his gun to fire. The third and fourth bullets smashed into his chest with such force he bucked backward and crashed through the saloon window. A blizzard of glass shards rained onto the street.

The spectators behind the yellow line roared applause, thinking they were witnessing the greatest western drama ever enacted, with astoundingly realistic special effects. The tiny "on" lights of video cameras glowed like constellations of red stars.

An Asian man leapt at him from the side, stabbing with a knife. Nat twisted hard to avoid the thrust and fell backward. The blade ripped through his vest and shirt and scraped a gash along his ribs. The impact with the ground knocked the pistol from his grip. The man stabbed at him again as they wrestled in the dirt. Nat grabbed the wrist of the knife hand with both his hands. Their scrabbling bodies knocked down a knot of costumed customers. The glinting point of the knife bore down toward Nat's left eye, his arms too weak to save him.

Suddenly the thick barrel of the Winchester rifle jabbed the assailant's temple. *WHAM!* The impact caved in the side of the man's face, splattering Nat with glops of brain like scrambled eggs. The body collapsed on Nat. He squirmed out from under it, choking back his gag reflex.

"Where's Jazz?" he said.

"Hiding in a rain barrel."

Standing in the interior behind the swinging doors of the saloon, another assailant opened fire

262

with an AK-47 assault rifle. A swarm of bullets buzz-sawed the wood-slatted doors to splinters. Nat reached for the Winchester and Aria handed it to him. But when he squeezed the rifle's trigger, it was out of cartridges. Someone in the crowd broke the rules and trained a camera spotlight on the saloon doors and when the would-be assassin burst into view the brilliant glare blinded him. The attacker squinted into the light and squeezed off a short burst of automatic fire—*kakow kakow*. A groan. A thud. The irritating light was no more.

Abruptly the audience hushed. Something was terribly wrong. The actors weren't supposed to pretend to kill the *audience*. And a fully-automatic weapon did not belong in the Old West.

When the truth sank in, a woman screamed piercingly. Then the camera crowd bolted like a stampede of terrified cattle, joined in the next instant by fleeing actors and role-playing customers. Nat had drawn his Colt Frontier revolver from his left-hip holster, but in the pandemonium he could not fire a clear shot at his assailant. People stormed out of the saloon, unaware that the gunman was standing on its porch, searching the street, having temporarily lost sight of his target in the escaping horde. A large man in a sheriff's outfit ploughed into the Asian gunner, shoved him forward into the street, where the river of panicked people surged around him, buffeting him. The gunner took a wide-legged stance in the center of the street, like a lone tree resisting a flash flood. His eyes darted left and right, seeking Nat, assault rifle at waist-height.

Nat found him first.

263

Lunging from a crouch behind him, Nat reached around and plunged the big Bowie knife underhand, thrusting up through the hollow of the diaphragm. As the man folded over from pain Nat jerked the blade to the side, severing the aorta, and a gusher of warm blood drenched Nat's hand to his elbow. He yanked out the Bowie knife as the dying man crumpled. Main Street was now empty of life and movement, except for Nat.

"Aria!"

She stepped out with Jasmine in hand from the alley between the saloon and dry-goods store. They ran to him, their eyes huge with fright. "Are you hit?" Aria said, gaping at Nat's bloody shirt.

He shook his head, panting heavily. "Most of it's not my blood."

"*Most* of it?"

"Guy with the knife cut me, not too bad." He used his wool hat as a rag to wipe the slick blood from his skin. Sweat stung his eyes as he stooped and retrieved the Colt six-gun from the dirt and re-holstered it.

"Let's get out of here," Aria said.

"Wait." Nat bent over the body and searched the pockets for identification.

Nothing.

"Asian," Nat said. "That's all we know."

"They're Korean," Jasmine said. "The guy who tried to stab Aria shouted something in Korean."

Aria and Nat looked at her with raised eyebrows.

"Kim Sook goes to my school; she's from South Korea," she said. "I've been over to her house a bunch of times. I know how it sounds."

"Okay. Korean," Nat said. "What's that tell us?"

"That the gadgets you implanted in my head have become a major tourist attraction."

An alarm warbled loudly, high-pitched and repeating.

"C'mon," Nat said. "We can talk in the car. Let's get back on the highway and keep driving."

The three caught up to the exodus of terrified customers who had bottlenecked at the gate. They merged with the others and squeezed through the narrow exit.

The parking lot was a chaos of gridlocked cars and tour buses. Horns honked. Angry and frightened people shouted.

A white Ford Explorer crumpled the rear bumper and left rear fender of a red Porsche Carrera; the Explorer was rammed in turn by a blue-and-silver Toyota Camry. The driver and passengers inside the Camry wore the blue uniforms of the mid-19th-Century U.S. Army Cavalry. No one stopped or got out of their cars. Wailing sirens approached from a distance.

At last the three reached their Volvo station wagon. Nat tore off his bloody cowboy shirt and vest. So much for the museum-quality wardrobe. The knife wound on his left side burned like a strip of stinging fire ants wrapped partway around his ribs. Medically, it amounted to only a long, deep scratch—probably could use a few stitches at the

265

center to close the spreading edges of flesh, but no big deal. Aria handed him a clean T-shirt and he winced as he lifted his arms to pull it on.

Now that the immediate danger of the gunfight was gone, Nat's hands shook from the cocktail of adrenaline and endorphins the battle had set loose in his bloodstream. From the time more than a year ago when he was told that Roan had been murdered, Nat knew that he *could* kill to protect his family. But knowing it and *doing* it were universes apart. He was not by nature a violent man—at least that's what he had always told himself. On the other hand, he'd met the enemy in a life-and-death battle and the bad guys were now corpses. On some primal level, he felt damn good about that.

I'm not a victim. Not powerless. Try to hurt my family and I'll stop you dead.

Aria had to step out of her hoop skirt to fit through the car door. She climbed into the back seat next to Jasmine and hugged her tight. Once inside the car, Jasmine broke down into sobs. Her chest heaved and her shoulders shook in Aria's arms. Nat glanced back at them. Minutes earlier, on the walk to the car, Aria had stopped suddenly and vomited; but now her amber eyes shone with strength in order to care for Jasmine.

Nat drove out of the parking lot and attached the Volvo like a caboose to the train of bumper-to-bumper vehicles that choked the narrow lanes leading from Wild West Territories. As the traffic crept forward, Nat realized Jasmine had been right, he *did* stink. He cranked down the window,

266

preferring gas and diesel fumes to the reek of anxious sweat, blood, gunpowder and hundred-year-old leather chaps.

"This whole thing is insane," Nat said. "An attack on American citizens, on their own soil—*in public*? Can you fathom the political repercussions? We're allies with South Korea, for chrissakes. This could break off all our ties. Are they totally nuts?"

"Could be *North* Korea," Aria said. "Already our enemy."

"Even so. It's lunatic. This kind of shit could start a war."

"They're desperate," Aria said. "What they're after is more important to them than worrying about starting a war."

"Why?" Jasmine asked, her cheeks wet with tears. "To help the blind to see?"

"No baby," Nat said. "This sure as hell has nothing to do with healing the blind. But it *is* about Aria's special vision." Nat looked at Aria, shook his head grimly. "Such an important advance—I just don't know why it's so *deadly* important."

Aria shrugged. "All I know, their leader, I'm going to call him The Creep, said it has nothing to do with conventional spying."

"Right," Nat said. "So it's about using your super vision for—what?—some military purpose, gotta be, but a mission other than remote reconnaissance. Something we can't even guess at, maybe."

"Someone who is on *our side* knows," Aria said. "That's who we need to talk to."

Nat nodded and glanced up in the rearview mirror at Jasmine. She clung to Aria for comfort the way the little bonobo, Mojo, had clung to him. Aria caught his eye. "It's time we told her," she said.

"Jasmine," Nat said, "Aria has wonderful news."

Aria told Jasmine how she had found Roan. "Your mommy is alive, baby. Mommy is alive!"

34

Aria rested her forehead on the buzzing Plexiglas window of the twin-engine turboprop on the early morning flight from Miami to Curacao. Nat had managed to sell his vintage guns and other collectibles to an eager buyer in Miami. They had abandoned the Volvo at the airport and caught an early bird flight to the Dutch Antilles on Caribbean Air. Now the southern coast of Cuba was slowly passing below, framed by the sea which sparkled pink in the rising sun like a rosè wine.

Jasmine slept with her head in Aria's lap, red braids splayed over Aria's caramel thighs. They had all taken turns in a hot shower at a Coral Gables motel and with the cash from the gun sale, they each had purchased a small wardrobe at a GAP clothing outlet store.

Nat napped in a seat across the aisle of the Brazilian-made Embraer propjet. He features looked raw-boned, but Aria had noticed a renewed spirit in him, a return of some of his strength, both physical and emotional.

Of course he's feeling energized, she thought. *The love of his life is alive.*

Aria ran her fingertips over Jasmine's cheeks. The girl's smooth warm skin was the color of café-con-leche, her freckles imitating the mocha sprinkles on top.

Aria had never felt so much love for a child. She glanced across at Nat. Or so much love for a man. But they were flying to Curacao to find a way to rescue Roan. If their mission was a success, Aria would soon be an add-on to this family portrait.

Julia Roan McKenzie. From what Aria had heard and seen, she could not help but admire the woman. Beautiful. Gifted. Brilliant. Such words were made for geniuses such as Roan.

The lush green northern coast of Haiti slid by 18,000 feet beneath the airplane's port wingtip. Aria gazed down, thinking of parrots; a species that mates for life. She thought of passion flowers, powder-white beaches, making love in gentle surf.

Maybe after this crisis has passed Nat will recover fully from his cancer. Then all four of us can go live in some culture where men are allowed to have more than one wife. Together, happily ever after.

"Yeah, right," she whispered. "What a dreamer."

The lush tropical canopy far below had given way to ragged patches of farms and villages hacked out of the rainforest, which in turn were eaten up by the crowded, dilapidated sprawl of Port-Au-Prince. Aria sighed and turned away from the blighted view. She gazed again at Jasmine and Nat.

Aside from her husband's brain tumor and his *other* wife, there was the little problem of the techno-wizardry lodged in Aria's eyes and brain. She shifted her visual focus and looked at the baby floating head-down in the womb of a bleached-blonde Hispanic woman four rows in front. A boy, with black hair. He sucked his thumb, opened his eyes and blinked, then closed his eyes and returned to his undersea dreams.

270

As with many of her visions, Aria gasped in awe at the miraculous insight into the deep wonder and beauty of the living world. Such perception was truly godlike. Yet she was simply human.

Aria felt as if she were the heroine of a mythic tale. *A blind girl is given the new eyes of a goddess; now she must understand the great responsibility that comes with her gift.*

"That about sums it up," she told herself.

For her, the story bore the sense of profound destiny but Aria had no idea what it might be.

I'm a visionary. Maybe I'm supposed to go around telling everybody how gorgeous the world is. From subatomic particles to galaxies, I can see it and describe it.

But I'm no poet. Why couldn't this have happened to a poet? Or a saint.

Aria began thinking choreographically, wondering how she might interpret some of her visions as dance. She gave up after a moment. The whole shining universe was dancing. What a view! But to try to convey it to those who could not see it for themselves would be like trying to describe a rainbow to the blind.

What is my mission, here? What am I supposed to do with this blessing?

And what about evil?

Through a starboard window Aria saw the glinting coin of the full moon. Evil looms in all myths, sure as the moon sets in the west. Aria couldn't afford to ignore the danger. Untold numbers of government agents, domestic and foreign, were hunting her now to steal the secret of her magic eyes.

And with their stolen magic, the malevolent ones would—what? *What did they plan to do?*

The only thing Aria was certain of was that the violence was far from over. More people were going to get killed.

She prayed the coming destruction would not claim the adorable girl asleep in her lap.

35

Roan realized something major was happening at the underground base. Ten times as many footsteps as usual tramped across the floor above the ceiling of her room. The sound of equipment being rolled out on hand trucks and the hammering of nails (on crates?) told her the base was being rapidly dismantled, evacuated.

She went to the wall and pressed the talk-button on the intercom. It gave direct access to the office of the man who had been her primary personal contact since she had arrived at the secret base more than a year before.

"John?" she said. "You there?"

"Hello, Doc," a husky male voice replied.

"What's going on?" she said. "Is the party finally over?"

"Guess you heard all the commotion."

"How many times do I have to remind you guys I'm not deaf?"

"Can't talk now. I'll call you back." He clicked off.

"Yeah, thanks for all the insightful news, pal."

After an hour or so of commotion on the upper levels, a brisk knock sounded on the steel door of her room and without waiting for her reply, the lock turned, the door swung open and a group barged in. She counted the footfall of six or eight men. She was escorted into a corner, where she was asked to sit on the floor and stay out of their way.

Without another word, the team began working all around the room, dismantling her bedroom office and hauling it away.

"Excuse me," Roan said. "Would any of you gentlemen care to tell me what's going on here?"

Tramping and shuffling boots, sounds of furniture and desks being hauled out of the room. More men entering the room as others exited.

"Isn't anyone going to have the decency to answer me?"

"Ma'am we have orders not to talk with you," a male voice replied. "We're clearing out your room; everything is leaving with us today. That's all I'm permitted to say."

Now she heard them emptying her desk drawers, floppy disk files, dumping the contents into bags or cartons of some sort. Her computer died with a soft whine as the plug was pulled from the wall socket. The silence that replaced the buzz of the computer rang through Roan's head ominously.

I'm no longer needed. She gulped at the implications.

"If everything leaves with you today," Roan said, "does that go for me, too?"

"Ma'am, we can't answer any of your questions, so just don't talk to us okay?"

In an hour, Roan's room had been stripped bare. She stepped into her bathroom and was amazed to find they had hauled away the sink, the toilet, the fiberglass shower stall, everything.

Roan paced from wall to wall, thinking, thinking, but unable to come up with any scheme to

274

save herself. By late-afternoon, the din on the floors above her head had slowed to sporadic foot traffic and the occasional swoosh of elevator doors. Through the soles of her bare feet, she felt the heavy drone of engines vibrating down through the lava rock on the surface.

Helicopters? Amphibious landing craft? Whatever the vehicles, the rats were abandoning ship.

Roan tried the door to her room. Locked. She fought against a nauseating rush of claustrophobia. *Is everyone just going to take off and leave me here to die?*

She ran to the wall intercom unit and punched it to call John. A terrible moment passed in silence.

"I'm still here, Roan," said the husky voice at last.

Roan tried not to let him hear the sigh of relief she exhaled. At least he hadn't deserted her.

"Please tell me what's going on, I'm scared."

"The uh, project…" he sighed…"the project has been shut down."

"No shit," she said. "But you sound really sad. I didn't realize your heart was so into it."

"It's not that. Look…I mean, listen."

"I'm listening."

He hesitated on the other end of the line. Clearly something was troubling him and that scared her most of all.

"John, what is it you want to get off your chest?" she said, unable to keep her voice from quavering.

"The project is over, Roan."

"You said that already."

"You don't seem to understand."

"Apparently not, but being that I'm not a total idiot, I take it from your manner that you're not going to let me go home." A teardrop balanced on her eyelid then ran down her cheek.

"They left me behind with a few, uh, other agents, to..."

"Just tell me, goddamn it."

"These guys are demolition. The clean-up crew. They're gonna blow this whole warren, all traces of our operation here."

"Keep talking."

"Roan, I have to follow orders."

The pressure of her anger squeezed in on her like six atmospheres. Tears streamed down her face. "Do I...do I get to listen to the fireworks from a sailing yacht off on the horizon, or am I strapped to this powder keg?"

"They're not going to let you go, Roan."

"Fuck 'they.' What about *you*, John? I'm asking *you*. Will you give me a chance?"

He sighed. "Got my orders."

Roan gritted her teeth to hold in her sobs, her panic. The piped-in air in the underground room was suffocating. "Remember our walks on the beach?" she said.

"Of course I do."

"Do your orders mention anything about refusing a condemned woman her last request?"

"No. I can make you comfortable. We've got—we *had*—a pharmacy here. You won't have to suffer. You can go to sleep."

"I was thinking more in terms of catching one last picnic on the beach with you."

A hesitation.

"John, let me feel the sand on my feet, the waves on my ankles once more."

"I got until 19:00 hours to vacate this island and leave it sanitized."

She slapped at the button on her talking wristwatch. *"Eleven-fifteen a.m."*

"John, we've got nearly eight hours. In eight hours we could walk all the way around this mountain like a couple of Hindu pilgrims. I'm only asking for a half-hour on the beach, on the last day of my life."

"Gotta think about it."

"*No!*" She said it louder than she intended. "John, please. Don't think about it. *Feel* about it. Feel it in your heart. You owe it to me. I cooperated. I gave you people what you wanted. Just let me have a final moment to make my peace with the Earth."

He sighed again. "Okay, Roan. Okay. I'll be down to get you soon as everything's squared away topside." He clicked off.

"Fuck you very much!" Roan smashed at the intercom with her fist like a hammer till her skin tore and bled.

She wanted her body to shatter into a thousand fiery darts of rage and make every whizzing dart strike down one of the bastards who had done this to her. She wanted to turn into a blazing lake of lava and burn a hole through the walls of her prison, rocket to the surface and erupt over all her tormentors, shooting sparks as she burned them down to soot.

All her life since her high-diving accident had been one long exercise of positive willpower, her ability to take charge of her moods, her actions—to *choose* freedom and happiness, to excel despite her disability. She had never wasted time cursing her fate or hating her life. Self-pity was for tragic characters with broken dreams. But Roan had made sure she *lived* her dreams, day by day, even moment by moment.

But for most of those days, Nat had stood with her. And Jasmine. And Seeker. And she had possessed her life's work.

Now she was alone and lost; an island mountain for her mausoleum. She felt utterly helpless, godforsaken. And for the first time in her life, she despised her blindness and despised herself for being blind.

Roan flung herself onto the tiled floor and sobbed uncontrollably. Her fiery anger had died and quick-rotted into despair. "I'm so pathetic," she wailed. "I can't *see*! Fuck me, I'm *blind*!"

Now she only wanted to melt into one big lonely teardrop and merge with the deep blue sea.

36

The propjet aircraft banked low and lined up with the airport runway on the outskirts of Willemstad, Curacao. Aria gazed down upon the gingerbread buildings of colonial Dutch architecture in the port city. Bright tropical pastels splashed the walls, gables and arcades of hotels, stores and homes: mango orange beside coral pink; sea-green beside hibiscus red; yellow moon beside African violet—all of them crowned with roofs of cinnamon-colored ceramic tiles.

The trio did not head into the city because Aria feared her relatives and friends might be under surveillance by the agents hunting for her. Instead, they took a taxicab from the airport toward the outlying fishing villages of the 36-mile-long island. Aria had a distant cousin in the smuggling trade who owned a legendarily fast boat. She was counting on her cousin's help in getting Roan off Isla Los Aves. Not that such a notion could be construed as a plan. She had no idea how they were going to pull off the rescue.

The cab passed a Shell Oil refinery that belched flames from tall flares like hideous candles. Massive tanker ships glided in and out of the deep harbor; those entering port rode high in the blue water; those departing the oil refinery rode low.

Scrubby palms and palmettoes, spiny aloes and several types of cacti dotted the rocky landscape. Clumps of divi-divi trees tilted their canopies in the same southwesterly direction, bent by the steady northeast trade winds. In some places, farmers had trained the thriving datu cacti into irregular spiky fences.

"I like those fences, they're cool," Jasmine said, her face pressed to the cab's window.

"Goats like them, too," Aria said. Four shaggy black goats stood by the roadway munching on the thorny green cactus railings.

"I thought all tropical islands were lush," Jasmine said. "This looks almost like a desert."

"Most tropical islands get lots of rain," Aria said. "But Curacao is semi-arid, like Arizona, say. It never gets too hot here and the nights are cool even in summer. It'll get a lot greener as we go higher."

As if on cue, the taxi began climbing a knob and tamarind trees sprouted up thickly, forming arches over the potholed asphalt road. Sailing over a set of billowing swells, the cab climbed a final steep hill. Aria tapped the driver's shoulder and said something to him in a lilting patois. He pulled over onto the shoulder of the road and came to a stop beside a cliff.

"This is it," Aria said, as she handed the driver twenty American dollars. "We get out here."

The three travelers stood poised above a blue-green lagoon framed with gleaming white sand. Wooden ketches and catboats lay at a tilt on the beach, their painted plank hulls as colorful as the fairy-tale buildings back in Willemstad. A group of dark-skinned men and women sat on the shore mending nets. To the west of the lagoon, houses huddled shoulder-to-shoulder climbing the steep

280

slope, their corrugated steel roofs streaked and blotched by a riot of orange-red rust.

"My cousin lives in that village," Aria said, pointing. "Let's go."

After a half-hour of scrambling down a switchback trail over boulders and gravel, the three arrived, dusty and thirsty in the little fishing village of Otrabanda—the "Other Side".

A flock of pink flamingoes flapped overhead, absurdly long necks counterbalanced by unreasonably lanky legs, looking beautiful, graceful and comical all at once.

"Wow!" Jasmine said. "Flamingoes. Must be a hundred or more."

"Gorgeous, huh?" Aria said. "We call them *chogògos*. They breed in the salt marshes on Bonaire, a nearby island."

A group of boys on the beach played soccer with a floppy ball that had seen better days. The boys possessed every shade of brown skin and many different hair colors and textures. Aria called out to them in Papyamentu, the hybrid language of the Dutch Leewards. They stopped their game and stared, smiling. Several older boys jogged over to greet them.

Aria talked with a slim boy named Tommy who had chocolate-brown skin, gray eyes and blond dreadlocks. He spoke rapidly in sing-song patois, gesturing with a slender muscled arm toward the houses riding up the hill. He kept staring at Jasmine and smiling with bright white teeth.

"He says my cousin Balboa lives in the house with the TV antenna," Aria said. "Oh, and he

281

says he loves your hair, Jazz. Says it reminds him of fire coral."

Jasmine smiled back at the boy. "Thanks. I think your dreadlocks are way cool."

The boys led the newcomers up a footpath to Balboa's house. Black chickens with red-speckled feathers squawked and strutted out of the path of the homecoming parade. A man in his early thirties stepped out on his porch, drawn by the clamor of laughter and shouting. He was heavily muscled for his petite frame, with waist-length black dreadlocks and a short black beard, skin as dark as Dutch chocolate, which by contrast made his blue eyes shine from his face like electric lights.

"Balboa!" Aria shouted from the footpath below.

A smile of recognition lit up his dark brown face like the crescent moonrise beams in the night. "Aria Carmen! Me beautiful cuz." He hopped off the porch and ran down the path to embrace her. "*Wansalawata!*" Balboa said.

"Wansalawata." Aria answered the traditional greeting, pidgin English for "One salt water." It referred to the unity of all the peoples of one ocean planet, the saltwater of their ancestral birthplace still flowing in their bloodstreams.

"W'happen? You was in the U.S. I heard last."

Aria introduced Nat and Jasmine and explained their dire situation to Balboa. Without going into detail about her enhanced vision she admitted she and Nat were being hunted by U.S. agents and others and were in mortal danger. "I

282

need a boat to us get to Isla Los Aves. We've got to find a way to get Roan off the island."

Balboa frowned. "Das some heavy shit ya got yaself into, cuz." He chewed his lower lip. "I gotta fast-fast boat, mon, but ya friend is in dat freaky place. Spooky lights, bad spirits. Nobody don' go near it no mo'. Ya get too close, ya don' come home."

"It's people on the island, not ghosts."

Balboa held up his hands. "Yeah, but such people, mon! I don' know...I mean, running a coupla kilos up the Florida Straits is one ting, mon, but messin' wid de CIA, dat's another ting."

"Please. We've got to rescue her," Jasmine said. "She's my mommy."

"We can lease your boat," Nat said. "You don't have to come with us. I've got American cash..."

By now, every member of the village had gathered in a throng around the visitors, hearing their story.

"Come, cuz, we get ya'll fed," Balboa said. "We need talk 'bout dis mo'."

He led her into his house. It was twice as roomy inside as she had imagined, partly because the house had no interior walls, only curtains separating the living spaces. An impromptu welcoming committee crowded into the one room bringing fresh coconut milk; lemon-marinated raw grouper called *ceviche*; a sweet cold soup made of jellied *kadushi* cactus; and slightly bitter *casava* pancakes made from breadfruit flour. Aria felt

283

pleased that Nat and Jasmine relished the native foods.

A yellow-breasted bird, the size of a robin, flew in through an unscreened window, stole a nip from Jasmine's dark yellow finger-banana, and flitted out again. Jasmine laughed with delight.

"We call them *ladrones de azugar*—sugar thieves," Aria said. "They're bold and greedy and they raid anything sweet."

"He's cute," Jasmine said. "I'll share my banana with him if he'll come back."

Tommy, the blonde-haired boy from the beach, stepped forward and held up a milky piece of green coconut flesh. The bird flew through the open window again and tried to snatch the treat from his hand. When the boy wouldn't part with the fruit, the sugar thief flitted about, then finally landed on the boy's outstretched finger.

Tommy then slowly transferred the piece of coconut to Jasmine's hand and the bird hopped over to her outstretched finger, still pecking at the sweet. Jasmine beamed. Aria chuckled. The local boy had just earned gold stars in Jasmine's eyes.

Aria talked with Balboa and the villagers in Papyamentu, a blend of Portuguese, Dutch, Spanish, English, African and Awarak Indian. Suddenly, a feeling of dread washed over her like a foul wave. Goosebumps rose on her arms and neck.

Nat stopped chewing in the middle of a bite of sun-dried mango. "What's wrong?"

"I just got a real bad feeling, out of nowhere. I think it's Roan. Something's happening, Nat."

"It's Roan?"

She nodded. "I need to quit second-guessing myself just because I don't know how this power works. I *know* it's Roan. No question. And she's in trouble. I've got to try to contact her."

He stood. "Let's go out. These people might think you're a witch or something."

"Right. Good idea." Aria spoke to the crowd in their musical hybrid tongue. The people nodded knowingly.

"What'd you tell them?" Nat said.

"That I'm a *bruja*, a witch. That I can see things from far away. They respect people with such gifts here, it's a very old part of their culture, going back to Africa. I told them I need to check on a friend who has called to me from a distance."

The crowd hushed to allow Aria to concentrate. A skinny girl fanned Aria with a round fan of woven palm fronds.

Aria breathed deeply and relaxed her body. She opened her amber eyes wider and shifted her focus and the tin roof overhead became as transparent as a clear window. Her vision tunneled through ordinary space and expanded into a vaster, more inclusive space, into which easily fit the big, blue sky—even all the skies of all the worlds.

With amplified vision Aria could now see herself and Nat and Jasmine and all the folks in the room and the sailboats beached in the white sand and the turquoise curve of the sea and the sphere of the Earth and its orbit around the sun and on and on, in the illuminated realm of hyperspace. She was now free to select any point, within or without, in all of ordinary space-time, as her viewpoint.

285

She quickly located Isla Los Aves and found Roan, lying face down on the floor of her room, sobbing. The first time Aria discovered Roan, the room had been dimly lit by the glow of monitor lights from four video cameras mounted high on opposite walls and by the on-lights of a computer, CD-player, stereo speakers and other electronics. The equipment was gone now and the room was lightless, but heat-wavelengths revealed Roan's form in glowing red detail.

The underground base was all but deserted. The mainframe computers, telecommunications gear, furniture and other equipment, all gone. Aria swept her vision through the five underground levels. She found a man sitting alone in an empty room, his back to the wall. He seemed to be waiting nervously. On the second level down she found two men attaching small packages to the support beams in the corners of each cinderblock room. She studied the packages more closely. Each looked like a brick of plastic modeling clay wrapped in clear cellophane tape, wired to a battery-powered radio receiver.

Bombs. The men were planting plastic explosives with detonators. Aria found more bombs on the lower three levels. The demolition team was working its way from the bottom to the top and had nearly finished its task.

Aria returned her viewpoint to Roan's room. Roan had stopped sobbing and was sitting up now on the floor in the dark, legs drawn up tight, hands folded around her ankles.

Aria wanted to contact Roan, send her a message of hope. But how?

Aria always had believed in telepathy, of sorts. She had been close enough to a few of her best friends to be privy to their unspoken thoughts and moods many times, in uncanny ways. She regarded that level of intuition as a natural feature of intimacy. But surely such empathy was leagues away from *controlled* telepathy; *intentionally* sending a detailed message. How do you transmit thoughts?

"Roan, listen to me," Aria whispered, concentrating on beaming the thoughts to the woman in the dark room on Isla Los Aves. "I'm a friend. Nat and Jasmine are here with me. They know you're alive. We're close by and we're coming to get you off the island."

Roan still hugged herself, head lowered to knees, rocking gently, apparently unaware of the message Aria had tried to broadcast to her.

"Roan, can you hear? Don't give up. We're going to rescue you."

Roan looked up. She frowned, staring toward the door.

Had she picked up on something?

"Roan, I'm a friend. Nat and Jasmine are here, too. We're coming to get you off the island."

Roan stood and crossed to the door, pressed her ear against the steel.

Aria felt frustrated. Obviously, something had stirred in Roan's mind; maybe she thought she was hearing the mumble of faraway voices. But clearly she was not receiving the actual message.

287

Aria broke off the vision. Nat eyed her with a worried frown. "Roan is all right for now," she said, "but the situation there has gotten critical. The base has been evacuated, the equipment and all the personnel. Just three men are left behind on the island—"

"But that's great, now's our chance."

"No, listen. Two of the men are planting explosives. Nat, they're going to blow the place sky-high."

"Oh no." He ran his hand through his hair. "Can she hear your thoughts?"

Aria shook her head. "I don't know how to send them."

"What about telekinesis? Can you do something—anything?"

"Like what? Her room is empty. Even if there were objects in it that I could toss around like a poltergeist, I don't know what good that would do. It'd just scare her more; she'd think it was an earthquake or something."

"Aria, ask Mammy Mako. She know," Balboa said. "She a bruja like you. She contact spirits and all kinda magic."

"Who is Mammy Mako?"

The crowd parted. A fat, dark-skinned woman with short gray wooly hair shuffled forward. She wore a baggy burlap dress made of sewn-together *Schooner Brand* flour sacks. She gazed at Aria with kindness and her ancient, watery eyes crinkled into a smile. "I'm Mammy Mako."

Aria took her big, gnarled hands and kissed them. "Grandmother, I'm trying to send my

288

thoughts to a friend on Isla Los Aves," she said. "I think she feels something stirring in her mind, but she can't make out the message I'm trying to send."

Mammy Mako grinned, revealing cigar-stained teeth the colors of Indian corn. "Chile, don' be thinkin' of sendin' no message. Don' be thinkin' her far away. Ya see? Sendin' messages far away is for da postal mon, no? Spirit-talkin' is more like talkin' to da baby inside ya womb. She closer than ya breath. Ya see? Not *far*. Not 'send a message'."

Aria squinted. "You're saying, you just sort of talk inside your head to the other person—and they hear you?"

Mammy Mako shook her wooly head. "Don' be thinkin' *other* person. Dat an address for de postal mon, ya see?" Mammy Mako reached out with one bony black finger and tapped Aria's bosom. "Ya gotta meet dat person *here*, touch ya spirits inside. Then ya don' need no talk. Wad ya know, dey know."

Aria suddenly understood. And in hyperspace, it was certainly true that there was no distance between her and Roan. Every point in ordinary space was equally accessible from hyperspace, because ordinary space was *contained* within higher space. Roan had not been able to hear her because Aria had conceived the problem of communication as one of transmitting or shouting from afar. But the real trick was that of becoming one with Roan. Then even a whisper would not be necessary.

"Nat, hold my hand," Aria said. "Jasmine, take my other hand." They clasped hands. "Feel what it's like to be Roan right now. She feels alone and scared. So hold her inside your heart. Remember all your love for her and just *be* with her, *here*."

Jasmine softly cried. "Mommy, I love you so much!"

Aria glanced around the room. "Let's all be with her, here and now."

Mammy Mako nodded approvingly and closed her eyes. Aria sat on the rattan-carpeted floor. Mammy Mako's big black hands rested on her shoulders. The only sound in the room was the slow, hushed breath of the sea on the shoreline below.

Aria shifted her vision to super-spatial awareness. She re-contacted Roan and allowed their hearts to merge, sharing minds.

Suddenly Roan's eyes grew huge. She gasped and jumped up from the floor and ran to the door, but found it locked. "Nat! Jasmine!" She turned her head listening all around the room. Then she smiled and burst into tears, pressing her hands to her heart. "I hear you, I hear you! Yes, I hear you! You've found me! You're coming for me."

Aria wept, too, along with Nat and Jasmine. All wept the same tears of relief and joy.

"Balboa, ya take dis man and woman in ya boat to Isla Los Aves," Mammy Mako said. "Da little girl she stay here wid me."

"Gramma, a secret military base be on dat island. My boat fast-fast, but it ain' no match for dat kinda devil."

"Ya take dem, Balboa. I say so."

Balboa let out a sigh of resignation. "Yes, Gramma. I take dem."

37

"They're coming for me," Roan told herself. "They know I'm here and they're coming for me."

Her faith in life had been more than restored; it had leaped to a higher level. Somehow her family had found her, even in this hidden hell; somehow they had communicated with her. That said something amazing and wonderful about the power of love.

Unless the experience had been just some hallucination her mind had dreamt up in its lonely desperation.

"No, I can't let myself believe that. It was real. I felt them. It was *real*. They're on their way." She gathered up her strength and courage, pushed aside her doubts. She had to figure out how to help them get her out of there.

She began to pace back and forth when a fist rapped on her door.

"Roan, it's me, John." The lock turned and the door opened. "I've come to take you topside for a walk on the beach," said the husky male voice. "C'mon. We don't have much time. One last stroll, you and me."

38

Aria and Nat helped Balboa remove layers of palm fronds and a military surplus camouflage netting that covered his boat, beached inside a shoreline grotto in a limestone cliff.

Twenty minutes work unveiled a vintage U.S. Navy patrol-torpedo strike boat with a sleek and narrow, 80-foot-long plywood hull. Angular bands of blue, gray and white marine paint camouflaged her sides and visually broke up her low profile above the waterline. Small black letters on the stern told her name: *Blast from the Past*.

"This is *it*?" Nat said. "A PT boat? An *antique*? For chrissakes, she's—what?—sixty years old?"

"Dis baby outrun anyting, mon. Coast Guard patrol boats, dey eat her wake. Trust me."

Nat sighed. "Guess I've got no choice."

"Hey, mon, don' hurt her feelins'." Balboa's eyes roved over the boat from prow to stern with real affection. "She built at de Higgins Shipyard, New Orleans, 1944, and was de fastest strike boat of her day, mon—could hit 50 knots—and dat's wid hauling torpedoes, rockets, cannon and machine guns. Now she stripped bare, mon—no weapons, no ammo, no armor plating around de bridge—plus no crew of a dozen sailors. Dat make her lighter and faster dan ever."

Nat was not convinced. The modern U.S. Navy had turbo-powered interceptor boats—with hydrofoils. Who knew what they might be up against?

Balboa grinned. "Remember dat Beach Boys' tune, 'Little Deuce Coupe'?"

"Grew up with it."

Balboa sang in falsetto, "'Ya don' know wad I got!'" He nodded for Nat to follow and led him to the rear half of the wooden deck and lifted up one hinged section of an aluminum engine cover. "Looky here, mon." A huge, gray-painted engine block filled most of the hull. Its large brass nameplate identified it as a Rolls-Royce Proteus gas-turbine, generating 25,000 horsepower.

"Holy shit!" Nat said. "That's like strapping a rocket on a water ski. Where'd this come from? They didn't have gas-turbines during World War Two."

Balboa grinned. "Took de engine from a Dutch Navy patrol boat dat ran aground near here in Hurricane Danny. De boat abandoned and I claimed her, mon—law of the high seas—towed her off de reef at flow tide and stripped her for parts. Swapped me pistons for de turbine. Now she hit sixty-five knots from full stop in a minute flat."

It was Nat's turn to grin. "Now I hear you talking. She's 'fast-fast.'"

With a hydraulic winch connected to a launch dolly on steel rails they rolled the boat down the slope of the beach. The shallow-draft hull slid into the blue-green waters of the lagoon and Balboa instantly cranked the gas-turbine engine. It whined slowly up through three octaves and then screamed to mighty life, sounding like the propjet that had

294

flown Nat here, and giving off the same oily smell of jet-fuel-grade kerosene.

Balboa spun the bow around to head into the light surf at the mouth of the lagoon. "Hang on cuz." Balboa winked at Aria and shoved the throttle to full. The PT boat exploded forward as if fired from a slingshot, the bow leapt clear of the water, Nat plunked down hard into his chair on the bridge. Within seconds, the lightweight, overpowered wooden boat was hydroplaning. Only the last dozen feet of the 80-foot keel and the stern pitch stabilizer kept the three-bladed high-speed screw knifing through the sea.

Low clouds scudded in, riding fast on the freshening trade winds from the northeast. The *Blast from the Past* kicked up a wake like frothy champagne. Nat shared a look with Aria. She smiled, happy for him. He felt that he was with the most wonderful woman on earth, zooming across the sea to Isla Los Aves, to rescue the most wonderful woman on earth.

39

Roan followed John into the elevator. The acrid odor of ozone mixed with the smells of steel, plastic, and John's ever present cologne. Roan's heart thumped so loudly she worried the sound would echo from the walls of the elevator car.

We're going outside. This is it. My only chance. But what am I going to do?

They rode without speaking through the upper four stories and stepped out into a hallway that angled upward to the exit door. Sea wind and island sounds rushed forward to greet Roan as soon as she emerged outside. But this afternoon, she did not pause to relish their embrace. She was busy counting her footsteps.

During dozens of walks with John she had memorized the number of steps to various features of the trail, thinking such landmarks might serve her someday in an escape attempt. *One-eighteen, one-nineteen...* Now she was able to clearly picture their position on the trail in relation to the first tight switchback; the sea cliff; an oblong, tree-lined hillock; two more switchbacks; then a narrow ravine with a limestone floor like a steep staircase that stepped down to the sand dunes, which opened out at last upon a broad, flat beach.

She also knew about a sea cave on the south end of the beach. Roan had heard boats powering in and out of it and guessed it contained a hidden dock that served the secret base. During each of her beach strolls she had made it her goal to form a clear sound-picture in her mind of the cave's location.

This afternoon she sensed John was in a hurry, felt his nervous energy. He had his orders, and a beach excursion had not been planned in the schedule of sending the underground base—along with Roan—to oblivion.

The sea wind tossed Roan's hair behind her like a long, fluttering flag. Pumice gravel crunched beneath their feet. The two had just entered the first switchback when John spoke.

"Roan…"

He swallowed and could not get past her name.

One-ninety-two, one-ninety-three…

He began again a moment later. "Roan, it's not my idea not to let you go home. If I could, I would. I think you know that. My orders came down directly from Wolfe."

"What would happen if you got me off the island? Who would know?"

"Oh, he would find out, all right. He's got the implants, remember? He can see things, see *every*thing."

Two-thirty-one, two-thirty-two… "Why'd they shut down the project?"

"They got what they wanted. Got the vision system. It works. Now the mission is to keep anyone else from developing it. I've heard somebody else already has the technology, the implants in place, everything. Wolfe is obsessed with hunting them down."

297

Two-forty-four..."Somebody else has the implants in place?"

"Some woman. American."

Roan now understood how she had been contacted by Nat and Jasmine and...whom? Some woman with the power to touch any point in ordinary space-time. *Two-sixty, two-sixty-one...*

Roan's sole purpose during all her years of research had been to develop the technology to enable herself and others like her to see again. But her dreams had been twisted into a nightmare.

"The one thing I have never been told is *why*?" she said. "Why, John? Is all this part of a spying mission?"

"Don't know. Only the topmost agents on this project were briefed about its real purpose. But it's not any ordinary kind of spying they're after, I do know that. Scuttlebutt says it's got something to do with alien contact."

"*What*?" She stopped walking.

"Yeah, that's what I said—aliens—if you can believe that. Pretty weird, huh?"

Roan had been so startled she was not sure of the count, but she still had a good idea where they were. The break in the trail with the sea-cliff was coming up on their left in a hundred yards or so.

John took Roan's hand and led her to walk with him again. "You know, Roan, you're a beautiful woman. Very. All the guys in my barracks have been talking about you, fantasizing, all year long. I'm...well, you know, I'm trying to say I've grown...attached...to you over time."

298

Oh, god. Where was this leading? "That so?" she said. "Gee, then it must really make you feel kind of rotten that you're going to lock me in my room and blast me to smithereens. I mean, with you being such a sensitive human being, and all."

"I told you it wasn't my idea. I'm only following orders."

"Well, that's mighty consoling, John. When the death camp guards told that to the Jews, it made a world of difference."

"Cut the crap." He stopped and spun her toward him. "You know how I feel about you. You've been playing off my affection all year—"

"Only to get you to take me out of my cage for a walk on the beach."

"Been wanting you so long." His deep voice dropped low. "It's your last hour, Roan. I promise I can make it sweeter."

He tilted his head up to kiss her and she jerked her face away. He tightened his squeeze on her arms until it hurt. He was an inch or two shorter than her, but broad-chested and densely muscled.

"I don't want to force you, but you know I will if I have to. Use some sense, Roan. It's over. Your time on this planet is up. The other men are already in the last boat, waiting for me. Soon I've got to take you back to your room. I'm *asking* you, for now. But I'll take what I want either way."

"All right."

"What?" he sounded surprised.

"All right. But not here. Not in the gravel. Let's go down to the beach, to the sand."

"Sure. Sure. You won't regret this." They began to walk again and he grabbed a handful of hair at the nape of her neck and let his fingers comb through it, feeling the luxuriant texture. "I bet your muff is fiery red like your mane," he said, and his voice cracked with sexual excitement. "Am I right?"

"Shut up, okay?" She took John's hand down from her hair, gave it a little squeeze and snuggled closer as she walked beside him.

"No problem."

Roan listened and felt for the subtle shift in air currents that announced the break in the mountain trail at the cliff's edge. In a moment, the breeze shifted and the path beneath her feet turned to a stretch of solid rock. She sensed the cliff edge only a few feet to their left. The cliff terrified her, but she knew what she must do.

She let go of John's hand and wrapped her arm around his waist. Then she paused in the trail and turned him toward her slowly, his back to the cliff. She closed her eyes and parted her lips slightly, eagerly. Just as his lips mashed into hers, she suddenly ducked and plowed into him fast and hard at waist height, driving with both her legs and all her strength. He rocked backward, off-balance, grunted with sudden panic.

His scream hung suspended in air then plummeted over the sheer rock ledge, dropping in pitch as it fell. Seconds later, a crashing wave swallowed the endnote, and the echoing wail was lost in the sea breeze.

Roan had stumbled onto her hands and knees at the lip of rock and sensed the black hole of space gaping before her. She scooted back from the cliff and rose to her feet on shaky legs.

She had just killed a human being. She had not even known his last name. She half-expected to be crushed by guilt for her mortal sin, but instead an emotional power surged through her veins that overwhelmed her earlier feelings of helplessness and despair.

"Nat's coming for me." She imagined herself in the arms of her husband and daughter again. The love she felt now was so passionate that, in her own way, she could *see* Nat and Jasmine, wrapped inside her heart. "He's coming for me, I feel it."

Roan turned and began descending the rocky footpath leading to the beach. She would wait on the shoreline for her beloved. Nat was on his way.

After a quarter-hour picking her way carefully down the mountain, orienting by remembering the features of the trail beneath her tennis shoes and the location of the switchbacks, Roan heard voices below her. She nearly cried out with joy, but a sudden instinct kept her quiet.

Male voices.

Roan crouched low, listening. Boot steps tramping up the mountain, scattering loose stones.

"It was John, I'm sure of it," one voice said, huffing with exertion.

"Just because you heard a scream don't mean it was John."

"Had to be. Nobody's left on the island but the woman."

"So maybe *she* screamed. John said he wasn't gonna let her go to waste."

"No, it was a man's voice, a male scream. Women *shriek*. It was John, I tell you."

"Well, check your watch. Let's hurry the fuck up. I'd like to be a mile or two away from shore when this firecracker goes off."

Roan's heart drummed in her chest. She realized the men couldn't see her because clumps of trees covering the hillock blocked their line of vision.

"Can you believe that asshole can't even handle a blind woman?" the first voice said.

"Fuck. We now got less than forty minutes to put a bullet in her head, throw her back inside on top of the plastics and scramble back down to the cutter. Man, I ain't diggin' this countdown at all."

Roan spun, heart in her throat, and scrambled uphill, retracing her steps as fast as she could go. The map in her mind and the sensations of the trail beneath her shoes guided her. In ten minutes she stood at the breezy gap in the trees where the cliff overlooked the sea.

She wore a nylon windbreaker over a dance leotard and denim shorts. She yanked off the windbreaker, tennis shoes, and shorts. The rock felt gritty, damp and cold on the soles of her bare feet. Wind tousled her hair. She inched forward until her toes felt the hard edge of the rock ledge. There she poised, shivering, more from fright than cold.

302

Instead of the smell of chlorine and wet concrete, and the sound of the gurgling water breaking the pool surface below for visual reference, she smelled salt spray, wet limestone and heard waves booming in and rolling out again.

"*About a hundred feet, straight down to the sea*, John had said. Like the celebrated diving cliff at La Quebrada in Acapulco.

Before her accident Roan had made thousands of high dives while training for state, regional and national championships and the try-outs for the U.S. Olympic Diving Team. But those dives had been from 10 meters—about 33 feet. The highest dive she had ever made was about 80 feet, into a quarry, and it felt scary even though she could see.

It was not just a matter of executing a dive from a potentially deadly height, years removed from her training. Timing was now critical. She must launch from the top in order to hit the water at the instant it would be deepest and the splash back from the rocks at the base would sweep her out to sea, where she could outswim the reach of the currents. Even if she cut the water perfectly with the kind of dive that would earn a straight 10 from Olympic judges, if her timing was off by more than a couple seconds the incoming wave would grind her against the rocks.

It was a matter of doing all this without benefit of eyesight. No visual references. Just a black vault of space before and below her like a hole in the universe.

303

A leap of faith. To make the dive of her life. Or her death.

But either way, I'm not helpless. I choose.

"Look! There she is! C'mon! Stop her!

The voices startled her and she wobbled. She regained her balance, reoriented her mind, concentrating on timing. She must take her cue not from the danger above, but from the waves far below.

Pow! Gun fire. *Pow! Pow! Zing!* Rocks popped and scattered high behind her on the rocky wall. Someone was shooting at her from below, but they had an awkward line of fire. Her heart jumped into her throat, but her feet stayed planted on the ledge.

Pow! Plink! Getting closer. Zeroing in on target.

Wait. Wait! Listen to the surf.

Pow! Plink! Too damn close.

Waves surged in far below, rushing to attack the base of the cliff.

"Now!"

Roan shoved off with her calves and flexed tiptoes and sailed into space, arms outspread like swan wings for balance. Her hair whipped behind like a banner of flames in the slipstream as she knifed through the sea salt air.

Long seconds passed and she could not tell if she dived or if she flew, only that she smiled.

40

The *Blast from the Past* skimmed at sixty-plus knots toward Isla Los Aves and in less than an hour the island's conical silhouette poked up from the horizon.

Aria was huddled behind the helm against the dashing spray of water over the bow. Nat trained binoculars on the island. "Aria. We need your help to find her."

Aria shifted her vision into hyperspace and focused on the small island, scanning. She gasped and held in her breath when she located Roan balancing barefoot at the cliff's edge. Roan pushed off straight outward from the ledge and hovered for an instant like a floating swan. Then she plummeted with perfect form into the sea below and slit the water with a small splash. The crashing wave rebounded off the cliff base and swept her seaward, away from the rocks.

"Oh my god!" Aria shouted. "Roan just dove from a cliff into the sea. It was the most beautiful, most graceful thing I've ever seen in my life!"

"Is she all right?"

"Yes! The undertow dragged her away from the cliff and now she's swimming hard, straight out to sea."

"Thank god."

"There are men on the island. *Shit*. They've got rifles."

"Oh no."

"She's out of range for them to shoot her. She's a half-mile out. They're watching her with binoculars. Wait. She just turned. Now she's swimming parallel to the island. The black sand beach is to the north. I think she's heading toward it. The men are running down a steep trail. *Damn.* The trail leads right to the beach—they must know she's swimming back."

"How much longer will it take us to get there?" Nat said.

Balboa tried to push the throttle forward but it was already shoved to full. The PT boat skipped and flew over the light swells. "Ten minutes? Twelve? Hell, I don' know, mon." He glanced behind. "See dat handle?" He pointed to a metal handle on a large rectangular door just behind the bridge. "Dat's a cargo hold. Open it up and start dumpin' everyting inside overboard. We lighten our load."

Nat yanked the hood off the cargo hold and found bale after bale of marijuana stacked like hay in a barn. He lifted the heavy bales and slid them toward Aria who levered them up and shoved them over the gunwale. The bales splashed into the sea and tumbled and spun in the foamy wake. In five minutes the cargo hold lay empty, and more than fifty bales of marijuana bobbed in a long trail behind.

The PT boat had gained another knot of speed.

"Aria, check on Roan." Nat shouted. "Are we going to make it?"

306

"As soon as she makes it to the beach they're going to have a clear shot from the lower part of the trail. Maybe five minutes to where they can see her and shoot at her."

"Roan!" Nat yelled. "Roan!" His body shook with raw passion.

"Wait, she's swimming into a...like a grotto. She's safe from their line of fire for now. Oh. There's a dock inside, a secret dock, hidden from the air. There's a boat at the dock. One of those ...uh, amphibious things... those landing craft that can drive right up onto the beach. Must be their getaway boat.

"Hey, one of the men just stumbled and pitched off the trail, down into a deep gulley. He's hurt, he's clutching his leg—"

"Good. One down, one to go," Balboa said.

Aria gasped. "The other man shot him. Just shot him. Now the guy with the rifle is scrambling as fast as he can down the trail toward the beach."

"C'mon. C'mon. Move, PT boat," Nat said.

"Roan just climbed aboard the boat inside the cave."

"What's she doing?"

"She's groping around. I don't know. Maybe for a weapon."

"How's she gonna aim a weapon, for chrissakes?"

"No. She was searching for the starter. She just started the engine."

"Yes!" Nat shouted. "That's my babe. Go! Go! Go!"

"The guy is now at the beach. He's running toward a...it's a door into the grotto. He's almost there. Damn it, Roan. Get out of there!"

"Throw it in reverse," Nat shouted, though he knew it was impossible for her to hear him. "Back out of the cave."

"What...?" Aria said. "She's climbed out on the dock. Oh. She unwrapped a bow line."

"Smart girl," Balboa said.

"Has this PT boat got an air horn?" Nat said.

"Gotcha," Balboa said and began to blast the air horn.

"Here, let me do that," Nat said. "Roan and I have a special knock." Nat punched the air horn button in the pattern the two used to identify each other: the funky five-beat rhythm Bo Diddley had made famous in his hit, "Hey, Bo Diddley!"

"She hears you," Aria said. "She looked up. Now she's smiling and crying. But the guy's almost there. He stopped to look toward us. He probably can make out our bow spray."

In desperation, Nat cupped his hands and bellowed, "Throw the transmission in reverse and ease back on the throttle handle." The sea spray tossed his voice back in his face.

"She know how to drive a boat?" Balboa said.

"Maybe. Yeah. Fuck. I don't know. I think her dad had a cabin cruiser when she was a kid."

"I can see de cave mouth," Balboa said. "We almost dere."

"Uh-oh, the guy's stepping through the doorway," Aria said. "He's running along the dock.

308

She heard him. She ducked down under the pilot house. Oh! She threw the engine into forward. She's going the wrong way!"

Aria watched as the landing craft's props churned the water to boiling and the boat surged forward, ramming the dock. The impact hurled the man face down in a sprawl. He rolled onto his back, drew up his assault rifle and opened fire. Roan kept her head down as a swarm of bullets ripped through the Plexiglas windshield and chewed the top of the aluminum pilot house into whizzing shrapnel.

Still crouching, Roan reached up with one hand and slapped at the control levers. The transmission shifted to neutral as the throttle raged to full. The engine revved to a high-rpm scream of protest. The flat bow slipped off the dock and the landing craft drifted backward a couple dozen feet in the canal. Roan clawed at the controls and the transmission shifted to full ahead. The landing craft lurched forward, gained momentum fast and slammed the dock. The flat-bottomed hull tilted upward halfway out of the water. It looked to Aria like a killer whale driving itself up onto the ice to snatch an unwary seal in its jaws. The man screamed and squeezed off a final burst of automatic rifle fire as the landing craft rode up over his legs, smearing them like crimson crayons. Then the vessel's tonnage crushed the dock and the man together in a splintering of wood and bones.

Roan cut off the engine and the landing craft settled back into the water amid a slosh of floating debris. She collapsed on the deck.

"She did it!" Aria shouted, jumping up and down. "He's dead. She's safe."

"My god, Roan," Nat whispered. "You're alive. You're safe." Tears streamed down his cheeks as he tapped the air horn repeatedly with the familiar pattern as if it were the world's happiest music.

Balboa cut the throttle back to idle, shifted to neutral. The dark grotto gaped like a maw as the PT boat glided inside. The cave stunk of seaweed, dead fish and diesel fumes. Balboa shifted to reverse and the *Blast from the Past* came to a stop alongside the landing craft's starboard gunwale.

Nat leapt onto the deck of the landing craft and scooped up pale white Roan into his dark brown arms. Her wet red hair spilled over him as they hugged and kissed and wept. And the expressions on their faces was so beatific that the jealousy Aria worried she might feel was quenched by her own tears of joy.

41

The PT boat had put several miles between its stern and the island when the explosives inside the underground base detonated. Aria squinted at the brilliant flash of light seconds before the deep boom and concussion of the explosion hurtled against her ear drums. Everybody on board flinched at the impact of the pressure wave of sound.

Aria watched the mountain spew fire high over its black cone, briefly reviving the glory of its volcanic past. Soon the flames died to a dull orange glow that flickered in the darkening distance.

Balboa slipped a tape of Bob Marley's Greatest Hits into a CD player as the *Blast from the Past* headed home at high speed. Nat and Roan snuggled together under a blanket, deep in their private communion.

Night fell on a lampless sky. It would take another few hours for the late-rising moon to shine over the dark curve of the sea. On the throat of heaven a necklace of stars broke and scattered diamonds across black velvet.

Aria huddled next to her cousin behind a windscreen to stay out of the spray from the PT boat's prow. Her intuition nagged her. *We're not out of danger yet*. She turned in a full circle, scanning the sea and sky. Her heat-sensitive vision spotted a glowing red sliver moving off the stern at horizon level. She tracked it with her eyes, focusing its infrared wavelength: a ship in pursuit, slicing along the sea.

"Balboa, we've got company." She patted his shoulder and pointed. "Look."

Balboa searched with a pair of night-vision binoculars. His dreadlocks whipped along his broad back as he leaned outside the shelter of the windscreen. He shrugged. "Where?"

"Near the horizon line, two-o'clock. Closing fast."

"Okay. I see dem now. Dey far. Just a speck."

"Trouble?" Nat said, joining them at the bridge with Roan.

"Not from dat distance, mon." Balboa grinned and laid his hand on the throttle handle. "Dey never catch us. Only ting on de wata faster dan me PT boat be a hydrofoil."

"Hydrofoil," Aria said. "Looks like a ship flying along on wings jutting down into the water?"

Balboa's blue eyes flashed big. "Aw shit. Dat's wad chasin' us?"

"Like I said, closing fast."

In another five minutes, Balboa confirmed with the night vision binoculars the ship was a hydrofoil strike boat. To Aria the interceptor looked like a giant steel version of a water-strider beetle skimming the sea surface on jointed legs at high speed.

A minute later an incoming shell shrieked overhead. *WHUMP!* The warhead exploded underwater. *SPLAKOOOSH!* A white plume geysered sixty feet into the air off the port bow like Old Faithful blowing its top. Balboa veered and

312

narrowly missed the eruption. The spray sloshed the deck with buckets of cold sea water.

Seconds later, another shrieking projectile detonated nearby. *WHOOOMP!* This time the plume geysered off the starboard bow.

"They're bracketing us," Nat said, "looking for a firing solution."

Balboa took evasive action, weaving erratically, which slowed the progress of their flight.

"They're gaining a lot faster now," Aria said.

"Dammit. Just me luck, de sea calm as glass."

"What do you mean?"

"Hydrofoils can't fly in rough seas. Dey have to slow down and ride de hull."

A hail of heavy-caliber machine gun fire stitched a line of small plumes across the sea to port. Balboa whipped the PT boat hard starboard.

"Keep zig-zagging, I'm going to try something," Aria said, keeping her eyes on the pursuing strike boat. A radar dome loomed above the bridge, a twin machine gun poked from a bow turret beneath a very nasty-looking cannon, and rocket launcher tubes crowded the sides and stern. The gray steel boat zipped along the smooth water, its hull towering a dozen feet in the air atop knife-like struts attached to three hydrofoils—one in the center under the bow and two jutting to the sides near the stern. The trailing struts were kicking up thirty-foot fishtail sprays. The boat was approaching fearfully fast.

313

Aria reached with her mind to the water just in front of the strike boat. As she had done when she moved the refrigerator with telekinesis, she did not struggle with or shove at the water, but imagined the sea leaping up like a custom-made tsunami directly in front of the boat, and she calmly but fervently beseeched the water for help, as one friend to another.

After a moment's concentration she felt the eerie and euphoric sensation of sympathetic rapport with the seawater, and again she felt awed that at the fundamental level of *essence*, far below thought and self-awareness, the water possessed a degree of mind, now in communion with her own mind. Aria surrendered herself, feeling deeper into the unity, entering a mood where she could no longer tell where she ended and the water began—or where mind ended and matter began.

Then it happened.

A seething wall of whitewater gushed out of the sea in front of the speeding strike boat. The boat slammed headlong into the isolated tidal wave. The steel bow plane snapped with a loud crack like thunder, and the stern planes twisted into junk. The keel plowed down into the sea with a mountainous splash. The effect of the sudden drag on the hull was like dropping sea anchors and the boat yawled sideways into skid, slinging men and loose equipment overboard, very nearly capsizing.

"Yeah, dat's me cuz!" Balboa yelled, watching the action through night-scope binoculars. He punched the air above his head. "Don' nobody mess wid de mighty *bruja*!"

314

In another moment the disabled strike craft had come to a dead stop, listing heavily to port. The crew began manning inflatable rafts.

Aria sat near Balboa's bare feet on the deck of the pilot house, her back against a bulkhead that buzzed in resonance with the gas-turbine engine whirring underneath. She recalled a line from the Roman poet, Virgil: *Mens agitat molem*—Mind moves matter. It seemed to Aria that Virgil had stopped short of the whole truth. She would have stood in his toga and proclaimed, *Mens* est *molem*—Mind *is* matter; or more accurately, Mind is matter-energy—*molem-energia*. She had found that matter-energy is a permutation of a higher, unified field. Whether that single field was called *Mind*, or *Spirit*, or *Tao*, or *God*, was beside the point. One could name it *Hortense*, if she liked.

Again Aria felt a sense of obligation riding on her blessings, her powers. But what was she supposed to do? Go around proclaiming the insights that were now her daily experience? Yuck. Preachers and preaching turned her off intensely.

Nat scooted next to her and touched her hand. "You okay?" he shouted above the engine roar. Water droplets beaded his wooly hair. His black eyes were shining and alive.

"I'm fine," Aria said. Nat's eyes searched hers, trying to read how she was dealing with her emotions about his reunion with Roan. Aria glanced over at Roan. She was wrapped in a gray wool Army Surplus blanket, her wet hair as earthy red as the juice of beets. Roan and Nat were mates— interlocked like jigsaw-puzzle pieces in the quantum geometries of their scientist souls. Aria and Nat loved each other, yes, but this *other* love...this *other* wife...

"Her Kung-Fu is stronger than mine," Aria said, imitating a heavily-accented voice-over from a martial arts flick.

Nat laughed.

"I'm very happy for you," she said. "For both of you."

Nat squeezed her shoulders and his soulful eyes said thank you stronger than any words.

A half-hour later, as the *Blast from the Past* approached the lagoon at Otrabanda village, welcoming bonfires burned on the beach. Several men helped Balboa guide the PT boat onto its steel dolly with controlled nudges from the boat's engine. They hurriedly winched the dolly and boat along the railroad tracks into the cave and covered the boat with the camouflage netting and layers of palm fronds.

Balboa and Aria, Nat and Roan walked up the footpath toward Balboa's house. Nat and Roan raced ahead, eager to see Jasmine. Aria was exhausted and held onto her cousin as they climbed the slope. Not till she was nearly at his porch did she notice the worried looks on the villager's faces.

Inside Balboa's house, the sunken look in Nat's eyes and the agony of Roan's sobs foretold terrible news.

"He took away Jasmine," Mammy Mako said, tears making her round black cheeks shine like polished obsidian.

"Who?" Aria demanded.

"Da wicked one. Wolfe. Jack Wolfe." Her sobs shook her pendulous breasts. "He say he wanna make sure ya come him. He be waiting ya at de harbor park in Willemstad. Come noon, he say. He got Jasmine." She cringed and buried her face in her hands.

"I'll go," Nat said.

"Let me go," Aria said. "You and Roan have each other now. Don't risk losing that again."

Mammy Mako glanced tearfully from Nat to Aria. "He say, ya *both* must come. De doctor and de lady. Both, he say."

"I'm going, too," Roan said.

"No. You're staying right here," Nat said.

"Aria is willing to risk her life to save our daughter. Don't you think I also deserve the chance to help?"

Nat only stared at Roan and swallowed hard.

"Nat, it's not a request," Roan said. "You're going, so I'm going."

"Jasmine," Mammy Mako sobbed. "Poor girl, she wid' da devil hisself."

42

Aria, Nat and Roan arrived on the outskirts of Willemstad in the morning driving a borrowed '68 Dodge Dart with the back half of its body cut away and a wooden frame built over the chassis to convert the vehicle into pickup truck. All streets into the capital city were roped off, closed to traffic. Today was the Monday before Ash Wednesday: Grand Carnival Day.

Nat was forced to park several miles from the downtown Punda district were Wolfe would be waiting for them at noon at Sint Anna Baii, a park at the harbor entrance. The three got out and hurried on foot into the city. But the closer they came to downtown and its main street, Queen Emma, the more tightly-pressed became the swaying throngs of dancers and revelers.

In contrast to the grim faces of the three who edged and wove their way through the crowd, the Carnival celebrators radiated a mood of happy madness. Bodies, bodies and more bodies. Singing, clapping, sweating, drinking, dancing, kissing. Everything, it seemed, but moving out of the way to let Aria and Nat and Roan pass. After an hour of squeezing through the crush of sweaty, undulating torsos and earning many angry glances, the three had progressed only four blocks.

"How much farther?" Nat said. "I've got to sit down and rest."

"Sit down here and you'll be trampled into cocoa butter," Aria said.

"He's really exhausted," Roan said.

"I can see that," Aria said. "And I'm beginning to worry we won't make it to the park by noon."

"Go on ahead without me," Nat said, hands on knees, panting. "Tell him I'm on my way."

"I'm not letting you out of my sight," Roan said to Nat, an old joke between them. She gripped his elbow more tightly.

The crowd dipped and bobbed, dancing, dancing; matching the pulse of the tin drums, heartbeat for heartbeat. Only the parade itself moved in the direction of the park, flowing down Queen Emma Street, a steady stream of swaying hips, shapely buttocks, jiggling breasts, and outrageously extravagant costumes.

"Gotta go with the flow," Aria said and tugged her companions into the middle of the parade, between two steel drum orchestras. Wheeled racks, each holding a dozen 44-gallon fuel drums discarded by the U.S. Navy during World War II, rolled along the cobblestone street, with panmen beating six drums each, tapping out an infectiously rhythmic calypso tune.

Costumed troupes pranced in front of and behind the tin-drum bands. One all-female squad, identified by a banner as the "The Erotiquettes" flaunted bare breasts and thong bikini bottoms under flimsy fringe skirts draped over their brown or caramel or black figures, each crowned with an elaborate, twenty-pound headdress—a six-foot starburst of tinsel, plastic, crepe, sequins, wire and *papier mache*.

319

Aria knew she and Nat and Roan stood out like gray clouds as they walked in the midst of the dancing human rainbow, not so much because they were plainly dressed and the gaudy headdresses towered above them, but because they did not laugh and join in the fun, the wildness, the exhibitionism set to music.

In an hour they reached the end of the parade at the entrance to Sint Anna Baii, a harbor park. Nat had grown so weak that Roan and Aria had to support him with their arms wrapping his waist, his arms draped over their shoulders.

It was eleven-thirty. They had a half-hour left to find Jack Wolfe among the park's milling throngs of spectators, parade troupers, assorted performers, and the hordes clustered around the many food booths. Beyond the park's green lawns and trees and soccer fields, steel-hulled freighters rode the low tide, fastened by massive ropes to their berths.

Mammy Mako said Wolfe had not been too specific about the meeting place. Aria had told Nat and Roan to keep their eyes peeled for a broad-shouldered man with white, spiky hair worn in a military crew cut, and one brown and one green eye. Now, for the third time, she tried scanning through hyperspace to locate The Creep, but even with her extended vision of the masses, she could not find him.

"He just said meet him in the park at noon," Aria said. "Doesn't tell us much."

"Your vision...?" Roan said.

She shook her head. "Doesn't help if I don't know where to focus it. Just gets more confusing."

Nat sprawled on a bench, his head in Roan's lap. She gently stroked his hair. "Maybe he wants to find us," Roan said. "Take us by surprise."

"What the hell does he want?" Nat said.

"Me," Aria said, and plopped next to Roan. "He wants me. He told me he thought about Seeker every day since the dog wounded his hand. He sought revenge, and he got it. Considering I dropped a refrigerator on him, escaped, and demolished all the spy equipment in his van, I don't doubt I've been at the forefront of his thoughts these past few days."

"He wants me, too," Nat said. "He wants to pick my brain." He laughed without mirth. "He's free to pick what's left of it. Won't be any help to him."

"Oh, baby," Roan said, and a tear dropped from her eye and splashed his forehead. "How could I find you only to lose you again?"

A chubby black man ambled up to their bench, smiling with missing front teeth. He was wrapped from neck to toe in an aluminum-foil costume that could have been the Carnival version of the Tin Man in the *Wizard of Oz*, but for the headdress of long white plumes that trailed to the ground behind. His breath smelled flammable, of 150-proof rum.

"De man, he give me money to tell ya he waitin' fo' ya." He wobbled as he pointed behind himself vaguely.

Nat sat up. "What man? Where?"

321

"See dat ship? De one with de yellow crane? Red hull?"

"I see it."

"He waitin' dere. He say, come."

Nat was on his feet. "Thanks."

The drunken man held out his palm, like a bellhop waiting for a tip.

"No spare change on me, pal," Nat said. "But here's my tip: don't get brain cancer if you want to live long and prosper."

Aria focused her vision inside the ship's wheelhouse and instantly found Jack Wolfe, dressed in tropical-issue military fatigues in green and brown camouflage, like the mismatched irises of his eyes. He sat in a tall captain's swivel chair, waiting.

Her sight flew to Jasmine, bound by her wrists with long strips of duct tape to a railing that ran along the bridge's wrap-around windows. The girl's breath was fast and shallow, her eyes big with fright, but she appeared physically unharmed.

By contrast, Wolfe looked in terrible shape; his eyes were savagely bloodshot as if they'd been rinsed with pepper gas. White stubble roughened his boxy jaw. His hands shook as they held a small-caliber Uzi machine pistol in his lap, its barrel trained on Jasmine.

"Hurry," Aria said, and she and Roan helped support Nat on each side as they shuffled toward the freighter. In a minute they reached the gangplank angling up to the ship's main deck. Streaks of dark red rust stained the hull at the anchor hole and reminded Aria of Seeker's blood splotched on

322

Wolfe's big serrated knife. Her gut tightened another notch.

When they stepped into the wheelhouse, Jack Wolfe grinned and said hoarsely, "Welcome to the bigamist and his two lovely wives."

Jasmine's eyes bulged when she saw her mother and she bellowed against her gag, making it sound like a muffled kazoo.

"And a very special welcome to you, Roan. I was most impressed when I remote-viewed the base evacuation yesterday and I watched you escape. That dive was pure movie-magic, put Johnny Weissmuller to shame."

"What do you want?" Nat said.

"To talk. To discuss with other brilliant minds the future of the human race." He wore an expression of bemusement and disdain, what a monkey must see from the other side of the bars at a zoo, Aria thought.

"Why don't you let her go?" Nat said, nodding his daughter. "She's just a little girl, scared to death. Let her go to her mother; then we'll talk."

"I presume you understand the endgame strategy of chess," Wolfe said. "That pawn is holding you in check, Dr. Colt. If you fail to cooperate—" He wiggled the gun in his lap—"Checkmate. Game over."

"Okay," Nat said. "You want to talk. So talk."

Wolfe turned his blood-red gaze to Aria. His eyes looked hot and sore and they glistened with tears.

323

"How do you like your powers? That was a pretty slick move you pulled with the refrigerator."

"My pleasure."

"The first thing I'd like to know is how you move things with your mind. I've got the crazy-enhanced vision, but I can't budge even a piece of lint. I've tried repeatedly to train myself. No dice."

"Yeah, well, it's a real knack," Aria said. "You kind of have to be born with it, like the ability to feel empathy."

Wolfe winced with pain and blinked back tears. "I don't believe you. Know what I think? I think you got a better set of gizmos in your skull than I do. Your electronics work better than mine."

"So buy an antenna."

"Maybe the award-winning doctors Colt can tell me why Aria, here, can perform telekinetic feats but I can't."

"I'm not sure," Nat said. "The two system designs vary. Different thresholds for wavelet quantization—"

"Spare me the jargon." Wolfe waved his free hand. "We'll get back to that. More important question: what do you do about the headaches?"

Aria and Nat glanced at each other.

"I take it from your blank expressions that I'm a lonely saint in my suffering," Wolfe said.

"I had headaches, at first," Aria said. "Bad ones for a few weeks. They went away."

"Fuck." Wolfe blew out his breath angrily. "Mine keep getting worse. Like someone twisting a corkscrew through my brain." He dragged his

324

muscled forearm across his eyes and wiped away tears.

Men like Wolfe don't cry, Aria knew that much. His eyes watered from excruciating pain. And he looked as if he hadn't slept in days.

"Third question. How do you shut off the voices and images?"

This time, Aria tried not to give herself away. She humored him. "That's a real distraction. I hate it. Kind of like—"

"Like having the tuner stuck between TV stations," he said. "Transparent ghost images, stacked one on top of the other, and voices all talking at once."

"Exactly," Aria said. "Drives me crazy, especially when I'm trying to sleep."

Wolfe chuckled, but it came out more like a whimper. "Sleep? I've forgotten what that is."

His eyes watered again and he wiped the back of his shaking hand across his cheeks, blinking, blinking. Then he giggled at some private humor. "Hang on I think I'm picking up *Seinfeld*—uh, never mind, just a re-run." He laughed explosively at his own joke. Then he smashed his fist into the white metal armrest of the captain's chair. Everyone else in the room flinched. The skin on his fist was already raw, and Aria noticed a maroon smear of dried blood on the white paint.

"This fuckin' computer-in-the-brain project ain't what it's cracked up to be." Wolfe groaned, breathing huskily. His whole body trembled.

"It's possible the pain can be treated," Nat said. "The implants can be removed, and that would

325

probably end the hurting. But that, of course, would leave you blind."

"I'm not going to go from gawking at the dark side of the moon—peering to the other end of the universe, for chrissake, to being *blind*!"

Nat shrugged. "Whatever you say."

"*Aghhhh!*" Wolfe screamed and jammed the heels of both palms into his eye sockets.

Aria lunged and snatched the Uzi off his lap, backed up, aiming it at his chest.

Wolfe forced opened his bleary red eyes, and tears ran down both cheeks. "Do you know the first thing about using an automatic weapon?"

"I do," Nat said, and smoothly took the machine pistol from Aria. "I'm quite a good marksman, in fact. At first, cardboard-target bad guys. Lately, flesh and blood. Either way, I usually hit my target."

Aria and Roan went to Jasmine and began cutting the duct tape free with the sharp edge of the key to the borrowed car. Roan covered Jasmine's face with kisses and tears of joy. Aria slowly peeled the strip of tape from Jasmine's mouth.

"Mommy!" she shouted.

Roan grabbed her daughter in a bear hug. They pressed their faces together and sobbed and their red hair fell and intertwined across their shoulders like scarlet weeping willows.

Nat kept his eyes and gun trained on Wolfe, his fingertip steady on the trigger. Wolfe had become absorbed by his private struggle with the agony inside his head. He gripped his temples and tears now streamed down his face beneath squeezed-shut eyelids.

After a few moments, Wolfe sat up straighter in the captain's chair, but all color had drained from his face, making his blood-red eyes seem darker and more clouded. His tight-pressed lips looked as ashen as a cadaver's. "Never should have volunteered for this mission," he whispered hoarsely.

"My turn to ask *you* a few questions," Nat said. "What *is* this goddamn mission? Why did you abduct my wife from our home and make her your slave? Who *are* you people? What's so important about all this? Tell me."

"I'm not at liberty to discuss—"

"Fuck you," Nat said. "You were at liberty to make me believe my wife had been murdered, you bastard. We're American citizens and we've got a right to know why our government has been playing us like pawns."

"Back to chess, eh?" Wolfe smiled in an ugly way. "You wouldn't believe me if I told you."

"Try us," Aria said.

"What can be so terribly important that you can dispose of people's lives at your whim?" Roan said, clutching Jasmine to her bosom.

Wolfe sighed raggedly. His lids drooped and he pressed the heels of his hands against his eyelids. "It's a race," he said, finally. "That's what this is all about."

"A race?" Aria said.

He opened his eyes and pinkish tears of watery blood snaked down stubbly cheeks. "An

327

international goddamn race, to gain access to a source of knowledge that'll make all mankind's technologies look like we're still sitting around in kindergarten, chewing paste."

Aria shrugged. "I haven't the slightest idea—"

"Ever read science fiction, popular astronomy, stuff like that?"

Aria shook her head, wondering where this was leading. "Not my thing."

"Me neither, but that was before I became a superhero." He blinked his horrible eyes and forced a harsh laugh. "I've learned that some big names in astronomy and physics and sci-fi have long speculated on a concept called the Encyclopedia Galactica."

Aria could not believe she had heard him correctly. "Encyclopedia... *Galactica*?"

"Holy cow," Nat said. Roan squeezed his arm.

"See," Wolfe said, "Your scientist pals know what I'm talking about. All the world's nerds have heard of it."

Nat nodded. "Aria, the idea is of a great repository of information, a kind of cosmic library, created—perhaps over eons—by many contributing technological civilizations throughout the galaxy."

Aria frowned and raised one eyebrow. "Are we talking *alien* societies?"

Wolfe barked a laugh. "Yeah, we're actually sitting in this rusty tub in the middle of Carnival talking about aliens. Alien societies! A super-civilization spread throughout the stars." His hand swept through an arc across the ceiling. Then he stabbed Aria with another bloody gaze that froze her marrow. "Yes, lady, *aliens!* And I'm as serious as death."

"That I'm sure of."

"So listen to what I'm saying," Wolfe said. "Encyclopedia Galactica: the recorded knowledge of a club of interstellar civilizations. To find it would be to find the cosmic Holy Grail—a store of unimaginably advanced technological and cultural data. Science, art, music, history—the works."

"I get the picture," Aria said. "But are you telling us this...thing...is real? It really exists?"

Wolfe nodded slowly. "I most definitely did *not* believe it, until I was shown the evidence. It's real. But nobody knows a thing about it beyond the fact of its existence. Nobody's been able to access it."

"Then how can you know it exists?"

"For decades NASA and a dozen universities have been running a listening program called SETI—stands for Search for Extraterrestrial Intelligence. They use radio telescopes to try to detect incoming messages from other worlds."

"That I *have* heard of," Aria said. "So you're saying, one day they downloaded the Encyclopedia Galactica?"

He shook his head. "No. Back in 1979, a grad student at Ohio State picked up a strong radio burst called the WOW! signal, because this guy got excited and scribbled WOW! in the margin of the computer printout."

329

"I read about that," Nat said. "Remember Roan? We were in grad school ourselves."

"I remember," Roan said.

"The signal contained ordered mathematical sequences, series of prime numbers, that sort of thing," Wolfe said. "Exactly the kind of signal everybody had been hoping to find—proof of an intentional, intelligent broadcast."

"Wait a minute," Nat said, "nobody said anything about prime number series. You mean—? No, the story I got is that it was simply an exceptionally powerful signal. Worthy of further investigation. But they tried and tried to re-contact the same radio source and never repeated their luck."

"That was the official story, yes," Wolfe said.

"A cover-up?" Roan said.

He nodded. "Pentagon yanked all copies of the data away from Ohio State and turned the project over to the National Reconnaissance Office, to a section we call The Shop. The project got instantly boosted to the topmost level of military secrecy."

"What about the grad students who knew the truth?" Aria said.

"Right. Two of them, plus one supervising professor. All were offered the opportunity to work for us. The students accepted and are still on the project today."

"And the professor?"

Wolfe sighed, as if recalling a particularly annoying day at the office. "She had kids, refused to

330

drop out of her little suburban dream. Let's see..."
His eyes focused upward to recall and their whites
looked tomato red. "I believe her car stalled on a
railroad track—no, her car went off a
bridge...whatever. Wasn't my assignment."

Aria seethed inwardly. This killer and his
secret organization had all the compassion of
hornets in a nest that had just been punted forty
yards. *Our tax dollars at work.*

"The spook scientists easily re-tuned to the
signal source and picked up a wallop of digital
code," he said. "Evidently, it's coming from a
transmitting station hundreds of light years away
that was built with the sole purpose of sending one
message. It's been beaming the same message—
waiting to get our attention—for god knows how
long."

"But how can we understand it?" Aria said.
"It's in an Earth-language?"

"To everybody's relief, it wasn't terribly
hard to interpret its meaning. The senders were
doing their damnedest to be understood. Used some
universal math principles to teach whoever picked
up the message how to decode it."

"I knew that's how they'd do it," Roan said,
nodding. "We've had this conversation, Nat."

"I'm totally stunned," Nat said.

Aria shook her head in wonder. "I'm not
believing this."

Wolfe was struck down by another lightning
bolt of agony. His breath escaped his lungs in a low,
tattered moan. A vein stood out in his thick neck
like a blue snake slithering up a tree trunk. He

331

pressed his palms to his eyelids and tear-diluted blood snaggled down the inside of one forearm.

When he had recovered, he looked up and pinned Aria with a hard-glinting stare. "Look at me," he whispered hoarsely, and his quietness and control made him all the more menacing. "I volunteered for this mission because it's *real*. Do I seem like a space-case to you? A fuckin' UFO-nut?"

Aria shook her head. *No, you seem like a trained killer—a cruel bastard who loves violence. A man to loathe and fear.*

He gestured to the deep creases etched in his pain-ridden face. "Think all this was for fun?"

"It was only a manner of speaking," Aria said. "I meant, it's an incredible revelation; mind-boggling."

He checked her eyes to see if she was mocking him. "Then just listen," he said, "and trust me that if none of this were true, I simply would have killed you earlier—all of you—rather than waste my time bullshitting you."

That's the one and only thing I do *trust about you.* "I'm listening."

"The message turned out to be a set of coordinates in higher geometry," he said. "They point to a region in hyperspace where *something* lies in wait for us to contact. No one's sure what it is. But the science boys think it's the location of the supreme prize, the Encyclopedia Galactica. The WOW! signal was just a calling card to get the attention of smart apes like us who're still tinkering around with radio waves."

332

Aria's felt dizzy with the immensity of the news.

"So a team of top government scientists has been pacing in circles for years now, giving themselves ulcers, trying to learn how to access information that's stored in a higher dimension. They were completely stumped until one of them studied the amazing work of Dr. Julia Roan McKenzie."

Nat glared at him. "So you kidnapped Roan."

"Wasn't my idea. I was in El Salvador, training government hit squads." He flashed an icy grin. "That's about as down-to-earth practical as it gets. They called me back and put me in charge of a special ops branch of the National Reconnaissance Agency, saddled me with a team of freaks who can read minds, levitate objects, all kinds of far-out shit."

"Go figure," Aria said.

"Next I volunteered to get gadgets stuck in my eyes and brain so I can hunt around the ether for the Encyclopedia Galactica. Like it or not, I'm now living in a science-fiction universe." He paused and grinned at Aria. "Just like you."

Aria nodded, and swallowed hard.

"So you're looking at the First Flyboy of Hyperspace," Wolfe said. "I was supposed to use my special vision, find this Encyclopedia, tap in, and tell the good scientists what I learned."

"Why not *share* the information?" Roan said. "Why not a joint project of the United Nations?"

"Can you imagine the possibilities?" Nat said. "We might learn how to live for centuries, star-hop through space, manipulate gravity—"

"Or feed the world, live in peace," Aria said.

"Ha. Ya'll sound like victims of too many deep conversations while stoned," Wolfe said. "The real world ain't so neighborly as the utopians would have you believe," he said. "We're talking about the ultimate opportunity for technological advancement in human history. You don't just *share* that or *give* it away."

"Yeah, I can see where the Pentagon is going with this," Aria said. "Maybe learn of some energy source that makes nuclear bombs seem like water balloons. Whatever nation taps the information first can dominate the Earth."

"Look lady, if one group on the planet is gonna live like kings and queens, why shouldn't it be Americans?

She snorted. "Never mind."

Nat's breath had become shallow and he began to pant. He propped his back against the wall. "So I take it...you...failed to access...the Encyclopedia Galactica?"

Wolfe stared at him with swollen eyeballs. "Buddy, if I had tapped it, I would have asked it for some alien super-aspirin. But then, who am I to complain, eh, Doc? You got problems of your own," he said. "I'm sure you'd love to see how the squid-monkeys, swimming in liquid nitrogen on Planet Z, treat brain tumors. Am I right?"

"Probably some...elementary cure...we've ...overlooked..." Nat wobbled then sagged into

Roan who caught him and held him up. His eyes rolled up in his head and his gun hand went slack.

In a burst of motion Wolfe sprang from his chair and snatched the Uzi out of Nat's loose grip. Aria gasped and stepped in front of Jasmine to protect her, as Roan placed her own body between Nat and Wolfe.

Wolfe glanced from Aria to Roan, sweeping the barrel of the automatic weapon from one to the other. Neither woman budged.

"Good." Wolfe gave a nod of appreciation. "Good soldiers."

He stuck the Uzi barrel in his mouth. "What goes 'round, comes 'round," he mumbled, then clamped his teeth on the flash suppresser and squeezed the trigger, showering the walls and ceiling and his guests with the final bits of his headache.

43

Nat Colt drifted in and out of consciousness, lying on a futon mattress on the porch of Balboa's house, an alpaca-wool blanket bundling his emaciated frame. Just as the cancer had made his body less weighty and solid, it also made his mind less anchored and fixed, free to slip, ghost-like, in and out of place and time.

He rode palomino horses bareback again with his dad. Held his warm, slippery-wet newborn daughter in his arms. Beamed with pride as his mom pinned on his sportcoat the first-place medal for the National Junior High School Science Fair. Felt pain like he had been hit by a truck when his collie, Galileo, was hit by a truck and killed. Got his first chemistry kit, and later that same day launched a homemade rocket that set the barn roof on fire. Stood dripping in the shower of the men's locker room, eyes ignited by the fiery delta of Roan McKenzie.

Even when he was awake, Nat sometimes thought he was back on his own porch in Tallahassee, overlooking the palomino saddle horses in the pasture. A beautiful life. When he would remember he was on Balboa's porch in the village of Otrabanda, that was fine, too. Dying felt easy. Struggling against death, trying to hold on? Way too much work. He didn't have the energy for it. He only insisted that he be allowed to die outdoors.

During one lucid phase, he remembered a conversation with Aria just after they had wed.

"What do you think happens when we die?" Aria had asked one night, staring out the window of Jasmine's bedroom at a full, pumpkin moon, while Jasmine slept in her lap. Earlier the three had finished reading *The Education of Little Tree* aloud together.

"That's the big question, isn't it?" he had said. "Hmm. Have you ever experienced team spirit?"

"Sure."

"Neuroscientists tend to think of 'self' as an emergent phenomenon, like team spirit. Let's say a group of guys get together to play soccer. They pool their talent and skills, enthusiasm and so forth— they interact—and team spirit emerges. Follow me?"

Aria nodded, then suddenly pointed out the window. "Look! Geese."

Nat followed her gesture, but saw nothing. "Where?"

"There!" she said. "See? Two Vs of geese, heading south. Beautiful. The moonlight is so bright it makes their white feathers glow orange."

Nat leaned his head closer to hers and lined his eyes up with her pointing finger, but still saw nothing. "You can see a flock?"

"Two flocks. Clearly. Snow geese, with black bills. They're flying straight this way."

He shook his head in wonder. "I think you're seeing them with enhanced vision."

"Oh. I just realized that, too. I'm seeing beyond the wall, because the wall doesn't reach into higher space—it simply isn't there. Strange, huh?" she said. "Go on. You were talking about team spirit."

"I was using the example of team spirit to explain the concept of 'emergent' phenomenon. People get together to play a sport, and team spirit emerges. It's a natural process."

"Right."

"So the experience of team spirit is real enough while it appears—it's felt by all the team members and even by others—but team spirit has no vital essence that survives the breakup of the team. Team spirit has no 'soul.' As soon as the team disbands—*poof!*—the phenomenon, or process, called team spirit no longer exists."

"Okay."

"Now, did team spirit go *somewhere*? North, South, East, West? Off to heaven?" he asked. "No. It just stopped arising. Another specimen of it will emerge whenever the necessary ingredients come together."

"Two guys, a football game, and a six-pack of beer," Aria said.

"In the same way, the *self*—the sense of 'yourself' as an independent entity—is an *emergent* process. The self emerges from the synergism of the senses, language, memories, and so forth. These simpler parts interact to give rise to a working sense of selfhood. But the self has no essence that exists independently of these senses and thoughts and all the little algorithms busy making something wonderfully complex out of simple parts."

"What about the soul?"

"No such entity."

"So you're saying the self is just an illusion. This is Buddhism you're throwing at me, Nat."

"Actually, this is neuroscience I'm throwing at you. And no, I didn't say the self is an *illusion*. Like 'team spirit,' it's very real when it exists, even though it isn't eternally real at all."

"I'm not sure I follow you."

"In other words, it's real enough to say, '*I* feel angry,' and '*I* am an American,' and '*I* blew my driver's test,' and '*I* can't stand licorice.' It's also correct to say, '*I* do not exist aside from a temporary, emergent phenomenon. There is no *abiding substance* that is self."

"Yep. Zen Buddhism. Thought so."

"Not just Zen. Others have said the same thing. The Greek philosopher Epicurus said, 'Death is nothing to us, because when we exist there is no death, and when there is death we do not exist.'"

He paused, listening. "I hear them." Vigorous honking filled the night sky, approaching from out of the north. Suddenly two Vs of silhouetted geese sailed before the round face of the moon. "There!" Nat said. "I see them." The moonlight did make their white feathers glow orange.

"How very lovely," Nat had said, and in his full-moon heart—true self, false self or no self—Nat Colt sorely longed to live.

44

Aria, Roan and Jasmine had been keeping a bedside vigil on Balboa's porch all the drizzling morning and into the drizzling afternoon. Here in Curacao, as in all the world's arid climes, rain was considered auspicious, a lucky time to depart on a journey. But Aria wished the sun would lend its light for just a little while before nightfall.

Nat was unconscious, occasionally stirring or talking in his sleep. His mutterings fell somewhere between coherency and a tossed word salad. Aria heard his latest babblings as "found" poetry—something about the team spirit of lovely moon geese.

The girl and two women took turns giving each other shoulder rubs. Aria was surprised at the strength and sensitivity in Jasmine's hands; her fingers knew right where to go. As Aria began massaging Roan's neck, Roan reached up and back and touched Aria's face.

"It's just a crazy thought," Roan said, "but I imagined a way you could save Nat."

"How?"

"You have the ability to control matter with your mind. You could locate the blood vessels that feed the tumor in his brain and pinch them closed, shut down the blood supply. The tumor would die quickly from lack of oxygen and nutrients."

Aria sighed and shook her head. "I've only used the power twice, Roan. The first time, it made a refrigerator leap up and dent the ceiling; the second time, it hurled tons of water up out of the sea. That's not the same as doing microsurgery inside a living brain. I don't trust that my control would be precise enough. I could easily kill him."

"Yeah," Roan nodded. "You're right. I'm grasping at straws."

"I got an idea," Jasmine said. Aria and Roan turned toward her. "You could practice."

"On what?"

"An egg, a fertilized chicken egg," Jasmine said. "I saw some in a kid's science project once. There are dozens of tiny blood vessels swirled through the yolk. You can try to get good that way."

"That's not bad idea, Jazz." Roan smiled at her daughter. "Aria, what do you think?"

She shook her head slowly. "I don't know," she said, and chewed her lower lip. "If I didn't control...No. No way. I could shatter his skull." She shuddered at the image. "It's not like I'm a talented neurosurgeon who *also* has a psychokinetic gift." She shrugged and raised her arms. "I'm a dancer. I teach the mambo and the tambu. I wouldn't know what tissues I was staring at."

"Cancer cells have a much higher metabolism than healthy cells," Roan said. "If you tune to the infrared wavelength the tumor will be glowing like a neon spider. You can't miss that target."

"Please?" Jasmine said.

"Aria...I...have...nothing...to...lose," Nat whispered hoarsely.

All heads spun toward him. He struggled to sit up and Jasmine stuffed pillows behind his neck.

341

His eyes opened to meet Aria's. "Even...if you ...smashed..." He panted from the effort to speak. "You'd only..." He made a weak smile and feebly touched her hand. "Dying...is...boring." He closed his eyes. "The...scientist...in...me...I...want... ...try...try."

"Okay, darling," Aria said, blinking back tears. "I will. I'll try my best."

An hour later, Aria was sitting at a picnic table in the outdoor kitchen of Balboa's backyard. Several dozen eggs were mounded in a big wicker basket on her left. On the green-painted table in front of her the smashed remains of eggshells, splattered egg whites and blood-streaked yolks drooled in a slimy ooze through the spaces between the planks and dripped onto the sand.

Aria and Jasmine were covered with shell shrapnel and runny goo, resembling losers in a food fight. Aria plunked her elbows down in the mess on the table and buried her face in her hands, exhausted.

"Keep trying," Jasmine said.

"It's no use. I'll shatter his skull. I don't have delicate control. I tune in to the matter inside the yolk...I feel connected, but then it all flies apart...like...like"—she thought of a man ejaculating too soon from over-eagerness, and for the first time sympathized with the male experience of that frustration—"the matter is too eager to move for me ...it's *too* responsive."

Raw egg odor filled her nostrils. *Yuck*. She thought absently that she never *had* liked eggs—not fried, poached, soft-boiled, hard-boiled...

342

She suddenly remembered a news clip about a cancer treatment that uses radio waves to cook tumors to death.

She looked up, eyes bright. "Hard-boiled," she said. "That's it! That's the answer."

"Huh?"

"Your mom said it. She said the tumor would stand out like a lit-up spider, because the cancer cells are more active, warmer than the surrounding tissue. What if, instead of trying to close down the tumor's blood supply, I concentrated on giving the tumor even more energy, a whole lot more energy, until the cancer cells are destroyed by their own heat?"

"How?"

"The 'kinetic theory of heat'—one of the few things I remember from high school physics, probably because it always makes me think of dancing, of passion. See, all the atoms and molecules that compose matter are in constant motion. All matter is dancing. And the faster it dances, the hotter it becomes."

"Daddy explained that to me once, when we were boiling spaghetti."

"I can ask the molecules in the tumor to vibrate faster. It's a lot easier than trying to pinch off tiny blood vessels."

"*Ask* them?"

"It's a long story. Set another egg on the table."

Aria shifted her vision to the interior of the light brown shell. She could clearly see the dark yellow yolk inside the shell, and by subtly tuning

343

her mind—tuning her sympathy, her feeling presence—she joined her awareness to the matter at a fundamental level.

She asked the molecules within the yolk to vibrate. She gave them her full attention, her encouragement, inviting them, compelling them to dance faster and faster. The yolk grew rapidly hotter. After a few seconds, the liquid congealed and shrank into a solid ball.

Aria returned her focus to normal vision. The brown-shelled egg sat on the table before her. She cracked open the shell and a blob of clear egg white spilled out, then the hardened yolk-ball plopped on the table, rolled and came to a stop in a crack.

"You did it!" Jasmine said, and hugged Aria's neck so hard it choked her.

I did it.

"Aria," Balboa called from the back door. "Roan says come now. Nat's not gonna make it."

Nat's breathing had become shallow and fast, his pulse weak. His eyes had rolled up in his head.

"It's now or never, Aria," Roan said.

"Everybody else, please leave," Aria said. "Let me be here alone with him."

Roan hesitated. Then she said, "Right," and took Jasmine's hand. Balboa led them inside the house.

Aria sat cross-legged on the porch and laid her hands over Nat's forehead. She focused her view inside his skull, immediately could see the greedy tarantula of the tumor, pulsing voraciously as it robbed blood and nutrients from healthy brain tissue. The cancer had taken over a large portion of his left frontal lobe, shoving his brain down and to the right, compressing vital nerve centers, killing him slowly but inexorably.

She shifted her focus to a deeper level and saw the molecules shimmering, dancing, vibrating. How strange to see that the molecules that composed the tumor were of themselves neither good nor evil—just as the molecules that made up the body of Hitler were not fundamentally different than the molecules that composed Jesus.

Communion with the molecules wasn't a matter of projecting her mind, moving her mental energy "outward" to meet the molecules. It wasn't a matter of overcoming distance at all, but, rather, of overcoming the *illusion* of distance, of separation. It was a matter of deeply intuiting and feeling the single field in which the molecules and her mind were already unified.

As her awareness became more gathered, deep and vast, Aria entered into the sense and mood of the essential unity of mind and matter. She asked the molecules to cooperate with her will. It felt not radically different than asking her hand or foot to move, it was only a subtler version of mind directing matter.

Aria pictured the molecules dancing more and more energetically, producing greater heat. The infrared wavelengths amplified, giving off rich red rays. The molecules buzzed like maddened hornets in a hive as their vibratory energy increased. Hotter, hotter, glowing brighter.

On the next structural level above molecules, that of proteins, Aria felt the molecular bonds breaking loose, the proteins destroyed. And on the structural level above proteins, she felt the tumor cells shriveling, cytoplasm coagulating, cell membranes bursting.

Within seconds, the tumor shrank dramatically to a congealed lump of dead flesh. Then Aria went after the remnants that had metastasized to the lypmh nodes of Nat's neck and armpits. Soon those enemy outposts also withered and died from their own heat. Then Aria asked Nat's immune system to mobilize against any straggler cancer cells in his body. The white cells responded by launching an all-out assault like avenging warriors. Within hours, every trace of cancer would be eradicated.

Aria resolved her vision to normal view just as the late afternoon sun parted the gray curtains of the clouds. She saw Nat breathing steadily, his pulse strong, the life-force within him joining its rays with the sun to illuminate his peaceful face.

He opened his eyes for a moment, smiled serenely and instantly fell deeply asleep. Even the mingled kisses and tears from Aria, Roan and Jasmine did not rouse him from his healing slumber.

45

In the coral-pink dawn Aria strolled high up into the cactus-dotted hills overlooking the village of Otrabanda, where Nat and Roan and Jasmine were celebrating a belated family reunion.

Aria spread a blanket on a deserted hilltop and gazed out over the Carribean. The Earth awakened, sunny and cloudless, and the sea mirrored the sky's depth and purity of blue.

Aria mulled over the events of the past three months. She felt neither rejected by Nat and his family, nor jealous of their happiness. On the contrary, she was overjoyed for them. But she could see their paths diverging, which made her feel a bit of her old, familiar longing. She was, of course, not Nat's wife any longer. The paperwork for the annulment would be nothing more than an afterthought.

On the other hand, the four were now kindred souls forever, and Aria already had begun Jasmine's drum and dance lessons. What better setting to teach the mambo than the powdery sand at Otrabanda, with Jazz dancing with Tommy, the boy with the chocolate skin and blond dreadlocks?

Aria recalled a recent conversation with Roan. She had taken Roan's hand and walked with her to a private spot. "I just wanted you to know that Nat and I—"

"Shhh," Roan had said. "You don't have to explain a thing. It's all right."

"But I want you to know—"

"Really, it's okay," Roan said. "You saved his life. I owe you everything."

"Just listen," Aria said. "Nat married me because he saw that Jazz and I really hit it off, and he felt I'd make a good mother for her. And he was right. I think I would've been a great mother. I adore Jasmine. I'd be very happy and proud in that role, as you are."

"Yes I am," Roan said, smiling.

"And I fell in love with Nat," Aria said. "But my point is; he never fell in love with me."

Roan swallowed hard. "You don't believe so?"

"I know he didn't. He loves me, yes, very much even—but not as his lover. We never consummated the marriage. Never. And it's not because he was sick. Yeah, he used that as an excuse, but I knew better. The truth is; he was totally devoted to you."

"Really?"

Aria laughed. "You kidding me? Thought you were supposed to be a genius! Lady, he's been nuts about you since he was seventeen. He's *still* got a teen-age crush on you, and there's simply no room in his heart for any other woman. Period."

Roan sucked in her breath and began to cry quietly. "Thank you. Thank you for telling me. It's silly, I guess…but…it means a lot to me."

"*Duh.*"

Then they burst out laughing and hugged like sisters. The six-foot, fair-skinned, Celtic Goddess and the five-foot, caramel-skinned,

348

Curacao Cocktail; different pigments belonging to the same paint set.

Now Aria sat overlooking the distant rusted rooftops that hemmed the hill's long dusty skirt, wondering about her future.

Roan and Nat and Jasmine were together again, but the danger to all their lives was not over. When would it ever be over? So many nations wanted to gain the know-how to build their own cyber-optic vision systems in the hope of tapping the Encyclopedia Galactica.

"Whovever wins this race, wins the *human* race," Wolfe had said.

Why did it have to be that way? Why couldn't people planet-wide rejoice in the thrill of contacting another world—or a galactic club of civilizations—and share the wealth of culture and technology the historic meeting promised?

Aria picked up a limestone rock embedded with prehistoric seashells. *Wansalawata.* One salt water. We're all children of the same ocean mother. But even after millions of years of evolution, people still see themselves not as co-passengers of Spaceship Earth, but as members of isolated, warring tribes: nation-states. Rally 'round the flags, boys and girls. It's *Us* vs. *Them.*

She flung the rock homeward, toward the sea it came from, heard it skip and bounce down the steep slope.

The Encyclopedia Galactica, repository of awesome knowledge. Where was it? In hyperspace, of course, but *where*?

349

Aria contemplated what she had learned from her voyages in hyperspace. Mammy Mako had alerted her to the essential truth: No distance. No separation. If the Encyclopedia Galactica existed at all, it was definitely not "out there." It was indivisibly joined with her own life and consciousness, here and now. Aria decided to open her awareness as fully as possible and let the Encylopedia Galactica "find" *her*.

She closed her eyes, letting go of the tension in her shoulders and forehead. As she settled deeper into the present moment with each breath, an emotion of calm expectation filled her and her vision spontaneously expanded into hyperspace, the realm she called EveryHere. She surrendered completely to her heartfelt intuition of the unity of life.

For several cycles of breath she felt profound, oceanic peace, floating freely in space. All in one instant, the light of her mind increased to an absolute lucidity—perfectly clear, unqualified, original. Her viewpoint shifted from that of an independent observer peering into hyperspace, to the radical view of being *identical* to hyperspace. Her limited self had been transcended in one bound, and the leap had happened as naturally as getting the punch line of a joke.

All questions, all fears, all strategies were resolved in the dazzling singularity of being. The sense of expansion or ascent had vanished, for there was no more "up" or "down", "in" or "out"—but all of existence had become radically equal and *whole*, the same bright freedom and fullness. Aria enjoyed the consciousness of limitless radiant being, identical with the Life of the universe.

At dusk, when she strolled back down the trail to the village, she couldn't guess how long she had remained consumed in the ecstatic domain. The most strange and surprising feature of the experience was that it had not *been* strange and surprising at all. Awakening to cosmic consciousness had felt utterly familiar, like coming home to her Self.

Aria smiled at the obviousness of her revelation. The Encyclopedia Galactica, the ultimate reservoir of knowledge, was not a technology at all—not *constructed* by any civilization. It had not been built, but only discovered, in the same way she had found it. It was right to call it an intergalactic communications network; indeed, it was a repository of the experiences of all living beings. And it could be contacted by anyone in the depth of heart feeling—gizmos or no gizmos.

The Encylopedia Galactica was the reality that people on Earth had for centuries venerated as "God" and hung a thousand masks and concepts upon. But at origin, before the invention of all the dogmas and schisms of belief and disbelief, the Encyclopedia Galactica was simply the everlasting life and mind of the universe.

46

In the Orion Nebula, trillions of miles from Balboa's house on Curacao, waves of gravity lapped at tidal pools of interstellar dust, birthing new stars. In the Otrabanda Lagoon, a few hundred feet from Balboa's porch, waves of seawater lapped at tidal flats spawning new starfish.

Aria and Nat and Roan were sitting on the porch discussing Aria's experience on the hilltop. Jasmine sat nearby on a rattan couch petting a little mutt dog that had become her fast friend; the scruffy pet looked like the "Curacao Cocktail" version of a Jack Russell terrier.

The village lay in repose. Most of the men were out on the sea net-fishing for squid, using lanterns to lure them to the surface. Their lamps bobbed on the dark water like floating constellations. Sounds of quiet laughter and conversation drifted from inside Balboa's house. The soft air smelled like sea grape and red jasmine.

Aria was doing her best to report her vision as objectively and neutrally as words could manage. But it was hard to suppress her enthusiasm. The awakening resonated in her body and mind with the force of revelation.

"The best way I can describe the event is to say it was a kind of *spiritual* experience," she said. "The Encyclopedia Galactica is not an artificial technological marvel built by engineers from some alien super-civilization," she said. "It's *inherent*. The structure of it is the structure of the universe."

She spread her arms wide. "Hyperspace, ordinary space—it *all* belongs to the Encyclopedia Galactica. Every particle and organism and ecosystem and world comprises it. And all its parts are busy processing and storing and retrieving information—forever."

"Fascinating," Roan said. "You're saying the whole universe is one vast, living Encyclopedia—a Cosmic Computer or Mind."

"Yes, exactly," Aria said. "And all living beings contribute to it, not through some advanced communications technology, but spontaneously. Just by participating in life, you add your experiences to the great pool."

"Wonderful," Nat said. In the shimmering light from a kerosene lantern his healthy skin color echoed the rich mahogany of the loveseat on which he and Roan cuddled.

"For a timeless moment I actually *became* the transcendental mind, beyond the limited planes of appearances." Aria shook her head. "Gosh, that sounds so pretentious. You know I'm not religious. I wish I could explain better."

Roan touched Aria's arm reassuringly and smiled. "You're doing an excellent job. I'm fascinated."

Nat was smiling, too. "You've got to deal with all us Flatfolk who can't see. You've got to lift us up to your higher vision."

"You know, Carl Jung, the Swiss psychiatrist, had his own term for that higher realm of mind," Roan said. "He called it the 'Collective Unconscious.' And he also coined the term 'archetypes,' meaning universal elements of culture."

"Ah. Tell me more about archetypes," Aria said.

"They're symbols, myths and technologies that show up in diverse societies, far removed in place and history," Roan said. "Like the valentine heart and the swastika, the Fall from Grace and Expulsion from Paradise, the bow and arrow, and so forth. He believed archetypes tapped the Collective Unconscious and were evidence of it."

"Aria, this really is astounding," Nat said. "If I understand you correctly, you might be able to tap the 'database' of all human experience. You could, say, hold an arrowhead in your hand—maybe even just *think* 'arrowhead'—and you would suddenly *remember* all you'd need to know about how to knap a chunk of flint into an arrowhead, courtesy of our tool-making ancestors. The pool of information is there, waiting—"

"No, not *there*. It's *here*." Aria tapped her heart. "And not just available to me—but to *you*, to Roan, to all aware beings. When I walked down from the hill, I knew that this is what the saints and mystics of all religions have been talking about for ages. 'The kingdom of heaven is at hand—it lies within.' They're proclaiming that beyond the mortal self of our personalities lies a domain of transcendental life, or mind, spirit—whatever you want to call it."

"Think I'll just go on calling it the Encyclopedia Galactica," Nat said.

"As good a name as any," Aria said. "Once I'd accessed the wholeness, I couldn't tell the difference between it and myself. Like I'd swallowed the ocean in one gulp—or, more accurately, it had swallowed me. I *became* what I sought."

Aria smiled with the lucid memory of the revelation. "All living things are linked through the Encyclopedia Galactica," she said. "It's the underlying pattern in nature and it operates holistically: the whole guides all its parts."

Roan frowned in concentration and ran her hand through her long tresses. "If the Encyclopedia Galactica is *not* some manufactured super-communications system, but rather, it's built into the fabric of the universe—"

"It simply *is* the universe, itself," Aria said, "the whole shebang. Mind *is* energy-matter."

Roan nodded. "Yes. But that leaves me wondering... What was the purpose of the WOW! message received at Ohio State that alerted everyone to this?"

Aria laughed and knew her amber eyes tossed back the lantern's glow. "Don't you get it?" she said. "It was a missionary message. Beings on some distant world were proclaiming the Good News to all their Milky Way neighbors, hoping we'd access the Encyclopedia Galactica and realize our unity before we destroyed ourselves."

Oculoneural.com

INSIGHT Vision Research Corporation

Project V.I.S.I.O.N.
(Visual Input System, Implanted Oculoneural Net)

Oculoneural.com provides comprehensive diagrams and technical data along with complete instructions for building cyber-optic implants. These plans are offered as free, open-source hardware and downloadable software; additionally, clinical training in the implantation procedures is available for ophthalmic and neurosurgeons.

We who lived the events in the story you have just read strongly feel that all scientists and the general public need to be aware not just of the new technology, but of the human drama behind the artificial vision system developed by Drs. Roan McKenzie and Nat Colt.

By publishing on the Worldwide Web and freely sharing with all interested parties the technical know-how to manufacture cyber-optic implants, as well as providing all medical-surgical information pertinent to the V.I.S.I.O.N. Project, we have accomplished our goal of rendering obsolete any further criminal actions against us by government agents, domestic and foreign. Now, no secrets exist. No exclusivity. This website provides the engineering data *in full*—open and available to *all*. No one else needs to be harmed in the effort to acquire the technology and information wholly and freely presented here.

We can only ask that those who visit this website will appreciate the human cost of the material offered here. By telling our personal story, we have tried to impress upon everyone the burden of responsibility that goes with the use of this miraculous technology.

INSIGHT Vision Research Corporation is sponsoring clinical trials of cyber-optic implants in 36 formerly blind patients. All but two patients have regained their eyesight, and in all but four cases, have developed some degree of higher-order vision. These human trials began with Aria Rioverde and Roan McKenzie, who have each been using the V.I.S.I.O.N. system for more than three years. In addition, 12 patients in the second cohort have now passed the two-year mark without problems. A bonobo chimpanzee named Mojo has successfully used the implants for five years.

As with any new and powerful tool—from lasers to computers to satellites—artificial vision systems can be used to serve life on Earth, or to hasten its destruction. Therefore, if you have the intention and the means to create and use cyber-optic devices, may you do so for the good of humankind—and all living beings.

And may we all live with insight and higher vision.

- Julia Roan McKenzie, M.D., Ph.D.
- Nat Winchester Colt, M.D., Ph.D.
- Aria Carmen Rioverde, MFA

Author's Note

The various near-future technologies featured in this novel were inspired by present-day research. M.I.T., Harvard and Duke, among other universities, are conducting promising experiments with artificial retinas. A typical design uses tiny cameras mounted on eyeglass frames that transmit visual data to an array of electrodes placed over the retinas.

Other schools are at work developing a computer chip to interface with brain cells. Researchers at the California Institute of Technology, for example, have fashioned a "bionic" chip using silicon and standard integrated-circuit techniques. The chips are dimpled with multiple pits, each pit half the diameter of a human hair, and each tiny well is hooked to an electrode that links it to a computer. The scientists fill each pit with nutrients that feed nerve cells, then add neurons from embryonic rat brains, one to each pit, and let the neurons thrive. Soon the neurons grow outward over the silicon walls separating the pits and make connections with each other just as they would in a developing brain. As hoped, the built-in electrodes are able to detect signals firing between the nerve cells. This is only a first step. Within the next half-century, bionic computer chips may be implanted within the human brain to boost various brain functions, such as vision, memory capacity or foreign language acquisition.

358

The notion of a "data-cube" which could store and process trillions of bits of information (say, all the text in the volumes of the Library of Congress) in a space smaller than a sugar cube, was inspired by research into 3-D memory storage devices at the University of California, Irvine, and elsewhere. In one method, data is stored digitally as holographic checkerboards within a crystal; the patterns represent ones and zeroes. The human brain itself probably stores and processes information three-dimensionally within its dense webs of nerve connections called neural nets.

In December, 2012, the National Intelligence Council, a U.S.-based coalition of spy agencies, released "Global Trends 2030: Alternative Worlds," a 140-page report predicting major changes expected in just 18 years. "Future retinal eye implants could enable night vision, and neuro-enhancements could provide superior memory recall or speed of thought," say the experts in the spy industry. "Brain-machine interfaces could offer superhuman abilities."

As for the story's speculations on the nature of higher dimensional space, such conjectures are at least as old as religion, and are wide open to multiple interpretations from theologians, mystics, philosophers, cosmologists, mathematicians, physicists—and novelists. I will simply note that it would be hard to find a cosmologist, mathematician or physicist today who does *not* accept as reality the existence of higher dimensions beyond the familiar four of "ordinary" space-time. By permitting higher space in their equations, theoretical physicists hope

359

to discover an overarching "Theory of Everything," which would gracefully unite the fundamental forces of nature within one mathematical framework.

Stay tuned.

16638368R00213

Made in the USA
Charleston, SC
03 January 2013